DEATH'S COLD HAND

A DCI Will Blake Novel

J.E. Mayhew

Obolus Books

ISBN-13: 978-1-9998407-9-2

Cover design by: Meg Jolly
Photography by: Dave Mort

To my Dad,
Charlie Mayhew

Although the story is set on the Wirral, the names of some establishments and roads have been fictionalised to protect the unloved and godless...
but you can have fun guessing...

Prepare your hearts for Death's cold hand! pre-
pare
Your souls for flight, your bodies for the earth;
Prepare your arms for glorious victory;
Prepare your eyes to meet a holy God!
Prepare, prepare!

A War Song To Englishmen

WILLIAM BLAKE

Chapter 1

Paul Travis never contemplated his own death. Even in the heat of Helmand Province, he never for one minute entertained the idea that there was a bullet or an IED out there with his name on it. The graven images and names carved into Port Sunlight war memorial didn't make him pause for thought in his lust for life. While he recognised and honoured the sacrifice of the people remembered there, he wouldn't be following them. This self-assurance had served him well and allowed him to get on in life. He'd trodden on a few toes along the way, and a few faces, come to think of it but he didn't really care. Of course, that self-assurance only got him so far and everybody dies some time.

Paul Travis included.

The sky was clear and the night felt cold, even for early May. Paul's mind turned to Summer and the villa in Portugal. He couldn't wait. Just him, Rachel and little Danielle. He gave a soppy grin, the beers he'd knocked back at the Bridge Inn making him sentimental. They'd be asleep when he got in. Danielle all snuggled up with her teddy bear. Maybe if Rachel wasn't too dead to the world, there might be the chance of something more. No chance. Who was he kidding? He rolled his eyes at the thought of the earbashing that would ensue if he tried it on.

Things weren't good in that department. Not good at all.

Stumbling over an uneven paving slab, he swore. How much had he had? He'd lost track but he knew it was time to leave when Barry began singing, 'You'll Never Walk Alone.' Dave and George had promised to get the big man home safely. Paul chuckled again, remembering the fun they'd had wrangling him into a taxi. The taxi driver had issued the usual warning about paying for any mess and Paul wondered how far they'd get before they had to stop to let Barry out.

The lads grumbled about travelling down the Wirral once every couple of weeks for a pint but so what? Paul liked the walk across the village, especially on a night like this. And what Paul liked, Paul got. One way or another. In a few minutes, he'd be at home, tucked up and snoring. They'd still be driving. Anyway, they bitched about everything. Tomorrow, once he'd slept off his hangover, he'd have a word with George. Tell the bastard properly that he knew what his game was and it wasn't on.

The War Memorial loomed over him, its white granite washed blue by the moonlight. He'd always loved it, even when he was a kid. It dominated this part of the village. A huge cross enthroned on an octagonal plinth accessed by four flights of steps. Everything about it was symmetrical and perfect. Some people didn't like the bronze figures of soldiers and seafarers protecting children. They said they were too realistic with their fixed bayonets and grim, resolute faces. Paul thought it was fitting. He'd lost friends in Afghanistan. It did people good to see that real people fell and died to keep them safe. A bit of grim resolution wouldn't harm anyone.

"Paul," a voice whispered from the shadows.

"Hello?" Paul said, his speech slurring. "Who's there."

Lurching a little, he staggered up the steps to the foot of the cross. If those bloody teenagers were messing around again, he'd give them a good hiding. He frowned into the darkness that clung to the base of the memorial. It looked like there was an extra statue. Another figure, silhouetted, stood stock still amongst the crouching bronze soldiers.

Paul grimaced and he heard a foot scrape behind him as one of the statues came to life, dragging itself from the shadows. By the time he realised the dark figure was swinging a baseball bat, it was too late.

Chapter 2

DCI Will Blake had cornered many criminals who were desperate to escape the long arm of the law, but this was probably his biggest challenge. Generally, he could reason with the individual and make them see the pointlessness of trying to flee. Usually, his superior height and size would emphasise that argument. And usually, at the end of the day, there were other ways to take down a villain.

This character wouldn't listen to reason, though and a taser, however tempting, was out of the question. She had her own agenda, and it didn't involve being grabbed by Blake. To some, she might seem like just a large fluffy Persian cat but Serafina was capable of inflicting painful wounds along with abject humiliation. And Blake had been chasing her around the house for the best part of an hour.

To add another level of complication to the whole proceedings, Charlie, Blake's Jack Russell, found the whole exercise too exciting for words and bounced around the living room yapping joyfully. This was the best entertainment he'd had in his life.

"Come on, Serafina," Blake said, trying to sound soothing. "C'mon, girl."

Serafina put her ears back and hissed, lashing

out with her claws. Despite wearing gloves, Blake whipped his hands back instinctively. She hated being picked up and only came to any human on her terms. Plus, she had seen the crate that Blake had tried to hide under a towel when he sat it on the sofa. The crate meant the vet and Serafina was having none of that.

Blake had come back from work a few days before to find that Serafina was off her food. Her appetite hadn't improved since.

"You're gonna have to get the vet to look at her," Ian Youde, his neighbour had said. "I reckon she's got a gammy tooth." He usually fed her, walked Charlie and kept an eye on them while Blake was working. He was a sour-faced old man with a letterbox mouth and narrow, suspicious eyes but Blake liked him. Despite Youde's self-proclaimed hatred of cats, he obviously knew animals and wouldn't have said anything unless he thought there was a problem.

Blake had dutifully made an appointment with the vets and now here he was, crawling around his own living room trying to catch Serafina, Charlie tugging at his jumper with his teeth. It was early morning and the appointment with the vet was hurtling towards him, making the need to capture Serafina all the more urgent. The cat crouched in a corner, hemmed in by an armchair and the wall as Blake inched forward. "It's okay, girl," he said, softly and reached out again.

That was when Serafina took her chance and sprang up. Blake's eyes widened as the huge ball of blue-grey fur filled his vision.

Suddenly, the cat wrapped itself around his head, effectively blindfolding him with her body and sinking her claws into his scalp. Blake roared with pain and Charlie barked with glee as Serafina pummelled his cheek with her back paws, claws exposed. He shot to his feet, the cat still clinging to his head and stumbled backwards across the living room. This would have been painful enough but Blake was still recovering from bruised ribs and the other injuries he'd received during his trip to Scotland a couple of months ago. Although he was nearly better, pain still seared through his body.

Then, just as quickly, the lights were back on and the cat had sprung from his shoulder. But Blake knew why. She was leaping to safety. The room lurched on its side as he tumbled over a footrest and, with a roar of indignation, he fell heavily onto an old armchair. For a second, Blake lay still, face down in the seat, recovering. "Jeez, Serafina, we've got to get that tooth sorted."

Wincing, he eased himself up and scanned the room for the cat, touching his cheek with his fingertips. She'd drawn blood. Charlie leapt up at his legs yapping happily at the excitement. Blake wondered whether the trauma of all his adventures in Scotland had pushed the little dog over the edge. "That'd be all I need," Blake muttered looking down at Charlie, "two psychotic animals in the house."

Charlie barked again and Blake realised that the Jack Russell was staring intently at the crate. Blake blinked in amazement at the two glowing eyes that glared out at him from the darkness of the crate. Serafina had taken refuge in the very box she was trying to avoid. "It's some kind of trick, isn't it boy?" he said to Charlie as he edged towards the crate. "She's taunting me. Trying to lull me into a false sense of security..." He lunged forward and flipped the mesh door on the crate, heaving a sigh of relief. If Laura had been there, he wouldn't have had that problem. She would have thought of some clever way to entice Serafina into the crate without the unnecessary bloodshed. Blake dabbed his cheek again. It was still bleeding. He stared into the crate. "Maybe you miss her too, eh, puss?" Serafina growled and glared at him.

Laura had left him before Christmas, forced to flee after her ex-husband Kyle Quinlan, a violent and powerful criminal had returned from the US. Blake had begged her to stay, telling her they could face Quinlan together but it wasn't enough. He sighed, picked up the crate and looked around the room. Laura had been a fixture in his life for months now and she'd woken him up from what, looking back, had been a miserable existence. He'd even made plans to sell the house and move in somewhere else with her. Now, once again, he was trapped in his dead mother's house with all its ancient furniture. The place still looked as though she'd just popped out to the shops. But he'd changed. Laura had changed him, and that new part of him wasn't prepared to give up on her.

Blake's phone rang.

"Kath, is this urgent? I'm kind of busy right now..."

"Sir, It's not good. You better get over to Port Sunlight," Detective Inspector Kath Cryer said. "It's a messy one."

Blake pursed his lips and glared at the crate. He'd have to rely on Ian Youde once again. "I'm on my way, Kath."

Chapter 3

There was nothing like a crime scene tent and some blue and white tape to lower the tone of an area, Blake thought. Some places welcomed and revelled in the new accessories. Others wore a look of shock, like Port Sunlight. Blake was familiar with the village that nestled in front of the Unilever factory and Lever House, a huge building with a grand front entrance overlooked by a large clock. The old factory buildings and workshops had been torn down and replaced with modern units that hid behind the façade of the factory wall. The factory produced more than it ever did now but employed a fraction of the workforce.

Port Sunlight itself was what they called a 'model village,' made by a philanthropist entrepreneur to keep the factory workforce healthy, happy and productive. Port Sunlight certainly outshone the surrounding areas with its wide, tree-lined drives, numerous flower beds and mock Tudor houses. But a huge swathe of it around the war memorial was cordoned off now and the cars that normally lined the edge of the road by the garden centre were replaced with police vehicles and ambulances. Crime Scene Investigators in white coveralls moved in and out of the tent and uniformed police officers were dotted around the cordon, keeping a few curious members of the public back.

Detective Inspector Kath Cryer hurried over to Blake as he climbed out of the car then stopped and did a double take. "What happened, sir?" she said, looking at the scratches on Blake's cheek.

Blake frowned, but remembered his wrestling match with Serafina this morning and touched the scratches on his own face. "Oh, just cat trouble, Kath," he said. "What have we got?"

Kath shook herself and looked down at her notes. "Male in his thirties, tall, six three. Looks like his head had been caved in with a blunt instrument."

"Who found him?"

"A young couple coming back from a night out in Liverpool. They saw him from out of their taxi. They couldn't miss him, though."

"Makes a change from a dog walker, I suppose. Are they still about?"

"No, guv, but we've got their addresses. You sure you're okay, sir?"

Blake grunted, trying to ignore the ache in his chest and the scratches acquired from Serafina. "I swear to God, that cat is going to be the death of me, Kath." Blake signed into the crime scene and dragged on a set of coveralls. The material felt plastic and constricted him. He put the face mask on and pulled the hood up before ducking into the tent.

The metallic smell of blood hit Blake first, even through the face mask. He trod gingerly onto the stepping plates that prevented anyone from stepping in the blood that pooled around the steps of the war memorial.

Malachy O'Hare, the Crime Scene Manager squatted over the body, masking the top half. Blake could only see the crime scene manager's back and his head was shrouded by the hood of the coveralls but he recognised the bony frame straight away.

"It's a bloody disgrace," O'Hare said, without turning round.

"What?" Blake said.

"Killing a man here. On this spot of all places. A bloody war memorial," O'Hare spat. "I mean, bad enough anywhere but this just takes the biscuit."

Blake nodded. "Are we certain he was killed, Mallachy?"

O'Hare turned, his white eyebrows did the talking for the rest of his face. He wasn't happy. "I'm telling you. Whoever did this wants stringing up."

Blake frowned. O'Hare was normally the source of dark banter at a scene like this. He was the one who kept a sense of humour when others were swallowing down their breakfasts again. "What makes you so sure it's murder?"

O'Hare stepped back to reveal a male body lying on its back on the steps as though catching a few minutes rest. One leg was bent, and the arms lay loosely at the side of the body. The head was bruised and battered and a jagged, red wound gaped at the victim's neck.

"Jeez, Mallachy. I take your point," he gasped. "Any ID?"

Mallachy held up a wallet stuffed with cash and a local gym pass with the name Paul Travis printed on it. Blake looked at the photograph. "Whoever did this was a head-the-ball, Will," Mallachy said. "A monster." He shook his head. "I'm sorry. I lost a nephew in Iraq a few years ago. How anyone could kill a man in a place like this just…" Mallachy shrugged. "I've no words."

"We need to get them, then," Blake said. Looking at the dead man's feet rather than anywhere else. "Any prints?

"We have a bloody boot print on a lower step. Whoever did this would have been splattered with blood, too. The victim's mobile phone was on him. Otherwise, nothing. I'm no pathologist but I'd say he went down with the first blow and then what followed was just savagery."

"A big man like that could have defended himself if he had the chance," Blake agreed. "Let's see what the pathologist says."

"Knowing Jack Kenning, he'll probably crack a shite joke and twiddle whichever godawful bow-tie he's decided to inflict on us," O'Hare said, the appraisal of Kenning being a sure sign of recovery from his initial shock. "Oh, there's this, too. I haven't removed it yet because I want to get a picture."

Blake squatted next to Mallachy, trying not to look at the pulp to his left. Fortunately, the investigator's attention was focused on the victim's hand. "What is it?"

"It's a hand, Will," Mallachy said. Blake gave him a wry look. Having vented his wrath, the old Mallachy was back with them.

"Hilarious. What's that in it?" Blake peered at the closed, white fingers. Something green and shiny was clutched in them. "It looks like it's round at the top. Hard to tell what it is."

"Callum!" Mallachy yelled, almost deafening Blake. "Callum, will you get that camera in here? Blake wants a selfie with me."

Blake glanced at O'Hare. "A selfie?"

"It was the best I could do on the spur of the moment, Blake, don't hate me."

Callum, whom Blake always thought of as new but was probably pretty well-established by now, appeared at the entrance, panting for breath, camera in hand. He nodded at Blake.

"You don't really want a picture with Mr O'Hare do you?" Callum said, glancing from Blake to Mallachy and back.

"I didn't think Malachy showed up on photographs," Blake said.

Callum looked confused. "Why not?"

"Ignore him, Callum," Mallachy said. "He's trying to be funny. Take a picture of that hand there."

Callum took some photographs and then Mallachy tried to prise the fingers apart. "No good. Rigor mortis. Let's hope so anyway or we might have to break the fingers."

"Really?" Callum said.

Mallachy rolled his eyes. "I don't know, what do they teach you in college these days? Cadaveric spasm mean anything to you?"

Callum looked a little lost and glanced over at Blake. "Don't look at me," Blake said.

"It's not rigor mortis but often mistaken for it," Mallachy explained. "If the victim died traumatically, there's a chance the body goes into cadaveric spasm. The whole body stiffens instantly and often, it doesn't loosen up. If he died clutching that, then the grip could be irreversible."

"Let's hope not," Blake said. "I want to know what he's holding as soon as possible." He stepped out of the tent and headed to where DI

Kath Cryer was talking to a member of the public. Pulling his mask off, he took a huge gulp of fresh air. It never got any easier, having to look at the corpses of people who had died violently. Blake always tried to maintain a sense of clinical detachment but when confronted with the actuality of a brutal death, it always shook him. Kath Cryer finished talking and hurried over to meet Blake.

"Neighbour, sir. Lives just on the corner, there. Thought she might have heard shouts sometime around midnight. She spent more time grumbling about the Bridge Inn and the rowdy folk club they have on a Wednesday than anything else. I'll get a statement anyway."

"Nice one, Kath. Get door-to-door going. Someone must have seen or heard something. It's such an open space to have attacked anyone..."

"D'you think the setting is significant. Sir?"

"I don't think anything yet, Kath. It's pretty apparent he was killed on the steps, judging by the blood. Knocked unconscious and then his throat cut maybe." Blake scanned the area. "It's such a peculiar place to choose to ambush anyone. I mean, look around you, it's effectively a massive roundabout surrounding the memorial. Very few hiding places."

"Maybe the victim knew his assailant."

"That's a possibility. So what happened? Did

they have an argument?"

Kath thought for a moment. "Whoever did that to Paul Travis was equipped for the job, sir. It doesn't take a pathologist to work that out. Why was he carrying a blunt instrument and a knife unless he intended to use it?"

"It doesn't pay to assume too much, Kath. It could have been an argument on the way back from work. The killer could have been carrying tools or a bowling ball if they'd been for a night out at Bromborough Bowl…"

"A bowling ball, sir?" Kath said, giving him a sceptical frown.

"I'm just saying, we don't know for certain…"

"Yes, sir," Kath said, staring up the treelined gardens to the Art Gallery. "It's a pretty place, isn't it? Must have been great for the workers here…"

"My grandad worked for Lever Brothers as they were before they became Unilever. He refused to live here."

"Really, sir?"

"Yeah. Apparently, he thought that once you did that, the company had you, body and soul. They told you when to go on holiday, and where to go, too. D'you remember that case last year with the paranormal investigator? What was his name?"

"Trevor Long, sir?"

"Yeah. That caravan park over in Thurstaston where we thought we'd found a body, I think that used to be a Lever Brothers holiday camp."

Kath raised her eyebrows and grinned. "As ever, it's an education working with you, sir."

Blake smiled back. He liked Kath, she could be a bit of a blabbermouth and she rubbed people up the wrong way. That was a distinct advantage sometimes. Kath was a diligent officer with a mind as sharp as her eye and a tongue to match both. "We need to find out if there's family and get Tasha Cook involved. Come on. The game's afoot, as Sherlock would probably say. To be honest, it doesn't feel much like a game to me."

Chapter 4

There was blood on his hands, blood on his boots. The face in the mirror opposite the bed he sat on was freckled in red. He'd even walked blood in through the house when he came in last night. He could see it everywhere. Whether he'd slept or what time it was, he had no idea. Birds sang outside and light streamed in through the thin curtains, so it must have been morning. Slowly the memories of last night crept into his mind. The staring eyes, his battered face and his open throat. The blood.

For a second, the room vanished and, once again, he was trapped in the Foxhound armoured car with the roar of the explosion, the heat of the flames and Corporal Graves' pleading face in his. Graves' hand gripped his ankle and then slid away as the car rolled and rolled. Pressing his fists to his temples he curled up, trying to squeeze the memories from his writhing brain. Blood pulsed round his temples and his heart hammered against his ribs.

And then just as quickly, he was back in the bedroom. He knew what he must do and prayed it wasn't too late. Running into the kitchen, he saw that the chef's blowtorch was on the work-top next to the pliers. Maybe he'd remembered and put them there last night. Rummaging in his pocket, he found the toy soldier. It was green and almost featureless, a man wearing a tin hat and carrying a rifle in one hand. With the other, it was throwing a grenade. He struck a match and smiled grimly at the satisfying roar of blue heat that sprang from the end of the blowtorch.

Gripping the toy soldier's feet with the pliers, he levelled the flame at its head. Slowly, the arm bent as drips of green plastic fizzed angrily onto the work surface. He angled the soldier so that the molten drips slid down the body of the toy and pooled on the stand. The smell filled the kitchen, tickling his nose. It wasn't unpleasant. It calmed him.

He spoke as though he was chanting a prayer. "Go back to Hell. You aren't welcome here. You aren't meant to be here. Go back." Clicking off the torch, he looked closely for any signs that it had worked. God, he hoped so. The toy soldier cooled into a shapeless lump with a pair of legs. He knew what he had to do now. Bath. Bin his clothes. Clean the house. Then sleep. And pray he didn't dream.

Chapter 5

It was late afternoon by the time Blake got the team together. A number of uniformed officers and detectives ranged around the meeting room. DI Kath Cryer sat at the front along with Detective Sergeant Vikki Chinn and Detective Constable Alex Manikas. Someone was missing, though.

"Where's Kinnear?" Blake said, scanning the group. DC Andrew Kinnear was one of the detectives Blake rated and liked to have on the team. He was rarely absent.

"Adoption meeting, sir," Vikki Chinn said, looking up from her notepad.

"Adoption? He's a bit old to be adopted, isn't he?"

"Him and Chris have been going to meetings and stuff for months, boss," Kath Cryer said. "Didn't he tell you?"

"It didn't really come up in conversation. We tend to talk about work. Or biscuits, to be honest," Blake said. "I guess I need to have a word. I feel bad now."

"I'm sure there's no need, sir," Alex Manikas said. "He wasn't exactly broadcasting it about the office. The Super, knows. Wrote him a reference and everything."

"I see," Blake said, wondering why he felt a little bit offended himself at not being asked for a reference. He scanned the group. "Okay. I'm sure Kinnear will catch up, when he's back. Let's have a look at what we've got here, then. So, in the early hours of this morning, around three o'clock, the body of Paul Travis age thirty-six was found on the steps of Port Sunlight war memorial. Someone had set about him with some kind of blunt instrument and cut his throat. The post-mortem will reveal more but, for once, this seems like an obvious attack. You can view the pictures at your leisure." He looked over to Vikki Chinn for more detail.

"Thanks, sir," she said, standing up. "Paul Travis lived at Central Avenue, Port Sunlight. CEO of a non-profit-making organisation, Pro-Vets, which found work for unemployed veterans in Merseyside, amongst other things..."

"War memorial... veterans... a connection you think, sir?" Kath said.

Blake nodded. "It's a possibility. Keep it in mind. Was he a veteran himself, Vikki? I'm guessing he might well be."

"Yes, sir, served in the Mercian Regiment until six years ago. When he left the army, he set up the Pro-Vets organisation with George Owens, another ex-army colleague."

"Domestic circumstances?" Blake asked.

"Married to Rachel Travis, they have a little

girl, Danielle," Vikki said, looking down. "Tasha Cook is Family Liaison Officer. They've broken the news and gleaned some preliminary information."

"The poor woman, little kiddie too," Blake said, with a sigh. "Any ideas what he was doing around the war memorial?"

"His wife said he'd been drinking at the Bridge Inn pub with three mates," Vikki said, checking her notes. "One of them, George Owens, who we mentioned before, a Dave Jones and a Barry Davies. We're in the process of trying to reach them."

"What does the manager of the Bridge Inn, say?" Blake said, "Did they all leave together?"

Kath put her hand up. "The manager knows Paul and his mates, he said they're semi-regular, pop in there every couple of weeks for a few pints. One of them, Barry Davies, had a few too many and was singing loudly. The manager wasn't particularly alarmed as Paul had already ordered a taxi for them."

"So they left in the taxi and Paul walked across the village alone," Blake said.

"It looks like it, sir," Kath said. "Although the manager didn't actually see them drive off. He gave me the names of a few regulars. I phoned them and two said they saw the friends getting into the taxi. Paul Travis set off alone down

Church Drive in the direction of the war memorial."

"Timing?"

Kath looked at her notes. "Eleven fifty or thereabouts."

"So, unless they zoomed round the corner and lay in wait for him, which seems highly unlikely, then they aren't suspects."

"Paul's wallet and phone were still on his body which rules out robbery as a motive," Vikki said.

"Unless the attacker was disturbed," Manikas chipped in.

Blake shook his head. "In the time it took to knock Travis out and cut his throat, the killer could have snatched his wallet from his pocket and run for it. Whoever did this was disturbed all right, Alex, but not in the way you mean."

"Mallachy O'Hare called a while ago, sir," Alex said. "Apparently, the sole print left in the blood matches a size 11 Bates Ultra-lite Tactical boot. As used by the British Army."

Blake raised his eyebrows. "Are they commonly worn outside the forces?"

"Dunno, sir. They're a hundred quid a pair. You can get them cheaper online but only about twenty quid less. I don't know if you're allowed to keep your boots when you leave the army?" He looked around the room, searching for anyone with recent service experience.

"Dress uniforms have to go back, Alex," DC Sue Wooton called from the back. "The rest you keep. I've got a ton of stuff up in my loft from my other half."

"Okay, Sue, thanks. That goes into the mix.," Blake said, rubbing his chin. "But keep an open mind, people. I don't want us to go bolting off down some weird army rabbit hole and missing something else because of it."

"We can check if any of his drinking mates have similar boots. It sounds like a possibility if they're ex-army, sir," Vikki said.

"True, Vikki. Has anything come from door-to-door?"

"Not much sir. Some people heard a disturbance around midnight, somebody running through the village but didn't see anything. There aren't that many houses that actually face onto the memorial and they're all some distance away."

"CCTV?" Blake said, hopefully but he already knew the answer.

"None, sir," Kath said. "No cameras there. Only one on the garden centre carpark and he didn't go near there."

"Okay, Vikki, Kath and Alex, you talk to Travis's drinking buddies. I'll pay a visit to Mrs Travis," Blake said, his heart sinking. "I want to get to the

24

bottom of this as quickly as possible."

*****

The Travis' house lay at the northern end of the village, not far from the Lady Lever Art Gallery. It was a large end terrace with a red tiled roof and white walls. Every house in Port Sunlight seemed slightly different to Blake, some of them looked small but the Travis' was one of the larger ones. Parking his car at the side of the road, he knocked on the bright green door and waited.

Tasha Cook answered the door, her thick, honey-coloured hair tied back. She looked drawn and, once again, Blake couldn't help but admire those who stayed with the bereaved, bridging that gap between family and the force. "You okay, Tasha?"

"Yes, sir. I think it's just sinking in with Rachel…"

"Mrs Travis?"

"That's right," Tasha said. "The little girl, Danielle is with her grandma."

"Any information?"

Tasha shook her head. "Nothing note-worthy yet. They seem like a normal, loving couple. Planning holidays, more kids, you know." She pulled the front door back and Blake stepped in. "She identified the photographs of the tattoos as being those of Paul Travis. I don't think she's able

25

to formally identify him. Just go gently, sir."

Blake raised an eyebrow at Tasha. She had been critical in the past and not afraid to respectfully point out that he could be like a bull in a china shop in his eagerness to solve a case. "I'll do my best."

The house was stylish and minimalist without being too clinical or cold. Whoever had decorated had an eye for design, mixing the traditional features of the house with modern wallpaper and paint colours. It looked lived-in, too, a child's bike in the hall and coats hanging on the banisters.

Rachel Travis was a small woman, in her early thirties, with shoulder-length blonde hair. She had an almond-shaped face and a short, snub nose that was currently rubbed red with tissues. Her cheeks were streaked with mascara. Blake wondered how she managed to do the simplest of tasks with nails as long as hers. She sat in a cream armchair, cradling a pile of tissues in her lap. An untouched cup of coffee stood on the parquet flooring.

"Rachel, this is Detective Chief Inspector Blake. He'll be leading the investigation into Paul's death."

Rachel stood up, smoothing her dark skirt down. "Forgive me. I must look a proper sight."

Blake gave a pained look. "No, no," Blake said,

trying to figure out what to say next. You look fine? Hardly. You okay considering your husband has just been murdered? Jeez! "Just... have a seat."

She folded back into the armchair, hugging herself. Blake settled on the edge of the sofa opposite her. "I'm so sorry for your loss," Blake said. The words always sounded hollow and he wished he could show he meant them. "This must be a terrible time for you."

Rachel looked up at Blake. "I've had better days," she said, her fleeting smile decaying into a sob.

Blake waited for her shaking to subside. "So, Rachel, I know you've been through this, but can you tell me when you last saw Paul."

"Early evening last night. He gave Danielle a bath, read her a bedtime story and headed out for the pub."

"And how did he seem? His mood, I mean..."

Rachel thought for a moment. "Just normal. Quite cheerful, I suppose. He pecked me on the cheek and said not to wait up. Oh God, those were his last words: don't wait up." She started sobbing again.

Blake glanced nervously over at Tasha. "Rachel, this is a difficult question to ask and it might be upsetting but, can you think of anyone who might want to hurt Paul?"

"No," Rachel said, looking at Blake in horror. "Who would want to do that? He was a kind, generous man, full of life. Everyone who met him loved him…"

"Could anyone have been jealous of that?"

Rachel looked perplexed as though she was trying to work out an impossible equation. "I honestly can't think of anyone who had a bad word to say about Paul. I mean, he had the odd difference of opinion with George about Pro-Vets…"

"This is George Owens?"

"Yeah but he'd never harm Paul…"

"Nobody is suggesting he would, Rachel, but we just need to get a full picture of Paul's background, his relationships, that kind of thing," Tasha said, eyeing Blake.

"What did he and Paul disagree about?" Blake asked.

Rachel smiled. "Paul was always wanting to go large, to grow the charity and help more people. George was just cautious, that's all. He wanted to keep things manageable. George kept an eye on the finances while Paul was more the front man. But they never fell out badly over anything, really."

"Can you think of anyone else, either in work or around here who might have any kind of grudge against Paul?" Blake said. "No matter how trivial."

Rachel Travis sat thinking for a while and for a second, Blake thought he'd lost her to some kind of miserable daydream but then she looked up at him. "A week ago, he had to have a word with some kids. Well, I say kids, they were teenagers and old enough to know better. It was last Saturday, I think. We were just taking Danielle around the village for a walk. They were sitting on the war memorial steps, drinking cans of lager. There was a can crushed and dropped on the ground."

"I imagine Paul wouldn't like that."

"No but he was sensible enough not to just go wading in and barking at them. He asked them politely if they knew what the memorial was for and asked them to respect it. One of the younger kids picked up the crushed can and the others started to go but one lad held back."

"He wasn't happy with Paul's intervention, then?"

"Paul tried to reason with him but the lad was drunk and gobby. He took a swing at Paul but ended up on his backside..."

"Did Paul hit him?"

"Not really. He kind of kicked the legs from under him and sat him on the floor. It was quite funny really. His little gang thought so, anyway.

Then Paul just leaned down and said something in the lad's ear. I dunno what, but the lad jumped up and ran away."

"Did the lad look frightened?"

"Yeah or maybe a bit shocked. I asked Paul what he'd said to him, but Paul just laughed. Anyway, I thought nothing of it until now. Do you think it might have been the kids who did it?"

"It's certainly something we'll investigate, Rachel. Did you overhear any names when the kids were talking to each other?"

"Only the big lad. They called him Bobby. I think he's local. I've seen him around the village a few times. He had a long face, a bit spotty and his hair was cut in a French crop."

Blake looked blankly at her.

"Sorry, I'm a hairdresser. It was short at the back and sides, very short and long on the top, combed forward, yeah?"

"That's great, Rachel," Tasha said, seeing Blake was still trying to work out what a French crop was. "Really useful."

"Yes," Blake said. A picture of Rachel and Paul, holding a little girl that must have been Danielle hung on the wall. Blake felt a pang of sympathy for the child. To lose a parent was bad enough but in such a violent manner would be hard to bear as she grew up.

"Do you know, I used to pray for him every night he was away with the army. Pray that he'd be safe from harm. Looks like he was safer over in Afghanistan than back here." She stopped crushing the tissues and looked up at Blake. "I should have kept praying, shouldn't I?"

"I'm so sorry, Mrs Travis, trust me, I won't rest until we find who killed your husband, Danielle's father. We'll get them, I promise."

Chapter 6

George Owens lived in a modest semi-detached house on Clifden Close, just off Kylemore Road in Oxton. The close was a small cul-de-sac of new buildings nestled amongst the large, red brick villas that typified this area. Even so, Vikki Chinn reckoned the house would be worth a bob or two. She sat in the car for a moment, wondering why she always eyed up property, estimating its value. Maybe it was because of her parents who were always nagging her to buy something bigger than her lovely flat close to the Anglican Cathedral in Liverpool. She was quite happy where she was, but she always felt this need to impress her parents. They'd never really been happy with her joining the police, but Vikki had a mind of her own.

Owens had sounded horrified at the news of Paul's death and had agreed to meet her without hesitation. She climbed out of the car and he appeared at the front door immediately. He was in his thirties, short and carrying a bit of weight. His hair was cropped, but he had let his brown beard grow long. His bulbous nose was red as were his eyes and Vikki guessed that he'd been crying.

"DS Vikki Chinn," Vikki said, showing him her warrant card. "Thank you for agreeing to see me, Mr Owens."

"Call me George," he said. "And how could I not agree? My God, it's awful what happened to Paul. He was my best friend." He paused, swallowing down a sob. "Anyway, come in, come in," he said brusquely to fight off the wave of grief. Vikki followed him into a cluttered front room, where two armchairs and a sofa covered in throws competed for floor space with a huge coffee table, a footrest and a drinks cabinet. Framed pictures covered the walls, photographs of various mountain views, some snowy, some green and verdant. There was one of George and a big man standing on the peak of a mountain. George noticed Vikki looking at them. "I fancy myself as a bit of a photographer," he said. "That and a love of the outdoors means I end up taking photographs of everything, everywhere I go!"

Vikki smiled and nodded. "If I can go through the events of last night, George, it's purely routine but there might be something that might shed some light on what has happened."

"Okay," Owens said, taking a deep breath. "We were in the Bridge Inn between eight and about half eleven, when they kicked us out. To be honest, Barry had started singing which is always a sure sign it's time to go, anyway." He gave a brief smile and then the weight returned to his face.

"And how would you describe Paul Travis' demeanour?"

"He was fine. We had a laugh. Put the world to rights. We were all in the forces at one time or another. We have a lot in common."

"Did you all drink a lot?"

"Depends on what you call a lot, doesn't it? We had a few pints but the worst that ever happens is Barry starts singing. It's quite comical really." He stopped and shook his head. "I guess we won't be boozing all together like that again, eh?"

Vikki gave George a moment to recover his composure. "And you left the Bridge Inn around half eleven?"

George twisted his fingers in his beard. "Yes. We said goodbye to Paul and we all piled into a taxi…"

"Do you know the name of the taxi service?"

"I can't remember, Thunderbird? Eastham Taxis? Anyway, he took us home, we asked for Barry to be dropped off first as he seemed the worst for wear…"

"And who was next?"

George thought a little more. "Me, I guess. It was late and I'd had a few. Yeah, it was me. I went to bed and woke up to the horrible news this morning."

"Any ideas who might want to hurt Paul?"

"Paul was loved by everyone. I can't think of

anyone who would even think badly of him. Honestly. His work with veterans, his giving nature, everything about him was…"

"Saintly?" Vikki suggested, looking unconvinced. "Look George, I know you might be worried about speaking ill of your friend but, in my experience, even the nicest person falls out with friends and has arguments. None of us are perfect."

"I suppose he could be a bit of a big head sometimes, if you interpreted it that way."

"Go on…"

"It's nothing, really but he could brag a bit. About Pro-Vets, about Rachel and his physical fitness. We all took it in good part…"

"But?"

"It's nothing," George said, looking tortured. "Really. It's all history and we're all mates, now…"

"George, you never know if something is pertinent to the case, believe me. If nothing else, it gives us a fuller picture of Paul's personality."

"Okay. Dave used to go out with Rachel when they were teenagers, that's all. He used to get a bit funny when Paul ribbed him about it. But it wasn't like he stole her away from him or anything. Rachel and Dave had been finished for years before she met Paul."

"I see," Vikki said scribbling in her notepad furiously.

"And we all kind of resented always having to go to the Bridge every fortnight. It sounds stupid, really, when you say it, but we always had to get the taxi while Paul sauntered across the street home. But Paul was like that. He called the shots and if you didn't like it, you could jog on."

"What about the charity?

George frowned. "What about it?"

"Didn't that cause any tensions between you? I mean, it's one thing to be old friends but workmates as well, that must bring its own stresses and tensions, surely."

"I suppose so," George admitted. "Barry and Dave have their own roles within the charity, so they're pretty much a law unto themselves. We have a weekly meet-up and air any problems but there's no blame when things do go wrong. We're army, we solve problems."

"You and Paul worked more closely together, though, didn't you?"

"Yes," George said, defensively. "Paul did a lot of the public work, 'front of house' we used to call it. You know, meeting potential donors, receiving big cheques and smiling for the camera…"

"While you worked backstage, unseen? That must be hard to stomach sometimes. Paul attending those lunches and slapping backs while you did all the paperwork."

George shook his head. "It wasn't like that. I prefer doing the backroom jobs and Paul always gave everyone their due. It was an equal partnership."

"Except, you've already said that Paul called the shots, even when it came to choosing a venue for a quiet pint."

"I told you it wasn't like that. I don't know why you're giving me the third degree. Look, can we do this some other time? I can't get my thoughts straight, right now. Paul was a great bloke, a good dad, good husband but one of the lads, too."

"Right," Vikki said, feeling that she had outstayed her welcome. "Here's my card. If you think of anything else, please don't hesitate to call me."

George licked his lips and looked at the card. "Thanks, I will." He followed Vikki to the door and she could feel his eyes on her as she drove off down the close.

*****

The Dell was a sunken garden, shrouded by rhododendrons behind the Lyceum Club and bowling green. It was a place where office workers escaped from the bustle of the Unilever complex just a stone's throw away. A footbridge went across the middle and, beneath it, Bobby Price leaned against the inner wall of the arch, glugging from a can of lager. He looked down at the two, younger lads who licked their lips at the prospect of a mouthful of ale.

"Gizza swig, Bob, go 'head," Alfie Lewis said.

Bobby pulled the can away from their questing fingers.

"Have you heard about that fella getting his head caved in up by the war memorial?" Harley Vickers, his mate said.

Alfie's eyes widened. "Yeah, I seen the bizzies and the ambulances and everything. There was blood and brains all over the steps. I seen it."

"Get stuffed. You didn't see nothing," Harley said, giving Alfie a shove. "They cleaned everything up didn't they? How would you have seen anything, you prick?"

Alfie looked at his trainers. "Just did didn't I?"

"That'll fuckin' teach 'im," Bobby said, slurring slightly.

"Teach who, Bob? What you on about?" Harley said. He wished they didn't have to hang around with Bobby Price. He was older than them for a start and Harley's big brother said he was a loser. I mean what right-minded seventeen-year-old hangs around with a bunch of kids still in school? But Alfie hero-worshipped Bobby and Alfie was Harley's best friend, so he went along with it. Besides, Bobby looked older and could get served at the off-licence which was a plus and more often than not, it was Bobby who sought them out, not the other way around.

Now Bobby Price looked grimly at them. "It was that fella from last week who had a go at us," he said. "It was him. He won't be pickin' on us anymore." He looked to his left at a baseball bat leaning against the wall.

Alfie Lewis's eyes widened. "Is that blood on it, Bobby? Where did you get that?"

"Where d'you think?"

"Oh my God, Bobby. What did you do?" Harley muttered.

Bobby took another swig from his can and wiped his mouth with his sleeve. "I'm not saying nothing."

"Fuckin' hell, he was a vet and everything. He fought in Afghanistan. You shouldna done that…" Harley said.

Bobby threw the drained can on the ground and grabbed Harley by his jacket. "Don't tell me what to do, you little shit. I didn't say I'd done anything did I? Anyway, keep your gob shut unless you want the same. Don't you breathe a fuckin' word to anyone…"

Chapter 7

If it hadn't been for Ian Youde, Blake was pretty sure he would have gone mad months ago. Or he would have had to have rehomed Charlie. In the past, Laura would have helped give Serafina her antibiotics, but Laura wasn't here. Blake had come back to his house in Rock Park on the banks of the Mersey to look in on the cat and Charlie, the Jack Russell, before heading back to the office but he'd found Ian at his front door.

"I was just going to check on that cat of yours," Ian said. "Now you're here, I'll take you up on that offer of a brew…"

Blake laughed. "You must be a mind reader, Ian, come on in. I'm parched, I've been on the go all day."

"Is your face all right?" Youde said. "The cat had a right go at you, didn't she?"

"Too right, mate," Blake said, touching the scab on his face. "Thanks for taking her to the vets, Ian, you saved my bacon. Was she okay for you?" He opened the front door and went inside.

"Good as gold," Youde said, following him in.

"You're kidding me."

"Honest! Not a peep out of her. Purring at the vet most of the time."

Blake shook his head. "Jeez. It's just me she's got

it in for, then..."

Youde grinned and scratched Charlie behind the ear while Blake filled the kettle. "You involved in that Port Sunlight attack? I wanted to go to the garden centre to get some chicken wire, but it was bedlam. A murder, wasn't it?"

Blake nodded. "Nasty business. I haven't seen such a mess in a long time."

"It'll have people up in arms. Murder on the war memorial. It's not right."

"No," Blake said, getting two mugs from the cupboard. "It isn't. Shows a distinct lack of respect. Mind you, I don't suppose it mattered to the poor sod who was killed there."

Youde grimaced and nodded. "True. Was there any significance in it being the war memorial?"

"I don't know. Weird place to ambush him if that's what happened. I mean, it's not like there's anywhere to conceal yourself up on the memorial..."

"Maybe he was waiting to confront your man," Ian said, sipping at the steaming mug Blake passed him.. "Have a word with him about something."

"The victim was a big lad, Ian, you'd want to get the drop on him if you were going to try and take him out. But yes, it's all possible. That's the trouble with this stage of an investigation; every-

41

thing is possible. It drives me mad. Speaking of which…" Serafina slid into the kitchen, tangling herself around Blake's ankles.

Blake crushed the antibiotics into her food and put the plate on the floor. Serafina gave it a sniff and then looked up, meowing pitifully. "I think she's rumbled you, Will," Ian laughed.

"I'll leave it a bit and see if she has it later. It's times like this when I miss Laura. She'd have some trick up her sleeve to get the pill down her throat."

Ian folded his arms. "The cat will eat when she's hungry."

"Don't count on it. I'm pretty sure Serafina's capable of a full-scale hunger strike if she felt aggrieved enough," Blake sighed. He downed the hot tea in a couple of gulps and dumped the mug in the sink. "Well, I'd better get back to it. You all right feeding this fella and taking him out for a walk?"

"Yeah," Ian said, ruffling the top of Charlie's head. "You get on."

Driving back, Blake rolled the various facts of the case around in his head. He was trying to avoid making assumptions, but he couldn't escape the feeling that Travis had been targeted. It didn't feel like a random killing. Not the way he'd been struck and then had his throat cut. It clearly wasn't robbery as the man's wallet and phone remained untouched. He decided to get another door-to-door organised focusing on the teenagers that Travis had encountered on the memorial. It was possible they jumped him, but surely there'd be more signs of a scuffle. More footprints. From what Blake had seen, Travis was felled with one blow and then someone got busy with the blade. Professional, then?

The lights in the roof of the tunnel flashed overhead as Blake drove almost on autopilot. His thoughts switched to Laura and he wondered where she was at that moment. He'd intended to go and find her but had been distracted by his sister's plight up in Scotland. She'd been accused of murder and he had to clear her name. Now, he was just waiting for the next opportunity to take time off to go and look for her. But she didn't want to be found. And Blake felt ill at ease with himself, wondering if searching was the right thing to do.

He sighed as the corner of the Liverpool World Museum came into view. "Focus on the case Blake. It's all you can do for now," he muttered at his reflection in the rear-view mirror. "Laura can look after herself, wherever she is."

*****

Harley Vickers' heart thumped against his ribs. He didn't want any part of this. Bobby Price was a psycho, there was no doubt in his mind as he sprinted down Wood Street towards the railway station. The red brick facade of the old Lever Brothers factory ran along on his left, hemming him in. He wished he'd gone into school and hadn't bunked off with Alfie. He should have known they'd end up with Bobby and that would end up in trouble.

Bobby had thrown down another can under the bridge in the Dell when an old man walking his dog had said something.

"Pick that up you messy bugger."

Bobby had scowled at him. "Fuck off."

The old man was fat and wore a hooded jacket that was a horrible snot-green colour. "Don't talk to me like that, you cheeky little streak of piss. I said pick that can up. It's bad enough having to put up with all your rowdiness in the evening without you leaving your cans lying all over the place..."

"You pick it up if you're so bothered," Bobby had said, giving Alfie a sidelong wink. Harley had felt himself shrivelling up inside as he watched Alfie grinning back at his hero.

"I'll call the police if you carry on like that," the man had said, rummaging in his coat pocket for his phone.

"Piss off, you interfering old codger," Bobby had snarled, snatching up the baseball bat. "Call them and I'll fucking leather you. Got it?"

"Bobby, don't," Harley said.

"Oh, Bobby is it? I'll remember that," the old man crowed, finally brandishing his phone. "I'm going to take some pictures of this. My grandson showed me how..."

He didn't finish the sentence because Bobby Price swung the bat, hitting the old man on the side of the head. Harley could still hear the sickening crack as it struck the old man and the strange sigh he let out. The phone spun off into the bushes and the old man crumpled to the floor, groaning.

"What the fuck did you do that for?" Harley had said, staring down at the old man.

"Nobody calls me a streak of piss," Bobby said, raising the bat again. Harley leapt forward before he could think about it and grabbed Bobby's arm.

"Don't you fucking idiot. You'll kill him."

Stars had exploded before Harley's eyes as Bobby backhanded him, sending him staggering back against the wall of the bridge. The old man groaned and started to pick himself up but this time, Bobby turned and ran, flinging the bat behind him, like he was running for first base. Harley and Alfie did likewise, Alfie following Bobby.

Harley had skidded to a halt and looked back at the old man and then took the opposite direction from the other two lads. That was it, he was going home. He'd had enough of Bobby and Alfie to last him a lifetime. In that moment, Harley decided he could see where Bobby Price was heading and Alfie, too and it wasn't a bright future. Harley decided he was going to stay away from them.

Now his feet pounded along the street alongside the factory wall. Up ahead, he could see the long roof and black and white timber cladding of the Gladstone Theatre. To its left, the ground became cobbled once more and ran into a dark alley running under the railway. He ran past the main front door of the factory, with its huge green clock and down into the darkness. That was it, he was free. He'd keep his head down and never have anything to do with either of those two losers again. He suddenly felt light and happy. Leaping over the metal railings that stopped cars using the passage under the bridge, he ran out into the road. A car blared its horn and Alfie threw himself back as the wing mirror whizzed a fraction of an inch from his head. He sat, panting on the pavement, watching the car vanish. It was then that reality hit him. He might choose to dump Bobby and Alfie, but they wouldn't leave him alone. Not after what he'd just witnessed. He'd never be free of them.

Chapter 8

If he could do anything about it, Blake avoided post-mortems at all costs. It wasn't that he was particularly squeamish, although watching a pathologist cut open a cadaver wasn't his idea of a morning's entertainment. Sometimes it was hard to attend because of the age or background of the victim. A child's PM lived with Blake for years after and he felt heavy-hearted today because he knew that Paul Travis was a loved and missed father. But the overriding reason he disliked going to post-mortems was the pathologist himself. Jack Kenning fancied himself as a rather dapper man with a rare line in dark humour. In reality, it was almost universally accepted that he was a dull man no matter how loud his bowtie or how 'edgy' his jokes.

Sitting there with Vikki Chinn in the post-mortem theatre, watching Jack Kenning perform grated on Blake more than he could say. Kenning had them right where he wanted them and there was nothing they could do but take notes. Fortunately, there was a viewing screen between the pathologist and Blake so the burly policeman could grumble to Vikki without being heard.

Blake shuddered, looking at Paul Travis' battered face as Kenning busied himself about the body. He muttered to his technician in what Blake decided was another language spoken only by pathologists as he only understood every fifth word. Vikki was hastily scribbling notes, leaving Blake wondering why he'd come along.

"Do you get half of what he's saying, Vikki? It's all gobbledegook to me."

Vikki gave him a big smile. "Most of it, sir. I'm editing out the 'humour' though."

"Ah, it's not just me then. I think that comment about Paul having large feet followed by a reference to American redwoods was some kind of sasquatch reference or something…"

Vikki smiled and looked appalled. "Spare a thought for the technician, sir. She has to work with him all the time."

Blake nodded. "It's a wonder we're not investigating *his* murder, Vikki. Imagine being subjected to that all day whilst being surrounded by so many sharp implements."

"Hello, what's this?" Kenning said over the intercom. He was prising Paul Travis' fingers open to get the object out so it wasn't really a source of surprise. He held it up so Blake could see but it was too far away. "It looks like a plastic figure, of a soldier. It's a toy soldier. Interesting," Kenning said. Blake gave Vikki another mutinous look as though he wanted to charge down there and ring Kenning's neck. He hated playing Kenning's little games.

He pressed the red button on the intercom that let him speak. "What's interesting, Jack?"

"Come on down and I'll tell you," Kenning said, raising a hand to indicate that he'd finished. Blake jumped up. "Right. Let's get this over with."

Kenning was washing his hands vigorously when they found him, just as you'd expect to see on a TV crime drama. The technician was watching him with a confused expression on his face. Blake rolled his eyes at Vikki. He imagined Kenning had been scrubbing his hands until Blake turned up. He also imagined that Kenning's next words would be...

"Ah, Blake. Bit of a rum do, eh?" Kenning shook the excess water off his chapped hands and looked around for a towel. The technician pointed at the paper towel dispenser as if to say, 'I'm not getting them for you.'

"So what did you conclude? Just the headlines if that's okay."

"Well, he was definitely dead," Kenning said, grinning.

"Right," Blake said, flatly. "Cause of death was..."

"Stiletto wound to the heart. Could hardly see the puncture wound..."

"Really?"

Kenning's face fell. "No, Blake. It was a joke..."

"Right. Could you give us some kind of warning if you're going to attempt humour, Jack, maybe an air horn or a klaxon or something?"

"Or just a sign, sir?" Vikki suggested.

Blake nodded in agreement. "Yes. Practical, Vikki. It could just say 'joke' on it."

Kenning pursed his lips. "And I suppose you're being funny now," he muttered, pulling on his tweed jacket. "Well, you can whistle. I'll send you the report and you can read it when it lands on your desk."

Blake held his hands up. "Sorry, Jack. My apologies. Just give us the headlines, then."

"As you've probably already surmised, he was knocked unconscious by a couple of hard blows to the head, then somebody slit his throat. It's a neat cut. Surgical almost."

"They knew what they were doing?"

"I'd say so. The average member of the public would make rather a hash of cutting someone's throat. Travis bled to death. Wouldn't have felt a thing, thank goodness for small mercies. Samples taken from the body at the scene suggest the blunt instrument used to bludgeon him was wooden and varnished. I'd say a cricket or baseball bat. It's more your area of expertise but I'd guess that whoever did this knew what they were doing. It wasn't a heat of the moment job."

"Any sign of a toxicology report yet?"

"Give them a chance, Blake," Kenning said, looking at his reflection as he adjusted his purple and pink bowtie. "Headlines from that are that he was drunk, but we haven't had any other information back yet."

"So nothing particularly new, then," Blake muttered. He hated to do it but Kenning was waiting for him to ask. "So what about the plastic soldier. Why did you say interesting?"

"You don't think it odd that a grown man should be holding a toy soldier as he walked back from a night out in the pub with his friends?"

"It is unusual but he could have been given it as a joke by one of his mates. He might have found it in the street and picked it up out of curiosity. It could be a lucky charm for him or something. There are any number of explanations."

"True but I've seen this before," Kenning said.

"What do you mean?"

"A heroin overdose about six months ago. Ince was his name. Found dead in his flat with a toy soldier in his hand. Seemed like a deliberate act. He left a note." Kenning put a hand to his chin. "He was an ex-serviceman too. Seems like quite a coincidence, Blake."

Blake nodded. "It does, Jack, I agree."

"These toys are commonplace, sir," Vikki said.

"Kids pick them up in packets from pound shops and as prizes in arcade games."

"Two soldiers found dead with toy soldiers in their hands, Vikki," Blake said, dubiously. "It's worth looking into, just to see if there's any kind of significance given to these toys, it could easily be just some sort of in-joke, we aren't party to."

"hardly a joke, Blake," Kenning added, "but I'd imagine that 'toy soldier' is something of an insult for any ex-serviceman."

"We'll check it out," Blake said. "But we have to keep an open mind. Was there any doubt as to whether the previous death was a suicide?"

Two spots of red bloomed on Kenning's gaunt face. "I can't remember the detail. Which would suggest it wasn't suspicious in any way or I'd recall it. It's worth having another look, though, don't you think?"

Blake was about to put Kenning straight on areas of responsibility in an investigation when his phone interrupted him. It was Kath Cryer. "Boss, just had notification that an old fella was attacked in Port Sunlight yesterday. He was a stone's throw from the war memorial and the attacker fled leaving a baseball bat behind. A very bloody one."

Chapter 9

Having driven from the Royal Liverpool straight to Arrowe Park Hospital, Blake began to feel that strange sense of weariness that comes with these places. Even though it was some time ago, his body still ached from the punishment he'd taken in Scotland. His ribs were healing slowly but there was something about hospital environments that sucked his energy. Whether it was the constant waiting for things to happen in these places that exhausted him, Blake didn't know but he stifled a yawn as he made his way to the assessment ward.

He always got lost in Arrowe Park and wondered who designed hospitals to be so confusing and badly signposted. Or maybe it was just him. A uniformed officer stood outside the ward and Blake felt some relief as he recognised PC Mark Robertson. He was a mature officer with a greying beard and he was a safe pair of hands. Robertson even saluted when Blake approached him.

"Sir," Robertson said. "Eric Smith, pensioner. Admitted last night with a serious head injury. Apparently, his dog came trotting out of the Dell in Port Sunlight, trailing its lead and arousing suspicion amongst passers-by. Some youngsters were seen running away from the Dell a few minutes earlier. I haven't spoken to him yet but the doctor has just said he's conscious and able to take some questions."

"Great, Mark, well done. What was the score on the baseball bat?"

"Bagged and tagged, sir. It was lying by the victim and had traces of dried blood on it. Just an old copper's instinct but thought it might have something to do with the memorial killing."

"Great work. Hopefully, forensics will tell us if it's the weapon used on Paul Travis or not. Shall we?" Blake said, gesturing towards Eric Smith's bed.

Eric Smith filled the bed, his big round, red face was wrapped in bandages. The right side of his face was a swollen mess of blue and purple. One eye was shut in a painful wink. He looked miserable.

"Mr Smith, my name is Detective Chief Inspector Blake and this is PC Mark Robertson. We'd like to ask you a few questions if you feel up to it."

"What about Toffee?" Eric said.

"Sorry?" Blake replied.

"Toffee is fine. She's with your daughter, Mr Smith, being well-looked after," PC Robertson said, he glanced at Blake. "Toffee is Mr Smith's dog."

"Ah, right," Blake said. "So, could you tell us what happened, Mr Smith?"

Eric Smith blinked and swallowed hard, wincing as he did. "Bloody kids these days," he said. "Boozing and making a racket. Back when I was a nipper, you lot would have been out on the beat. You'd have clocked this lot and given them a clip round the ear but no… you all swan around in your patrol cars, too scared to get out in case you upset some scally and take away his 'rights.' Makes me sick."

"It was a gang of teenagers who set about you, then?"

"Of course it was. They were boozing under the bridge in the Dell. Three of them there were, two little kids and a big ugly bugger. He was throwing cans all over the place."

"What time was this, Mr Smith," Blake said.

"About five o'clock. I always walk Toffee at that time. Anyway, this big lad threw a beer can on the ground and I told him to pick it up. He gave me a mouthful and I said I was going to take a photograph of him. My grandson showed me how to do it." His face softened and his good eye glistened. "He's a good lad. Works hard at school, plays footie with his mates at the weekend. He did a charity bag-pack at Sainsbury's the other day with the Air Cadets. You don't see him getting pissed in public and attacking helpless old men."

Blake shifted in his seat. "Your grandson

sounds like a credit to you, sir. Some kids don't have a role model like yourself to set them an example. You threatened to take a picture of the lads. How did they react?"

"How do you think? That was when the big one picked up the baseball bat and hit me with it. One of the other kids panicked then and tried to stop him. He called the big one Bobby…"

"Bobby," Blake repeated. "You're sure about that?"

"Yeah, why?"

"The name has cropped up before, that's all. Do you remember anything else about them?"

"One of the little lads was a carrot-top, the other was a blondie and Bobby was dark-haired, his was cut short round the sides and longer on the top…"

"A French crop," Blake said.

"What?"

"Apparently that's what it's called," Blake said, blushing. "So I've been told."

"Well I wouldn't know. He was an ugly bastard, that's all I know, spotty with a face like a slapped arse."

Blake gave Mark a knowing look. "PC Robertson will take a fuller description later but you may have to be a bit more specific than that, Mr Smith.

What happened next?"

"What do you think? The little get smacked me with the bat and I went down. Next thing I know I'm being loaded into an ambulance with a thumping headache. If I ever get hold of the…"

"We'll get him, Mr Smith, believe me. It's a miracle you weren't more seriously hurt. I promise you, we'll pick this lad up."

"Aye and then what? Tea and biscuits with a social worker? I'd have him flogged in public. Say what you like about these Arab countries but I reckon they've got the right idea when it comes to toerags like Bobby whoever he is."

Blake stood up. "I'll leave you in the capable hands of PC Robertson. We'll need to build up a fuller picture of this Bobby if you're happy to give a detailed description."

"I suppose so," Smith grumbled.

Blake left, anger boiling in his gut. Generally, he could ride the predictable rants from the older generation about not being tough enough on crime but to hear it from a victim sitting in a hospital bed was particularly dispiriting. He wasn't angry with Smith, to some extent he could see Smith's point of view. Often their hands were tied when it came to arresting youngsters and Blake was left wondering what hope these kids had of ever breaking out of a cycle of criminality. Beating them in public wasn't the answer but then, putting them on an endless merry-go-round of offending and reoffending didn't seem to help, either. This boy had been mentioned in the context of two very serious crimes. One way or another, Bobby had to be picked up.

*****

The Major Incident Room hummed with activity but it had a softer edge to it today. Kath Cryer, Alex Manikas and Vikki Chinn all crowded round a grinning DC Andrew Kinnear who held his phone for them all to see. "She's called Niamh. She's just under one but has had a difficult start in life. There's a possibility of some developmental issues but we can't be certain yet."

"She's gorgeous," Vikki cooed. "When do you get to meet her?"

"We've got more adoption training sessions but, hopefully, we'll meet her in the next couple of weeks. Chris is over the moon."

"It's just great that you can give her a loving family," Kath said. "Think how many kids we meet who have terrible home lives."

"What about beer, mate?" Alex Manikas said.

"I think she's a bit young for that. Probably warm milk and the odd biscuit…"

Manikas gave Kinnear a pained smile. "I mean what about us going out for a beer. It's all well and good giving her a lovely home but not if it completely destroys my social life!"

"You can make the coffee at the parent and toddler groups, Alex," Kinnear said, smirking. "You'll be a smash with all those yummy mummies."

Manikas crumpled up a piece of paper and threw it at Kinnear who dodged so it flew onward and landed at Blake's feet. They all turned to look at him and Blake suddenly felt like the schoolteacher who had rumbled a smoking circle behind the bike sheds.

"Congratulations, Andrew," Blake said, suddenly feeling awkward. There was so much going on in his head; the case, memories of his own daughter, how fleeting her life had been, his younger self with dreams of what she might do, they all crowded around his head, strangling off what he really wanted to say. And worse still was the 'understanding' nods from the team. They all knew about Ellie, his daughter; it was part of the 'Tragic Story of Will Blake.' He could see it written on their faces, sympathy, a sense of guilt that they'd brought it all up again in his presence. But the truth was, he wanted to celebrate with them. "A great thing you're doing there," he managed to say.

"Thanks sir," Kinnear said, with a flicker of a smile.

"Right. Turning to grimmer matters," Blake

said. "The post-mortem on Paul Travis confirmed what we already knew. He'd had a few pints and was beaten unconscious with a blunt object and then had his throat cut. It was a premeditated act as far as we can tell. A fw week before this, he'd had an altercation with a gang of teenagers, one of whom was called Bobby. Last night, Eric Smith, a pensioner from Port Sunlight, was attacked with a baseball bat by a gang of youths. The name 'Bobby' cropped up again. The bat was abandoned at the scene of the crime. Vikki, any news on that?"

Vikki consulted her notes. "Given the circumstances, it was fast-tracked today and it seems as though there are traces of Paul Travis's blood on it and some bone embedded in the wood." A few officers winced and shook their heads. "There are also traces of Mr Smith's blood and DNA from another, unknown, person."

"Probably Bobby unless he was wearing gloves," Alex said.

"Possibly," Blake said. "But it looks like we have the murder weapon. Kath, Alex and Andrew, can you coordinate the search for this Bobby? I want door-to-door and ask at local schools and colleges too."

"What about Jack Kenning's concerns, sir?" Vikki said.

Blake paused, running his fingers through his

hair. "So that you're all aware, Kenning discovered a plastic toy soldier in Paul Travis' grip."

"Do you think it's significant, sir?" Kinnear said. "I mean it seems a bit odd, don't you think?"

Alex nodded in agreement. "Soldier killed on a war memorial clutching a toy soldier. Add the boot print and it's all kind of strange."

"When you put it like that, Alex, yes, it does. But there are a number of reasons why Travis could have been holding that toy. It could have been given to him as a joke, he could have just found it..."

"All the same, sir," Alex said. "You have to admit, there's a kind of... I don't know... theme building up here."

"I'm not denying there might be something in it, Alex, which is why I'm asking Vikki to review the circumstances surrounding the suicide of Richard Ince, who was found with a similar plastic soldier in his hand six months ago."

"Really?" Alex said.

"Oi!" Vikki snapped, giving him a playful jab with her finger. "Don't you think I'm up to it?"

"N-no, Sarge," Alex stammered, "I mean yes. I mean, another man has been found dead with a toy soldier in his hand? That's weird..."

"Weirder things happen, Alex. If you look for a connection, there's a danger you'll make one that isn't really there. Let's be open-minded but look for actual evidence of any kind of link, right? Oh and we keep this detail to ourselves. Nobody else knows about the toy soldier, so it could be useful during interviews. What else have we got?"

Vikki looked at her notes. "Pretty much as we expected, sir. I spoke to George Owens and he confirmed that he and Dave Jones took Barry Davies home in a taxi. Davies was a bit the worse for wear."

"Nope," Kath Cryer said. "The first bit was right. Barry was pissed and he wasn't a pretty sight today when I interviewed him. George Owens wasn't in the taxi, though."

"You're certain, Kath?" Blake said. "Alex, what did Jones say?"

Manikas checked his notes. "He said that Owens got the train."

"'Like he always does,' were Barry Davies' exact words," Kath added.

"He was quite specific that he got into the taxi with the others, he even said he got out after Barry." Vikki said. "He became quite edgy when I started asking him about his relationship with Paul, too."

Kinnear looked at the map. "If he walked to the station, he'd be going in the same direction as Travis at least part of the way. He could easily have diverted off, run ahead. Shall we call him in, sir?"

"No," Blake said, rubbing his chin. "I'll go and have a word with him, tomorrow at Pro-Vets. I want to see this charity of theirs, find out a bit more about that. Then I might get a better idea why Mr Owens lied to us about where he went on the night his friend was murdered."

Chapter 10

Some things seem like a great idea when you start, but the longer you spend on them, the less appealing they become. This was what Jeff Blake thought as he watched Josh Gambles shuffle into the visiting room, flanked by two prison guards. He was a young man with a scruffy black beard and glittering dark eyes. His pointed features made him seem like he was mocking Jeff and the guards and anyone else he encountered. Maybe he was.

Josh Gambles was a serial killer and Jeff, for his sins, was his biographer. Gambles had an obsession with Jeff's brother, Will, and the Searchlight programme. He claimed that he had only committed the terrible murders to make Will Blake famous and it had, for a couple of weeks. Jeff's own star as a novelist was waning fast and, when Gambles had invited him to write his biography, Jeff had jumped at the chance.

The agreement to write for the serial killer had angered Will and put their already creaking relationship under even more strain. At first, Jeff dismissed Will's objections as morally pedestrian, but as time went on, he realised just how manipulative Gambles could be; dangerous, too. Even though he was locked up in prison, he had a number of twisted followers and old friends only too keen to gather information for him and keep him informed of what was going on in the outside world. Even as he settled himself in the chair opposite, Jeff could tell that Gambles had some news to impart, another game to play that would turn the screw on Will and make his life even more uncomfortable. Jeff often wondered if Gambles actually wanted his biography to be completed or if he just kept his regular meetings as a means to get at Will.

"Good afternoon, Jeffrey, I trust you're well?" Gambles said an eager light in his eye. Much of the psychopath's genius was imagined and his pompous greeting gave that away, Jeff thought.

"Fine, Josh, you look excited. Like you've got some news to share with me."

Gambles' face fell. "Really? Oh. I may have," he said, his eyes sliding right and left as though checking for anyone listening. Nobody was, and Jeff was beginning to wonder just how long the killer's currency would last outside prison. His infamy was still fresh at the moment but, from what Jeff could tell, his outrages hadn't really caught the public imagination in the way the Yorkshire Ripper or some of the American serial killers had.

This weekly ritual of meeting up, Gambles relating some anecdote of his and Jeff dutifully writing down had become old very quickly. Gambles refused to talk about either his family life or the killings that had put him behind bars.

Writing up his notes at home, much of what Gambles told him was unpleasant but mundane. His early life in care, his misdemeanours in school, being put into secure units, none of it shone, whichever way Gambles presented it and Jeff polished it. The story came over as a litany of grievances made by a petulant monster against largely dull and petty people. Whenever Jeff did touch on something interesting such as family life or possible abuse at home, Gambles shut down. He didn't want to be the flawed monster to be pitied, he wanted to be the evil mastermind to be feared.

Jeff sighed and got his pen and pad out. "Well, you can tell me now, or you don't have to tell me anything. Sooner or later you'll spill the beans. You can't help yourself…"

"Can't I?" Gambles steepled his fingers, as he always did, in a ridiculous 'Bond villain' manner.

Jeff began to wonder if taking another tack with Gambles might be interesting. Sliding his pen back into his jacket pocket, he shook his head. "I've had enough of this," he muttered and closed his notepad. "I'm off."

Gambles eyes widened. "Wh-what are you doing?"

"I'm going home. This is a waste of time. I could get more information on you by interviewing members of your family…"

"No."

"There are probably journalists doing that right now, if they haven't done so already. Plastering all the gory details over the weekend papers. The time you wet your pants in school, what your first pet was called. What an odd little boy you were… all of it. And I have to sit here watching you doing your impression of Dr Evil, every fucking week, writing down some pearl of half-baked internet wisdom you've thought up in that addled mind of yours. I'm sick of it. Even if your impending trial picks up the public interest, this book with be as dull as ditch water and less appetising. Goodbye, Josh." Jeff stood up and extended his hand.

Gambles just stared at the hand, making Jeff wonder if he should pull it away before it was bitten. "Smidge."

"What?"

"My first pet was called Smidge. He was a rabbit," Josh said, staring off into some distant past hell. For the first time in Jeff's short working relationship with Gambles, he saw the real human being underneath all the bravado and showmanship. He saw a vulnerable little boy, tossed around on a sea of upheaval and cruelty.

"What was he like?"

"Small, black and white. My dad came home with him from the pub and threw him in my lap. I kept him in my bedroom."

"What happened to him?" Jeff hated to ask. He didn't imagine much good would come of being looked after by a psychopath like Gambles. Many serial killers were reported to have been cruel to animals during their childhoods and Jeff couldn't see why Gambles would be any different.

"Dunno," Gambles said, glumly. "He just disappeared one day while I was at school. Dad kept making jokes about having stew for tea. I didn't eat for weeks."

"I see," Jeff said, sitting down and slowly getting his pen out. "You were upset."

Tears glittered in Gambles' eyes. "Of course I was upset. Wouldn't you be? That rabbit was my only friend. I fed it and nurtured it. From the day he vanished, I swore I'd never be tricked like that again..."

"Tricked?"

"Into feeling affection for something or someone. That was a watershed moment for me, Jeffrey. That was when I shut down."

"I see," Jeff looked hard at Gambles. Was he serious? It was hard to tell, sometimes. It had started off quite genuine but now was rapidly sliding into the melodramatic. Jeff wondered if some other fate had befallen poor Smidge all those years ago. Perhaps he would investigate further and actually seek out Gambles' family. "What do you mean by shut down?"

"It was like a short-circuit in my emotions. I became numb. After that, I could hurt anyone or anything and not feel anything. No remorse, no pity just nothing."

"And you believe the incident with your pet rabbit was the trigger for all of this?"

"I know it for sure." The light returned to Gambles' eyes. "Just like I know other things, Jeffrey."

"I'm warning you, Josh, I'm not going to continue coming here if you're just going to play silly games. Now let's talk more about this early memory. This is what readers want."

But the old Gambles was back. "Don't readers want a romance, Jeffrey? A lovelorn hero, a handsome bad boy and a whore with a heart of gold? Isn't that what readers want?"

"You've lost me."

"She's back."

Jeff shook his head. "Nope. You're talking in riddles again. Who's back?"

Gambles flared his nostrils and widened his eyes. "The girlfriend…"

"Laura Vexley? Will's girlfriend? When?"

"I thought you didn't want to know. Ah well, Jeffrey, it's been nice talking to you but I'm feeling too tired to carry on. See you next week?"

"Come on, Josh, tell me. When did she come back?"

"Guards!" Josh called. Jeff watched, fuming, as they escorted the killer back to his cell. What was he going to tell Will?

*****

Rock Lodge lay in darkness when Blake finally reached home that night. It was late and he felt every aching muscle as he climbed out of his car, his feet crunching on the white gravel. The lights of Liverpool's suburbs twinkled on the black waters of the River Mersey. The house had belonged to his parents and Blake had planned to sell up and move when Laura was with him. It was only two or three miles south of the Birkenhead Tunnel. Here, the A41 widened into a dual carriageway, hemming in the old Victorian villas of Rock Park against the banks of the Mersey. It also cut them off from the estates of New Ferry and Rock Ferry and gave it a shabby, but strangely exclusive feeling.

Blake's house was small in comparison to some of the big properties in the area. His house had once been a gate house for a bigger property that had since been demolished. It had four bedrooms and an overgrown garden. The thick bushes around the tiny lawn meant that you'd easily miss it if you hurried past. But its relatively small size gave it a certain charm, given that it still boasted the ornate brickwork and tiling in the hall of the other, grander properties. To Blake, it was beginning to feel like a trap again.

For a brief few months, Laura had breathed new life into this place and into Blake himself. She'd woken him up from a nightmare and given him some hope. They'd started making plans and thinking about the future. Then she'd vanished, fleeing from her brutal ex-husband Kyle Quinlan. But Blake hadn't slipped back into his old lethargy. His first instinct was to go after her but lately, he'd wondered at the wisdom of this. She was a grown up and her own person, after all. Blake wondered if his instinct to go after her was partly the same need for control that drove him to solve crimes. In a work context, it was valuable but in his relationship with Laura, it had caused them to clash. Laura was a free spirit and sometimes, Blake hadn't taken account of that.

Blake let himself into the house and switched the light on in the hall. Charlie came bounding up to greet him. Youde had texted earlier to say he'd taken the dog out for a walk and Blake suspected that he'd been out for most of the day. Serafina lay curled up on his armchair. He checked in the kitchen, her bowl was empty and he just hoped that meant she had eaten her food and the antibiotics. It was just as possible that Charlie had helped her out but Youde would have watched out for that.

Blake scanned the fridge for anything edible and found a lump of cheese and some ham that was only three days past its use-by date. His bread was a bit mouldy but he picked the worst of it off and rustled up some cheese and ham on toast. "Hardly health food," he muttered to Charlie who watched intently for anything that might drop on the floor.

The little dog turned his head to the hall and gave a brief 'yip.'

"What is it, boy?" Rising from his seat, Blake followed Charlie who had scurried out to the front door and was scratching at it. He let him out and watched as Charlie bounded into the front garden barking into the dark lane beyond the bushes.

A dark BMW sat at the entrance to Blake's drive, its engine idling. The moment he stepped towards it, the car pulled away and drove off. Charlie gave a final yelp and started sniffing the ground. A wave of disquiet swept over Blake. Rock Park was something of a dead end and not a place you drove through. Sandwiched between the river and the A41, it was a destination and hardly anyone came here at night unless they were visiting. Or keeping an eye on someone. Blake was pretty sure it was the latter and he had an idea who it was.

Chapter 11

Sun streamed through Blake's bedroom curtains. His alarm clock bleeped frantically for the fourth time, this time loud and insistent, as though annoyed at having been ignored the last three times. Blake pushed an arm from under the duvet and jabbed an equally indignant finger at the clock. He leaned out and squinted at it. Then his eyes widened.

"Shit, shit, shit." He was meant to be meeting George Owens in fifteen minutes. Leaping out of bed, he grabbed a shirt off a nearby chair and re-coiled from it. "Jeez, smells like a dead otter."

He thundered down the stairs, two at a time and scrambled through the pile of shirts awaiting the attention of his iron. They all looked like unwanted betting slips, crumpled into a ball and dumped. Hissing with frustration, Blake grabbed the nearest and tried to smooth it out. Charlie bounced up and down around Blake barking excitedly at this new running-around-the-house game. Serafina wound herself around Blake's ankles just as he set off, sending him tumbling out into the hall with a yell.

"Right, Blake. Stop. Slow down," he muttered to himself. "Feed the cat and dog. Antibiotics. Phone ahead and tell them you're going to be late…"

As it turned out, Blake was only a few minutes late. Even with the rush hour traffic, it was ten minutes' drive from Blake's house. Pro-Vets head-quarters was an industrial unit down by the Birkenhead docklands. It looked like a large hangar in grey and blue with a few windows and a door in the front. He pulled up outside the main office, but at the side, he could see a larger opening with people carrying food parcels from a van and taking them inside. There was the sound of hammering and construction, too. The whole place was a hive of industry.

Blake pushed the office door open and stepped into the main reception where a smartly dressed young woman sat behind a counter. It was a small space, bordering on cramped. A few chairs stood in a line to the left of the door he had just entered by and a staircase ran up beside the counter to a second floor. A door at the bottom of the stairs led into the warehouse area, Blake presumed. The woman smiled at him, but Blake could tell her heart wasn't in it. Clearly the news about Paul Travis had filtered through the work-force and he was missed. "Welcome to Pro-Vets. How can I help you?"

Blake produced his warrant card. "DCI Will Blake, Merseyside Police. I have an appointment with…"

"DCI Blake," George Owens said from the stairs beside the counter. He was a stocky man with cropped brown hair and a straggly beard. He'd clearly relaxed his exercise regime since leaving the forces. "It's okay, Chloe, I'm expecting him. Would you like a quick tour, Inspector? It'll give you an idea of what we do and the legacy that Paul leaves behind. We made a decision not to halt business but to keep it going in his memory. It's what he would have wanted."

Blake nodded. "That would be great, thank you." He wanted to get an idea of what it was that Paul did, anyway and a tour would give him useful background.

"This way," Jones said, leading Blake through the door into the warehouse area. "So, upstairs, we have offices, we can have a chat there in a minute but through here are the food bank and workshops."

They stood in a large warehouse with a high ceiling. Tables laden with different kinds of food, packets, tins, dessert, savoury products, and a table for fresh produce. A small army of people hurried around, filling bags and boxes. "You've caught us at a busy time, we're getting ready for the rush."

"This can't all be for people who were in the forces, surely."

"No. Our aim is to provide useful roles and positions for ex-servicemen and women who might have fallen on hard times or are in need. The food bank is for anyone who needs it. There's Dave Jones supervising the sorting. I think Barry is out on a delivery."

They walked over to Jones who stood giving directions to a big man with a blank face. "Put these with the other cans, Terry, okay?"

Terry looked blankly for a moment then nodded. "Yes." He picked up the box and marched over to the table. Blake noticed a pale scar across the back of his head, barely covered by the baseball cap he wore. Dave shook his head.

"Dave, this is DCI Blake. I don't need to tell you why he's here. Problem, Dave?" George Owens said, looking concerned.

Jones laughed. "Nah. Just Whitey, there, God love him. He seems to be getting worse at following directions." Jones' smile faded. "Looked at me blankly when I asked him if he'd had a good weekend. I do think he needs more help."

"We'll have a chat with him and Nicola. Maybe we need to find something else for him to do," George muttered. He turned to Blake. "Not breaking any confidences, Inspector but some of our vets have very specific difficulties. The TV programmes might show you the guys who have lost a limb charging around a basketball court in a wheelchair, but you don't always see the Terries of this world. Acquired Brain Injury from an improvised explosive device. Changed his personality. Difficult man but we wouldn't turn our back on him."

Blake nodded. "That's admirable. This must cost a fortune to run all this support..."

"It's a constant headache," Owens agreed, walking across the cavernous space. "We have all kinds of charitable events and I spend most of my time searching for grants or preparing bids for them." He opened another door and Blake found himself in a busy workshop where circular saws whined, and the sound of hammering battered at his ears. Work benches filled this room and people leaned over them, making and cutting. "Here we make garden furniture, birdboxes, anything we can sell, really and our clients learn business skills as well as a practical trade."

"It seems like quite a set-up," Blake said. "And all this was Paul's vision?"

"And mine," Owens said, a little defensively. "We left the army six years ago and set up with a grant. We built it from there. Paul's mother died, leaving some money which he ploughed into Pro-Vets. Everything we earn goes back into the business."

"And you take a wage, I presume," Blake said.

"A modest one and the supervisors do too. We have to live, Inspector..."

Blake held his hands up. "It wasn't a criticism.

You provide a valuable service. I can see that and as you say, without a wage, you couldn't do it."

Owens smiled. "I'm glad you feel that way. There are some who don't. Usually, people who don't volunteer themselves. I'm not sure how they expect things to get done. I'll take you back up to the offices. We have some counselling suites up there that get quite a lot of use…"

"It's a proper wrap-around service then?" Blake said as they headed across the warehouse and back upstairs.

"We do socials too, outdoor pursuits weekends, family respite breaks, all kinds of things. I sometimes think we're too thinly spread but Paul, well, he wanted to do everything."

"Did that cause tension between you?" Blake said as they entered an office with two desks that, again, felt cramped. A huge rump covered in rather stretched brown fabric stuck out from under one of the desks.

"Quentin, what are you doing?" George said, stepping over the man's legs to get to his own desk.

Quentin reversed himself, bumping into Blake's legs as he tried to manoeuvre into a standing position. He was a large man with a mop of unruly brown hair, a straggly chin beard and horn-rimmed glasses. His face was red, and he looked sweaty and flustered.

"Sorry... sorry... I was just fixing a cable on Paul's computer. H-he complained about it last week and I was going to get it fixed but... so I..." Quentin's voice faded to silence. "Don't suppose I need to now," he said, bluntly.

"Probably not, Quentin," George said. "Inspector Will Blake, this is Quentin Ufford, our Accountant and IT technician. He keeps the books straight and fixes all the glitches in our hardware and software ..."

"Will Blake," Quentin said, grinning. "Tyger, tyger burning bright..."

Blake gave a brief, pained smile. "That's right. Carry on." If he had a quid for every time someone had quoted poetry at him, he'd never have to work again.

Ufford's face fell. "I don't really know any more. I was just making a joke... Your name... you know... it's..."

"Also the name of a famous poet," Blake said. "I know that, Mr Ufford. My English teachers used to love reminding me. I felt obliged to smile then."

"Right. Sorry. I'll just..." Ufford bustled out of the room, shutting the door noisily behind him.

"Sorry about that," George Owens said, wincing. "He's a good lad. Paul hired him as an accountant a few months ago. But he proved to be a whizz on computers too. He really does keep this place running. It's all computers these days."

"Paul sat here," Blake said, looking at a photograph of Rachel and Danielle on the desk Quentin had been rummaging underneath.

Owens nodded and gave a tight smile. "He did. I haven't touched anything yet. Plenty of time for that." The stocky man sat down at his desk and indicated that Blake should take the seat that leaned against the wall. It looked small and rickety, but he lowered himself onto it. "In answer to your question, Inspector, Paul and I did have our differences about the direction of the service, but we always resolved them amicably."

"I see," Blake said. "You said before that the only waged people on the team were the supervisors. Who are they?"

"Myself, Paul, obviously. Then Dave Jones, he supervises the foodbank and Barry supervises the deliveries and collections. Nicola Norton is a part time psychologist who does our counselling, and we pay her by the session. Sasha Hughes is our receptionist. Quentin gets a wage. Everyone else is a volunteer."

"So the majority of people who are paid by Pro-Vets were out at the Bridge Inn the night Paul was killed."

"They were," Owens said, nodding sadly. "If only we'd persuaded Paul to take a taxi with us.

Things would have turned out differently."

"It's funny you should say that, Mr Owens," Blake said. "Because I wanted to explore something in a little more detail. My team interviewed Mr Davies and Mr Jones and they both said that you didn't take the taxi but that you walked to get the train, and apparently this is a common occurrence. Would you mind explaining?"

*****

Detective Sergeant Vikki Chinn had commandeered one of the meeting rooms so that she could spread the files regarding the death of Richard Ince across the tables. Although she could understand why Blake had wanted to keep an open mind, she shared Manikas' feeling that it was more than just odd. Kenning was a pain in the arse but that didn't mean that he was wrong every time.

She frowned at the photograph of Richard Ince. He was a big man with a flat boxer's nose and a gentle smile. She the thought she could see a sadness in his eyes. Vikki thought he looked familiar somehow, but she couldn't think why.

Alex Manikas appeared at the door. "Mind if I come in, Sarge?"

"Of course, aren't you phoning schools asking if they have a pupil called Bobby?" Vikki said, grinning. She liked Manikas, not just because he was easy on the eye with his dark, brooding Mediterranean looks but he was quiet and thoughtful. He was a good copper too.

Alex rolled his eyes. "Kath and Andrew are out on that gig at the moment. I'm coordinating door-to-door. Just thought I'd look in before I went. Have you found anything?"

"Just started, really. Nothing remarkable yet. Richard Ince aged thirty-five, worked in a local Asda, happy-go-lucky guy on the face of it. Found dead in the bath. He'd been drinking heavily that night, but it was an overdose of heroin that killed him. He left a suicide note. The only link I've found with Travis apart from the toy soldier in his hand is that he went to Pro-Vets for counselling."

"So he must have been having mental health problems, then, Sarge" Alex conceded. "Who was the counsellor?"

Vikki flicked through the file. "Nicola Norton. She made a statement to say that Ince was depressed and having flashbacks from his time in Afghanistan. He had been to the doctor for anti-depressants but hadn't talked about harming himself. She adds that it saddened her to hear the news but didn't surprise her."

"Any sightings before he killed himself?"

"He was drinking heavily with someone in the local pub. According to the notes, regulars thought he was an old army pal, but they'd never seen him before. There's no description but I get the impression that it was seen as an open and shut case. No evidence of a struggle, history of mental health problems and excessive drinking. A hint from a professional that he might have been heading that way." Vikki shrugged.

"Worth talking to this Nicola Norton, though, eh, Sarge?"

Vikki thought for a second. "Yeah. It is."

Chapter 12

George Owens didn't look particularly surprised. He just sat back in his chair and sighed a little as though irritated at being caught out so quickly. "I didn't get in the taxi that night, but I didn't kill Paul. I wouldn't. He was my friend…"

"Would it surprise you to learn that a lot of murders are committed by friends, Mr Owens?" Blake said. "It looks very suspicious, to be perfectly honest. You were one of the last people to see Paul Travis alive and you've lied about where you were on the night in question."

Owens held up a hand. "Yes, yes I know but it's not what you think…"

"Tell me what it is exactly, then," Blake said. "It better be good; perverting the course of justice is a serious offence."

"I can't. Look, I went up Bolton Road and got the train. I never meant to hinder the investigation. It makes no difference."

"It makes a huge difference, Mr Owens, why do that when there's a taxi already waiting to take you home?"

"I don't know," Owens said, reddening and looking at the desk. "Maybe I just didn't like the idea of sharing a taxi with Barry. He was going to be sick. I was sure of it."

"I'm sorry, Mr Owens, but why lie about it?"

"Because I knew if I said that, it would get back to the others and I didn't want to upset Barry." Owens looked up at Blake.

"Really? Your best friend is brutally murdered and the first thing you think about is not hurting Barry Davies' feelings?"

"Please," Owens said pressing his hands on the desktop and leaning forward. "Yes. Well, no. I just didn't want there to be any ill will between us at this difficult time…"

"I'm sorry, Mr Owens, but that sounds like a feeble excuse. Firstly, they told me that you were in the habit of walking up to get the train. Surely they would have questioned why you did that."

A hopeful look spread across Owens' face. "If you know that I never get a taxi with the others, then you know that I was walking up to get a train." Blake wondered if Owens ever played poker. He hoped not. The man would have given his hand away in seconds.

"If you had told me where you went in the first place, then I might have been less suspicious. But if you walked up Bolton Road, you could easily have diverted and met Paul at the memorial. The fact that you lied to me doesn't make any of this look good for you."

"I just caught a train."

"We can talk about that later, along with asking staff for that night if they saw you, looking at CCTV at the station and appealing to the public for any witnesses to the fact you were where you say you were. Right now, I need you to accompany me to the station and provide a DNA sample, so we can check the murder weapon and the body for any traces."

"You've found the murder weapon?" Owens said, going pale.

"We think so, yes. We're following a number of lines of enquiry," Blake leaned forward. "Now, come with me and if you tell me you're busy, I'll arrest you for obstruction and perverting the course of justice, right?"

*****

Although History was probably the only lesson Harley Vickers was allowed to attend, he couldn't concentrate today. There was too much going on. Whispers in the corridor about Bobby Price and Alfie. People laughing or scowling at him.

Normally, he'd be hanging on Mr Lowry's every word. The History teacher had a way of bringing the past to life that Harley loved, and he didn't patronise or try to threaten Harley like other teachers did. Most lessons went badly for Harley, he'd say something or someone would say something to him, then the teacher would get involved and it was Harley who got sent to the Remove Room. Then, because he'd missed the last lesson, he'd be confused about where he was up to and get into trouble for not knowing things that he'd never been taught. It was a vicious circle, and the Remove Room had a revolving door.

Mr Lowry was different. Maybe it was because he was older. Some of the younger teachers seemed to have decided that Harley was a troublemaker as soon as they met him; before if they'd been told what a nuisance he was by other teachers. They saw him as a threat to good order that had to be neutralised immediately. Harley suspected that some of the younger teachers were a bit frightened of him, too. He could see it in their eyes. To them, he was like an unexploded bomb just waiting to go off, so they may as well just cut the red wire and be done with it. There was none of that with Mr Lowry. The first thing Mr Lowry had done was ask after Harley's dad. Apparently, Mr Lowry had taught him way back. He told Harley that his dad was a gifted student and he made a bet with Harley that he would be too. That wasn't to say that Harley had never had trouble in Mr Lowry's class, but he was always fair and even-handed and Harley respected that. Today was different, though. Today there was a distraction outside.

They had all piled into the classroom and Mr Lowry had given one of his weary, disappointed looks that meant that they all had to go back out and come in sensibly. Barely a word was said but they knew the drill. They'd all lined up outside the classroom and come in quietly. There was some argument between Pavel and Dominick about who sat where but Mr Lowry's brow furrowed slightly, and the two boys settled their differences quickly enough.

Harley had really enjoyed the first part of the lesson, Mr Lowry had told them the story of Arch-Duke Franz Ferdinand getting blown up and made a joke about a pop group who had the same name but nobody had heard of them so it didn't work. He'd made this kind of chain puzzle that linked the events to the start of the First World War.

"It's a bit like gangs, isn't it, sir?" Harley said.

Mr Lowry folded his arms and leaned on the desk, looking quizzically at him. "How do you mean, Harley?"

"Well, like, if my lads said they'd watch out for Dominick's chair and then Pavel took it, so we waded in…"

"I'd give you a fat lip, you skinny whelp!" Pavel always came up with these weird insults.

"He's just using you as an example, Pavel…"

"I'll make an example of him, sir."

"And if you do, I'll have to refer you to the Remove Room, won't I?"

"That's escalation, sir," Harley said, breaking the tension.

"Brilliant, Harley. It is. One comment led to a threat which led to an intervention. Not quite how the First World war got started but a good demonstration of how things get out of hand. It could have got nasty but you're both civilised gentlemen, right?"

Harley grinned and Pavel pulled a face that made everyone laugh. For the first time since Harley had seen the old man knocked down, he felt okay. Until Dominic spoke up. "Is that one of your lads out there, Harley?"

Mr Lowry's room looked out onto the front of the school and there was Price, hanging around the perimeter fence.

"Is that Bobby Price?" Mr Lowry said, squinting through the dirty window.

"Yes, sir," someone said. "He's waiting for Harley."

"No he isn't. Shut up," Harley snapped, slumping down in his chair.

"Someone told me he's after Harley," a girl at the back said in a quiet voice.

Harley turned round in his chair. "He's after your ma, you stupid cow."

"Okay, Harley, steady now," Mr Lowry said. "Let's not spoil things. I'll ring the office and see if a member of staff is free to go and have a word with Bobby. A lad his age shouldn't be hanging around the school gates."

Mr Lowry disappeared through the door that led into the faculty office and the phone. Dominic leaned back in his chair and whispered to the girl who had shouted out before. "Bobby killed that guy; you know, the soldier on the war memorial on Port Sunlight. He's a psycho…"

"Who told you that?" Harley said, scowling at Dominic.

"Everyone knows. Is it true?"

Harley groaned. Bloody Alfie Lewis had been blabbering about it. "No. It isn't. Bobby's probably heard that you've been spreading rumours about him and has come to do you in."

"Do you in more like," Pavel said. "I heard you grassed him up."

"Cheeky bastard!" Harley yelled and launched himself across the classroom, grabbing Pavel by the throat.

Mr Lowry appeared at the door. "Woah! What's going on here?"

But Harley couldn't hear him. All he could see was Pavel's jeering face. "He's gonna fuck you up, Harley boy! You dirty grass!"

Harley brought his fist down on Pavel's face and heard a satisfying crunch as blood spurted from the boy's nose. Then he felt himself being dragged back. It was worth the pain in his knuckles just to see the smug grin wiped off Pavel's face for once. Somewhere Mr Lowry's voice echoed in the back of his mind, telling him that he needed to get to the Remove Room, but Harley wasn't going to stay there, waiting until the end of the day for Bobby to get him. Without looking back, Harley ran for the door.

Chapter 13

Finding Nicola Norton wasn't difficult. A simple Google search brought DS Vikki Chinn to the psychologist's website. It was an impressive advertisement for her services; sleek and professional. Nicola's pretty, smiling face dominated the home page, her long, golden hair spilling over the shoulders of a well-tailored suit. It seemed to Vikki that Nicola Norton put a lot of store in her looks as her image was all over the website, sometimes listening earnestly, sometimes laughing with a client, there were even some pictures of her doing yoga poses.

One photo showed her in khaki fatigues, looking very young, the caption below it briefly outlined her time in the Royal Army Medical Corps, although there were no dates given. She claimed to have worked for a number of forces charities, specialising in PTSD and had been an expert witness in several court cases as well as 'advising Merseyside Police Service as a psychological profiler.'

"Ooh, she's pretty," said a voice at Vikki's shoulder. It was Madge the receptionist, holding a plate of biscuits. "She obviously looks after herself."

"Can I help you, Madge?" Vikki said, minimising the screen.

"Is Andrew about? I've got some biscuits for him," Madge said, scanning the room. Her dangly earrings clanked as she turned her head. Madge was one of two civilian employees who worked on the main reception. Both looked the same, with their dyed blonde hair and love of dangly earrings and they dressed identically. It didn't help that the other one was called Marge. Both also had a mission to feed Andrew biscuits until he exploded. Whenever a meeting ended and there were a few biscuits left on a plate, Madge or Marge would make sure they were squirreled away and sent up to Kinnear.

"He's out, Madge," Vikki said. "I'll put them on his desk for you if you want. You know he's on a diet, right?"

Madge's wrinkly face creased into a look of disbelief. "A young man like that? On a diet. I don't think so love. Here, make sure he gets them. There's a Jammy Dodger on there…"

Vikki looked shocked. "Who leaves a Jammy Dodger behind?"

"I know! I nearly had it myself, but I thought, 'No Madge, that Andrew Kinnear is going to be a dad. He'll need to keep his strength up.'"

"Okay," Vikki said, taking the plate.

Madge gripped it and looked at Vikki with a steely gaze. "They're for Andrew. Don't you go munching them all."

"Madge! What do you take me for?" The plate was released, and Vikki placed it on her desk. "I'll put them on his desk just as soon as I've done this."

"Make sure you do," Madge said, giving Vikki a stern look.

Vikki watched her leave and then bit into the Jammy Dodger, whilst dialling Nicola Norton's number. She was doing the poor man a favour, the women down on Reception seemed to be hellbent on feeding him up.

"Hello, Nicola Norton. How can I help?"

Vikki almost choked on the biscuit. From the slickness of the website, she'd half expected some kind of secretary to filter Norton's calls. "Hi, my name's Detective Sergeant Vikki Chinn of Merseyside Police. I wondered if it would be possible to chat with you…"

"Is this about Paul Travis?"

"Not exactly, I was reviewing the case of Richard Ince and wondered if I could pick your brains about it."

"Richard Ince. I see. Gosh. That was about six months ago, I'll try my best to remember. Fire away."

"Thanks. You told the investigating officers that you were saddened by the news of Ince's death but not surprised. Can you just elaborate on that for me a little?"

Nicola Norton gave a sad sigh. "On the face of it, Richard was a cheerful, fun-loving guy but like a lot of young men I meet, he put on a front. He was actually full of guilt and anxiety..."

"Why did he feel guilty?"

"For surviving," Norton said. "He'd been in a number of close calls in Afghanistan and lost mates there. He blamed himself. He thought better men than him had died."

"That must have been difficult for him..."

"Understatement of the year. Just to keep going every day, to get up for work and not let the whole thing consume him required a Herculean effort. In the end, it got him. He was strong to have lasted as long as he did."

"Did you share your concerns with anyone else?"

"I wrote to his GP, with Richard's permission. He increased his medication, and I was meeting him regularly through Pro-Vets for talking therapy. We weren't aware that he was taking heroin but then that isn't something people often reveal willingly unless it's got them into some kind of trouble. Oh, I also instituted a buddy system, whereby Richard could talk to someone who had been through the same kind of experience. I don't think we can imagine half of what some servicemen experience in the line of duty, Sergeant, I'm sure you can appreciate that."

"Absolutely," Vikki said. "And who was it that you teamed him up with?"

"I can't recall off the top of my head, Sergeant," Nicola said, her voice faltering slightly. "It was a few months ago and I've worked with so many other people since."

"Did you keep a record of who it was, by any chance?" Vikki said. "It might be very useful…"

"Is there some suspicion around Richard's death, Sergeant?" Nicola sounded worried. "I mean, as far as I remember, he left a suicide note. The previous investigating officer said it was pretty conclusive."

"No, it's just that I don't recall seeing any mention of a buddy system being set up in our records and it's important to ensure thoroughness even in what appears to be an open and shut case."

"Right," Norton said. "I see."

"So, would that be possible?"

"Would what be possible?"

"For you to consult the notes and call me back? I want to progress this case as quickly as possible," Vikki said, trying to reassure Norton.

"Yes, yes of course."

"Should I call you or you call me?" Vikki said, pushing her luck.

"I'll call," Nicola said, sounding deflated. "I'm sorry, Sergeant, obviously, with the terrible news about Paul, I'm feeling a little raw and now you're dredging up memories of Richard Ince. You'll have to forgive me."

"Completely understandable," Vikki said. "You knew Paul well then?"

"Professionally," Nicola said. "He hired me to do the counselling a couple of years ago, so we got to know each other. He was a good man. I can't quite believe what's happened to him. His poor family..."

"Indeed," Vikki said. "Did Paul have any enemies?"

"Not that I'm aware of, Sergeant. My interactions with Paul Travis were on a business level, apart from the odd casual conversation before or after meetings. If someone did want to harm him, he never confided in me."

"And you never noticed any kind of tension at Pro-Vets at all? No atmosphere between any individuals?"

"Not really. It's a friendly place to work on the whole."

"But not always?"

"It's just that there was a bit of tension between

George and Paul sometimes," Nicola said.

"How do you mean?"

"Oh, nothing much. Paul called me in to coach a couple of lads and George made a fuss about the cost. It was well known that they argued about stuff like that. George was always watching the money and Paul was always trying to find ways to spend it."

"Was it serious, do you think?"

"I honestly don't know, Sergeant. Listen, I'm a little uncomfortable talking about this. I hardly knew Paul and I thought you rang me to talk about Richard Ince," Nicola said, a hint of anxiety in her voice.

"Forgive me, Ms Norton, you're quite right. I'm just covering both cases. I'll leave it there. If you could call me back with the name of the buddy assigned to Richard, that would be great." They said their goodbyes and Vikki hung up, frowning. "So Paul and George had their differences but where does Richard fit in?" Vikki said to the dead phone.

*****

There comes a time in your life when you have to acknowledge that you just aren't going to outrun a seventeen-year-old, even if he spends most of his time smoking and drinking cheap lager. PC Mark Robertson had come to this conclusion some time ago which is why he walked to the school and sent his mate in the patrol car round the block so she could approach from the other direction.

He had been doing door-to-door in Port Sunlight when a call had come through that a young man was hanging around outside Bebington High School with the possible intent of harming a pupil. He hurried over to Alex Manikas who leaned against an unmarked car, scrolling through his texts.

"Just checking this call from Bebington High School, Alex. There's a lad lurking around outside. Could be something and nothing."

"Do you have to, Mark? He's probably got a hard-on for some sixth form girl and is waiting to pick her up. I'd rather get this murder sorted. You know priorities?"

"I know, Alex but if he is waiting to have a go at someone, what then? Don't want some poor kid stabbed on our watch, do we?"

Alex had looked pained. "Fair enough, mate. Any way of getting a bit more detail, first?"

"Maybe," Mark had said and pulled his mobile out. "I know one of the teachers there. We go for a pint every now and then. Put the world to rights, you know." He scrolled through his contacts until he found Frank Lowry. The phone buzzed for a while. Mark didn't expect an answer, he knew that phones were banned in lessons for both pupils and teachers. Mark just hoped he had a free lesson.

"Mark, how did you know?" Mr Lowry said, his voice animated.

"Know what, Frank?"

"About Bobby Price... the kids are full of rumours to do with that poor man who was killed the other day."

Once Mark had apprised Alex Manikas of that particular nugget of information, he had been less reluctant about letting Mark go.

"Bloody Jacks, standing around all day, why didn't he knock on a few doors?" PC Julie Irwin had muttered as they drove past Manikas on the way to Bebington High School. There were various reasons why uniformed officers called detectives 'Jacks' some kinder than others, depending on who you asked. "What did you ask him for anyway? He doesn't outrank you."

"Yeah, but I'd hate for him to miss out any houses because I'd done a flit. Anyway, stop your grumbling, he took over from me, so it's all fine."

Julie had dropped Mark off at the bottom of the road and he had start to walk slowly towards the school while she drove around to the other end. He wanted to jog but if Bobby Price saw him hurrying towards him, the boy might leg it before Julie was in position. He just prayed she'd be there in time.

Bebington High School stood on a long road comprised of what looked like nineteen fifties semi-detached houses. It was a nice, leafy area and for a few seconds, PC Robertson felt lucky to have a job that allowed you to walk out in the spring sunshine. Of course, the pimply youth at the end of his journey was less appealing.

The school had been modernised over the years, but Mark could tell that originally it had been built around the same time as the houses. It was a brick-built building that was largely on one level and surrounded by bushes and trees. Bobby Price was leaning against the red railings, his hands stuffed into his jacket. At that moment, Irwin appeared at the other end of the road, driving steadily towards him. Bobby seemed to be daydreaming because he made no attempt to move. Robertson got close. "Hi Bobby," he said, genially. "Nice day."

Bobby Price's face fell, and he turned to run. Seeing Irwin getting out of the car, he whirled around and threw himself towards Robertson. "Ah, come on, Bobby, I just want to have a chat..." whatever else Robertson planned on saying was crushed as Price's shoulder smashed into his stomach, winding him.

Gasping for breath, Robertson wrapped his

arms around Bobby's body. Price's face twisted with anger and he smacked his forehead hard into Robertson's face. Stars exploded before Robertson's eyes and he staggered back against the school railing. He vaguely heard the thud of Price's footsteps receding up the road.

"Bloody hell, Mark, are you okay?" Irwin said, peering at his face.

"It'll heal. Get after him!"

Irwin looked up the road at the disappearing boy and shook her head. "In these shoes, luv? I don't think so. He's got away."

"Bugger," Robertson snapped. "We won't hear the end of this now."

"Come on," Irwin said. "Let's get you patched up and then we'll have a word with your mate at the school while we're here."

Chapter 14

There seemed to be so many loose ends that Blake wasn't quite sure where to begin. They had gathered to share and sift through any information but at this stage, it always felt like overload. A small group of them sat in the Incident Room and Alex Manikas fed back on initial findings from the door-to-door which was limited. "Seems like nobody in Port Sunlight Village saw or heard much on the night Travis died, sir. Some residents had seen him arguing with the teenagers the previous weekend and the descriptions fitted with those given in relation to the assault on the old man. But nobody really knew where they came from though, and the general consensus was that they 'weren't from the village.'"

Blake nodded. Port Sunlight was comprised of listed buildings but was hemmed in on one side by New Ferry. Once a bustling little town, New Ferry had fallen on hard times and a lot of shops had closed. Things hadn't been helped by a huge gas explosion that had damaged a lot of property a few years back. It turned out to be an insurance job and someone went to prison for it. Houses in the village were listed buildings and highly sought after, something not reflected by the properties surrounding it.

So it didn't surprise Blake that the residents of Sunlight would see the kids as coming from elsewhere. "What about this Bobby character?" he said. "The one who was said to have hit the old man and was arguing with Travis?"

"Possibly Bobby Price, sir," Alex said. "He was hanging around outside Bebington High School, waiting for one of the pupils there. A lot of the kids are saying he killed Travis and this pupil grassed him up…"

"If only," Blake muttered. "Do we know where he lives?"

"Working on that now, sir. From what we know, the boy he was after is called Harley Vickers. He ran from the school once he realised Bobby was waiting outside for him. We have Harley's address. Mark Robertson nearly had Bobby Price, but Price assaulted him and made a run for it…" Alex nodded to the bruised PC who leaned against a wall at the back.

Blake looked over to him. "Are you okay, Robertson?"

Robertson sported a brilliant shiner. "I'm fine, sir. A bit battered and bruised. Been given a head injury letter to take home to my mum."

"So, this Bobby Price. Is he known to the school?"

"Ex-pupil, apparently," Robertson said, picking up the story. "He's done the rounds of schools that would have him and settled in Bebington

Secondary where they managed to keep hold of him until he was old enough to leave. He got a Food Technology GCSE..."

"Food Technology?" Blake said. "Is that cooking and stuff?"

"So I believe," Robertson said. "That was a couple of years ago. The family moved so we're having trouble finding his address. Since then, rumour has it that he's dropped out of a couple of apprenticeships. Some of the pupils I spoke to didn't like him. They called him a creep for hanging around with younger students. Or words to that effect. He hasn't got a record but that could just mean he hasn't been caught yet."

"What about this other lad, Harley?"

Robertson looked at his notebook. "Thirteen. Troubled kid with a temper problem. Some mild learning difficulties. On the verge of exclusion several times."

"I wonder why Bobby thought this Harley had grassed him up," Blake said.

"It seems that another friend, Alfie Lewis, had been telling the world, his wife and their dog that Bobby had murdered Paul Travis and assaulted the old man in the Dell. Bobby blames Harley for some reason."

Blake hissed and shook his head. "Bloody kids," he muttered. "How do you make a situation ten times worse in seconds? Just add teenagers. Jeez."

"I hope you're taking notes, Andrew," Kath Cryer said, grinning and giving Kinnear a nudge. "Ten years' time and you'll be running after a teenage daughter. Tearing your grey hairs out over her."

Kinnear blushed. "Hopefully, we'll give her a better moral framework..."

"Ooh, get you," Kath said.

"I'm sure Andrew will make a great dad, Kath," Blake said, awkwardly. He wasn't a great one for banter. "Anyway, Alex..."

"We've got Harley Vicker's home address, sir," Alex said. "We could go and talk to him. If he's afraid of Bobby Price, he might talk..."

"Or he might run away," Blake muttered. "Yep. Let's go for it. The sooner we find Bobby Price, the better. Have a chat with this Alfie Lewis, too. Have we managed to unlock Travis' mobile phone, yet?"

"They're still working on it, sir," Kinnear said.

"His wife doesn't know the pin for it?" Blake said. "Again, I can't help thinking that there's more to Paul Travis than just wholesome war hero and all-round good egg. What else have we got?"

"Sir, I called Nicola Norton, the psychologist who works for Pro-Vets, about Richard Ince. She was his counsellor before his suicide," Vikki said. "She told me that Ince had been assigned a buddy from Pro-Vets. I'm waiting for her to get to me with the name of the buddy, but she hasn't got back to me, yet."

"Do you think Ince's death was something other than suicide?"

"He left a note and overdosed on heroin, sir. It looks pretty conclusive. But Ince was drinking with someone the night he died. I think it might be the buddy. It could shed a different light on the case, that's all."

"Might be worth badgering this Norton woman a bit, Vikki. Did you mention the toy soldier?"

"No, sir. I thought we were keeping that quiet for now. Do you want me to?"

"Use your judgement. Norton might have some insight..."

"One thing she did say was that Paul and George often argued about money..."

"That's come up before but it's worth pursuing. Owens dismissed it but maybe we should push him on it along with where he was on the night in question," Blake muttered. "We can't leave him waiting for a formal interview all day. Though, to be honest, I feel like wasting his time like he's wasting ours."

"Want me to have a chat with him, sir?" Kath

Cryer said. "A fresh face might just put him off guard..."

"Terrify him more like," Kinnear said under his breath.

"Oi!" Kath said, elbowing Andrew in his side. "Who rattled your cage? You taking a breath between biscuits, soft lad?"

"Did you see that, boss?" Kinnear said, grinning. "That was assault, that was..."

Blake gave Kinnear a pained look but secretly he liked the fact that Kinnear and Cryer got along so well. At one time, they could easily have been enemies. "What about the baseball bat. Any indication where that came from?"

"Forensics indicated that there were no old scratches on the bat. All the impact damage done to it was associated with the attack as far as they could see," Kinnear said. "That would suggest it was recently bought or bought a while back and not used."

"They couldn't determine which?"

"Sorry, boss, no. There's no branding or logo on it, either. I checked with the major outlets and a baseball specialist in Birkenhead. Sports Direct and Argos sell wooden bats, but they're painted. Our murder weapon is natural wood colour, never been painted as far as forensics can tell. The specialist said that the bat was probably some kind of composite rather than maple or ash. It hadn't come from them and he suggested it was bought online."

"Good work, Andrew, I just wish we'd been able to glean more from it," Blake said, glancing at his watch. "Right. Let's focus on Bobby Price and this Harley character, see if we can't pick them up. I've got to talk to the Super' but Kath, if you and Andrew could talk to George Owens, that would be great. Let's see if we can move things forward, even if it's just by eliminating suspects."

*****

Superintendent Martin listened thoughtfully, as Blake listed all the things he hadn't found out yet and then sat back in his chair. He was a tall, vigorous-looking man, having served his time as a beat officer when there was a minimum height requirement. "This is a tricky case, Will," he said, narrowing his eyes. Martin was a fair man but his sharp features made him seem stern and unforgiving. "I've already had the Port Sunlight Village Trust asking me questions about what happened and the damage to the memorial. The British Legion aren't very happy either."

"I completely understand that, sir. A murder is bad enough but to have one in such a sensitive location. Our officers have treated the crime scene with the utmost respect..."

"You don't have to give me the official line, Will,

just tread carefully. I noticed in the report about your shenanigans up in Scotland that you managed to bring a whole valley side down…"

"I have to give the credit for that to the rain and snow, sir," Blake said, groaning inwardly. Martin could never get past the idea that Blake was some kind of grandstander, hungry for the publicity he used to get during his days on Searchlight. "I'll keep this low key, I promise."

"Be sure that you do. Paul Travis was something of a local hero, by all accounts, and people will be hungry for an arrest."

"Believe me, sir, nobody's hungrier than me," Blake said. "I just can't help feeling that this is more than an act of random street violence…"

"There you go, Will," Martin said, throwing his hands up. "Why couldn't it be that? A young lad with a grudge after Travis humiliated him lays in wait and springs out on him. Travis is drunk, can't defend himself and the boy gets carried away."

"With respect, sir, whoever killed Travis got more than carried away," Blake said. "They knocked him out and then cut his throat while he lay defenceless…"

"All I'm saying is follow the obvious leads first before you start getting tangled up in any far-fetched conspiracies, okay?"

"I'll do my best, sir," Blake said, through gritted teeth.

"Good," Martin said and lowered his eyes to the paperwork on his desk, a signature move that indicated the meeting was over. "Keep me posted."

If the door dampers hadn't stopped it, Blake would have slammed the door on his way out. Something needed to move on this case and soon.

Chapter 15

George Owens didn't look very happy to see DI Kath Cryer and DC Andrew Kinnear enter the room. It could have been the fact that they'd kept him waiting so long or that he expected to see Blake again, Kath couldn't tell. The delay had given him enough time to call for a brief to sit in on the conversation.

Kath recognised Gareth Cornell, the brief, straight away. Since representing a suspect a year or so ago, he had chanced his arm at a couple of criminal cases. It made a change from conveyancing and selling mortgages, she supposed. He was a tall, slight man or a streak of piss, as Kath thought of him, but that was more down to his demeanour than his size or shape. His pale complexion and long, droopy face didn't really inspire confidence. His light brown suit seemed a size too big for him, especially around the shoulders. His slick, mousey hair seemed to be caught between styles and it stuck out in all directions so much that Kath wondered quite what he was planning to do with it.

"Mr Owens, Mr Cornell," Kath said, nodding to them as she entered the interview room. "I'm DI Kath Cryer, this is DC Andrew Kinnear. We're sorry to have kept you waiting but, as you can probably appreciate, this is a complex case and it's important that we get things right..."

"Just as long as you acknowledge that Mr Owens has done no wrong and is cooperating fully with your enquiries," Cornell said, trying to coat his voice with a sense of gravitas and failing. Kath and Andrew sat down on the opposite side of the table.

"Well, that isn't strictly true, is it, Mr Owens?" Kath said, by-passing Cornell and making the point that he wasn't to interrupt again. "DCI Blake has asked you where you were on the night that Paul Travis was murdered and you declined to tell him. Are you prepared to now?"

"I just got the train," George Owens said.

"What time train did you get, sir?" Kinnear said.

"The last train, twenty to twelve. I had to run because it took so long to get Barry in the taxi."

"What station did you get off at? Only I looked and none of them seem even remotely conveni-ent for your house."

"I got off at Green Lane. It takes me twenty minutes to walk from there to my house."

"So you would walk up Bolton Road with Paul, surely." Kath added. "At least part of the way."

"No, he turned right up Church Drive al-most immediately after leaving the pub. I went straight on."

"Giving you the benefit of the doubt," Kath said,

"let's assume you didn't walk away from the pub with Paul and murder him…"

"I didn't…"

"Okay. You went to the station to catch a train that would drop you off miles from your home. A twenty-minute walk after a skinful. That just doesn't sound sensible…"

Owens looked down at his expanding waistline. "I'm trying to keep my weight down. Get some exercise, you know how it is."

"What *would* make sense was if you were going that way to visit someone between Green Lane and your house. Tell me if I'm getting warmer, Mr Owens."

"It's hard to explain," George Owens said, tangling his fingers together in front of him. He looked trapped.

Kath fixed her eye on Owens. "Harder than explaining to Mrs Travis what happened to her husband and telling her we can't track down his killer because his so-called friend thinks his personal life is more important than the investigation?"

"That's not fair," George Owens snapped.

Kath gave Kinnear a sidelong glance as if sharing a derogatory thought about Owens with him. "No, Mr Owens, it isn't fair, is it? You do realise that what you're doing makes you look like a prime suspect?"

"I didn't kill Paul," Owens said, glaring at Kath.

"So you say, but where were you?"

"I got the train and walked home."

"Did you and Paul argue, much?"

Owens looked from Kath to his brief and back. "A little. Mainly about business things..."

"Money," Kath said.

"Yeah. Money. Paul liked to spend and was always 'thinking big,' as he liked to call it. The trouble was, 'thinking big' cost a lot of cash. Cash we didn't always have."

"You sound bitter, Mr Owens."

"No. It was just annoying. You probably get annoyed by your work colleagues. It doesn't make you a murderer."

"It might if one of them turned up dead, I was the last person to see them and I wouldn't account for my whereabouts when he died."

"He didn't annoy me so much that I'd want to kill him. All I had to do was show Paul the bank balance and he'd realise we didn't have the funds to do whatever he'd dreamed up."

"That must have annoyed him."

"Yeah, I suppose it did," Owens said.

"And how did he show his annoyance?"

"I dunno. He grumbled a bit maybe or went off in a huff," Owens said.

"Went off in a huff," Kath repeated, looking at Kinnear. "If his reaction was so low-key, how come it was common knowledge around the charity that you argued a lot over money?"

"Maybe I grumbled to other people. Maybe Paul did."

"So you were bad-mouthing each other around the business? Doesn't sound very wholesome, George..."

"You're putting words into my client's mouth, now, DI Cryer," Cornell said, suddenly.

"No," Kath said, looking at him levelly. "I'm making an observation and you aren't in court now, Perry Mason. Another interruption and I'll have you kicked out."

Cornell shrank down in his seat.

Owens gave a frustrated sigh. "Look, Paul and I had our disagreements about how the charity spent its funds. That's no secret but I didn't kill him."

"So you keep saying but we don't know where you were on the night he was murdered."

"I got the train," Owens said through gritted teeth.

Kath sat back and folded her arms. "There's

117

something else, though, I can tell. Let's assume you are telling the truth for a moment and you got the train. It's well out of your way. I reckon the only reason you'd do that was if you were meeting someone and you're trying to protect them for some reason. Whatever you're hiding, I doubt it's worse than murder. Your secret will come out one way or another, so you may as well explain to us what it was you were doing because we *will* find out."

*****

Jeff Blake had spent most of the day trying to wrangle a few hundred words into coherent sentences that didn't sound like excerpts from a particularly dull stately home tour guide. It was hard to concentrate after Gambles had mentioned Laura's name. On one level he was annoyed with himself for letting Gambles snare him once again. Obviously, the killer had more information about where Laura was but once he'd realised that Jeff was hooked, Gambles had taken great pleasure in holding that back. Jeff was worried about Will, too.

It was possible that Will would keep it from Jeff if Laura had come home. They weren't the most communicative of brothers but also, Will would be aware of Jeff's link to Gambles and, therefore, to Quinlan. But what if Will didn't know? What if Laura had come back and been taken by Quinlan?

Gambles would love it if Jeff tipped Will off because it would drive another wedge between them, adding to the little psychodrama that the serial killer liked to keep going. Gambles was always trying to insert himself into the Blake family story. If Jeff and Will were arguing, at least they were arguing about Gambles. It made him the centre of discontent even if Laura was the main concern.

On the other hand, if he said nothing and Laura was in some kind of danger, Will would never forgive him. Jeff stopped typing. He had to let Will know. "I'm damned either way," he muttered to himself and picked up his phone. "It always goes to voice messaging anyway."

"Jeff, I'm busy," Will said, tersely. Jeff almost dropped the phone.

"I'm fine thanks, Will. How about you? Recovered from your jaunt up north?"

"What do you want?"

"I was talking to our mutual friend…"

"Gambles. Jeff, I've told you before, I don't want to know anything about that monster. You trade off the misery and horror he's caused in the past by all means but don't make me an accessory…"

"He told me Laura has come home," Jeff said. He would have skirted around the issue, but Will's tone had annoyed him. Jeff had helped Will with his investigations in Scotland and hoped he'd cut him some slack at least. A mean part of Jeff hoped his revelation hurt Will.

"What?"

"You didn't know?"

"No, I didn't. What did he say?"

"He said she was back but wouldn't give me any more details. You know what he's like…"

Will heaved a sigh down the phone. "Yes, Jeff, I do know. So he could just be winding you up."

"He could be, yes but there's generally a grain of truth in what he says at least. I didn't know what to do for the best, Will. Was I wrong to call you? Should I have just ignored it and then, God forbid if something terrible happened…"

Another sigh. "What you should do for the best, Jeff is have nothing to do with that psychopath. But, yeah, I can see your dilemma. He didn't say anything else?"

"He went on about Romance stories. He said something about 'a lovelorn hero, a whore with a heart of gold and a handsome bad boy…'"

"Kyle Quinlan," Blake muttered.

"Do you think he's been in touch with Quinlan? I mean they were friends in the past, weren't they?"

"Anything is possible with Gambles, Jeff. If

Laura is home, then I'm sure she would have got in touch. She could be in danger. Although Quinlan has been very quiet. She took off the moment she realised he was coming back, and I haven't heard anything amongst my colleagues about him. Listen, thanks for letting me know and... I'm sorry I bit your head off. I'll check it out." Will hung up and Jeff sat staring at his phone for a second, hoping he hadn't just lit a fuse for a powder keg of Gambles' making.

Chapter 16

Blake sat at his desk, turning a biro over and over in his fingers. The news that Laura was back on the Wirral disturbed him. He hadn't expected her to come running to him for protection but at the same time, she could have let him know. What had changed to bring her back of her own free will? Or had she? Had Quinlan caught up with her?

DCI Matty Cavanagh had been looking into the whole business of Kyle Quinlan, but Blake was sure it had all been put on the back burner now. Still, it might be worth chatting to Cavanagh in case anything had come up recently.

Cavanagh had a reputation as a young DCI who cared more about his appearance and popularity than actually getting to the truth of things. He and his trusty DS Dirkin also had a knack of cutting through the crap and getting speedy arrests. There was a suspicion, too, that Dirkin had pulled Cavanagh's fat out of the fire on many occasions. How true any of this was, Blake didn't know. If he was honest, too, he disliked Cavanagh more for his easy manner and ability to charm almost anyone. Blake rarely felt comfortable in his own skin. Cavanagh was a scouser through and through, and he wore it like a badge of honour to the point of it becoming almost stereotypical. He loved his football and his banter, especially if he was teasing Blake about being from the Wirral.

True to form, Cavanagh was leaning back in his chair, his feet up on the desk when Blake entered his office. "All right, Blakey," he said, not altering his relaxed position.

"Sorry, Matty, are you busy?" Blake said, maybe with a little too much edge in his voice.

Matty Cavanagh tapped the side of his head. "Thinking, Blakey, mulling stuff over. Got to have time to think, eh? How are your turnips growing over the water, eh? Good harvest? Sheep all healthy?"

Blake rolled his eyes. "Hilarious. Listen, have you heard any more about Kyle Quinlan? Last I heard you were looking into it..."

"We were, Blakey, then your Laura did a runner, didn't she? We were chasing shadows, to be honest. I blamed that bloody Gambles character for sending us on a wild goose chase."

"So you closed the case?"

Cavanagh stretched in his seat. "We were going to but then Kyle Quinlan showed up..."

"Showed up? What d'you mean, showed up?"

"Obviously, we knew he was around because of what Laura told you but nobody had eyeballed him. Then he bought a house up in Caldy, bold as brass. I think it belonged to that mate of yours off the telly. The one Gambles murdered."

"Ross Armitage? Kyle Quinlan bought Ross Armitage's house?" Blake dropped heavily into the nearest chair. "Jeez, that's bizarre. How would he be able to afford a property in Caldy?"

Cavanagh raised his hands and his eyebrows, displaying a disturbing lack of knowledge or care. "Who knows, Blakey? We can't just go barging into people's houses asking them why they're rich, can we?"

"Not unless they're massively wealthy and can't account for it, no but…"

"And Quinlan hasn't been down to Harrods on a shopping spree for handbags and shoes, recently. So we're stuffed at the moment. But we're watching him."

Blake rubbed his chin. "Ross Armitage's house," he muttered. "Jeez. Why didn't you tell me?"

"Why would we tell you, Blakey?" Cavanagh said, leaning forward. "Have you heard something?"

Blake nodded. "Laura is back, according to Gambles…"

"According to Gambles? Has that nutter been pulling your little brother's strings again, mate? You wanna have a word about that. Listen, you've got to stay away from Kyle Quinlan."

Blake looked up. "What? Did you know? About Laura?"

"I can't tell you anything, mate," Cavanagh said, red spots appearing on his cheeks.

"You're a crap liar, Matty. What's going on? Where's Laura? Is she safe?"

Cavanagh rubbed his forehead. "'Kin' 'ell," he muttered. "She's fine, Will. More than fine. Thriving, okay?"

"What are you on about?" Blake said, planting his fists on Cavanagh's desk. "What do you mean she's thriving?"

"I didn't want to be the one to break the news, mate. She's living with Quinlan. We've seen her coming and going freely from the house, sometimes with Quinlan sometimes without..."

"Jeez," Blake threw his arms up. "Why didn't you tell me?"

"Why do you think? Look at yourself. Nobody likes news like that. This is a delicate operation. We're just at the information gathering stage and..."

"He must have some kind of hold over her," Blake said. "We've got to get her away from there..."

"Will, she's fine. There's nothing we can do. You know that. Just stay away. I told you. Quinlan came back from the States and, from what we've gleaned, he was working for a pretty heavy outfit over there: drugs, extortion, protection and gambling rackets. Our theory is that he's setting up on the Wirral. We're watching him. If you go wading in, then he'll cotton on right away."

"But if Laura could be in danger. I need to..."

"You don't need to do anything," Cavanagh said, "apart from keep the fuck away from Caldy and that house. I'm warning you, mate, if I have to go to the Super about this, I won't hesitate. This could be big."

"You thinking about your career again, Matty?"

"I'm thinking about the tidal wave of drug-related crime and misery that we might stop if we catch Quinlan before he gets going. If you don't like that, then go and have a word with Martin yourself. He'll give you a flea in your ear, too. Now, if you don't mind, I've got more thinking to do."

Blake stalked out of Cavanagh's office. If he couldn't get any information here, then he knew somewhere he could.

*****

Despite being told to go home, PC Mark Robertson had insisted on accompanying DC Alex Manikas to Harley Vickers' home address. The boy had information that might explain why PC Robertson had ended the day with a black eye and a headache. Harley was running for a reason.

Harley lived across the A41 from Port Sunlight.

These houses were clearly once Lever's property too but hadn't been protected in the same way as those in the main village. These houses had been pebble-dashed, double-glazed and extended over the years. Some had small front gardens and others had carports. The Vickers' house was a small semidetached on a curiously-named road called The Anzacs.

"Australian and New Zealand Army Corps," Mark Robertson said to Manikas who was frowning at the road sign. "First World War. Must have been named in their honour."

"Were they the guys who fought at Gallipoli?" Manikas said. "I think I saw the film. God, what a mess, eh?"

"Indeed," Robertson said. "We don't know we're born, do we? You know, part of me hopes these kids weren't involved in Travis' murder. I still like to have some faith in future generations."

A large privet hedge screened the Vickers' house from the road. Alex and Mark climbed the steps into a small garden with an immaculate lawn and a little Wendy house on one side of the path. It was a semi-detached property with a modern extension to the side that would never have been permitted had the house been built a few hundred yards across the road. It looked well-maintained and tidy. Alex rang the doorbell and glanced at Mark as Greensleeves echoed inside the hall.

"Classy," Mark said.

A petite woman in her thirties with dark hair opened the door. "DC Alex Manikas, Ma'am," he said, flashing his warrant card. "This is PC Mark Robertson. Would we be able to talk to Harley Vickers by any chance?"

She looked harassed before they had asked her about Harley but the mention of his name seemed to make the blood drain from her face. "What's he been up to now?"

"Sorry, Ma'am, your name is?"

"I'm Jane Vickers, his mum," she said, scowling. "Some days, I wish I wasn't. What's he done, then?"

"He ran out of school today and we think he may be able to help us with our investigation," Alex said. "As far as we know, he isn't in any trouble. He may have witnessed something, that's all."

The woman turned and bellowed up the stairs. "Harley! Get down here now!"

A slight, blond-haired boy appeared at the top of the stairs. When he saw Mark's uniform, his eyes widened and he vanished out of sight. "Harley! Back here, now!"

"With your permission, Mrs Vickers, could we come in and talk to him?" PC Robertson said. "It might be more fruitful."

"Fruitful?" Mrs Vickers said, looking confused.

"I mean, better than us standing here while you shout up the stairs," Mark said, as he glanced up and down the road for effect. "It'll stop the curtains twitching, too."

"Come on in," Mrs Vickers sighed.

Alex and Mark nodded, wiping their feet and squeezing into the tiny hallway. Mark climbed the stairs. Harley's room was obvious by the huge 'Keep Out' sign on the door and the fact that his name was emblazoned all over it. He tapped gently. "Harley, my name's PC Mark Robertson. I wonder if we could speak with you for a minute. You aren't in any trouble. We just want a quick word about Bobby Price." Silence. Mark gave the bedroom door a gentle push and it swung open.

A cool breeze greeted him, wafting a pungent combination of body odour, spray to cover the body odour, and cigarette smoke in Mark's direction. The room lay empty and the window open. Mark hurried across a floor littered with dirty clothes and poked his head out of the window. Harley was down in the street limping away as fast as he could, his mum screeching at him from the front door.

*****

The Seraph was an old street corner pub in the

North End area of Birkenhead trapped between the park and the docks. The area was a strange mixture of Sixties infill buildings, old Edwardian terraces and more modern remodelling. It was an area that had experienced great hardship through the Eighties but was quiet nowadays. These were the old houses of dock workers and the shipbuilders, ravaged in the Blitz and rebuilt. It was a tightknit, friendly community that looked after its own. Many of the corner pubs had gone to the wall in recent years as people took to drinking at home or preloading before going over to Liverpool on a night out.

Shunned even by locals, The Seraph managed to keep going because it had an underworld clientele of its very own. Reviews for it online made it clear it wasn't the kind of pub you dropped in on unexpectedly and outsiders weren't to expect a warm welcome. Coppers were even less welcome. And yet, the pub was always quiet. It was a place where criminals came to talk and no crime was tolerated on the premises.

Blake took a breath and pushed on the brass doorhandle, inhaling the heady alcohol-infused atmosphere. It took a moment for his eyes to adjust to the dingy interior of the pub and in that time, the small number of drinkers had clocked him and were heading out of the other door. It was a tiny pub, no bigger than an average living room. Anyone sitting in here, had to squash onto a stool over a copper-topped table. Years of polish had blackened the wooden beams and the flock wallpaper could easily be from the early days of the pub. The landlord, Boredom McClague, stood crammed behind a short bar that housed three pumps and several lager taps. The bottles and optics on the wall flanked a hatch through to what seemed like an even smaller back room.

"Will Blake," McClague said, flatly. "What a pleasant surprise." The man's face looked as though it was about to lose its fight with gravity entirely. The bags under his eyes, his jowls and even his ears seemed to sag, hence the nickname, Boredom. Looking so uninterested in the world was something that Boredom played to his full advantage. But to fall for that was to underestimate the wily landlord. Behind that mask of tired indifference glittered a pair of razor-sharp eyes.

"Evening Boredom," Blake said. "Sorry to scare off your customers."

Boredom shrugged. "They'll be back. Anyway, I've been expecting you for some time now."

"You sound like a Bond villain. Should I be worried?"

"Dunno, Blakey. Depends if you've come in here looking for a certain young lady..."

"Laura Vexley?"

"Aye. She was in here a month or so ago."

"In here? But that's like…"

"Sticking your head in the lion's mouth? That's what I thought. Then she pulled its bloody tail, just for laughs."

"What d'you mean?"

Boredom leaned over his bar, bringing his face close to Blake's. "I'm telling you this because it's common knowledge, right? She came in here and told me to spread the word that she was sitting in the corner of the pub, sipping a cider like she was on holiday."

"She wanted Kyle Quinlan to know she was here?"

Boredom gave another shrug. "I couldn't say whose attention she was trying to grab but I know it wouldn't be healthy…"

"Did Quinlan come for her?"

"Nope. A big guy called Nick picked her up. He's not a regular, Blakey. Okay, last wee bit of information for free and then I'm going to have to kick you out. She came in here as bold as you like. If you ask me, she looked like a woman who had a plan. Rumour has it she's fine, living in a big house…"

"In Caldy?"

"I wouldn't know. Okay DCI Blake. Your time's

up. I want my customers back and they don't like your company."

Blake nodded. "Thanks, Boredom. Listen, Quinlan, what's he up to?"

Boredom McClague gave Blake a look of appalled disgust at the very idea he'd answer such a question. His glass cloth squeaked on the pint pot he dried slowly and steadily, whilst gazing at the door. Blake needed more answers but he wasn't going to get them here.

Chapter 17

It was late and Blake sat at his desk back in the Major Incident Room chewing on a stale digestive that he'd taken from a plate on Kinnear's desk. He'd picked it up hoping it would go some way to easing his hunger, but it just made him want a steak pie and chips. He vowed to himself that he'd keep that particular promise on the way home, if he could. Kinnear and Cryer sat opposite him. They looked exhausted.

"I thought I'd let you know as soon as I could, sir. It looks like Owens met his dealer outside Green Lane regular as clockwork," Cryer said. "A bit of coke and some dope. He didn't want to bring the charity into disrepute." She rolled her eyes.

Blake chewed slowly. Cryer always loved to draw out the tension. "The dealer, anyone we know?"

"We're checking now. Probably. I think he's telling the truth. He says he uses it to calm his nerves. Apparently he suffers from anxiety."

"I've a good mind to turn his house upside down and charge him if we find anything," Blake said, spraying crumbs everywhere. "Jeez. What a waste of time."

"D'you think there might be some kind of drug link, sir?"

"It doesn't feel like it," Blake said. "He could still be telling porkies."

"We should have more information by the morning, sir," Kath said. "CCTV from the station will help. I've let Owens go for now."

"Okay, Kath. We'll have the DNA results too, hopefully and that will tell us something."

"Says something about Owens, don't you think?" Kinnear said, through a mouthful of custard cream. "To be so self-absorbed that you'd think about your dealer and your reputation before your murdered best friend."

"Yeah," Blake muttered. "Do you think he's hiding anything else?"

"What like, sir?" Kath Cryer said.

"I dunno," Blake sighed. "I can't get away from the idea that Travis's death has something to do with Pro-Vets. Money is always a stronger motive than revenge in my experience. The idea that those teenagers waited at the War memorial seems farfetched to me. They might give him a good hiding, fair enough but to slit his throat? That's cold and calculating. He lay there unconscious, and someone took a knife to him. They weren't frenzied stab wounds from a street brawl. Just one neat cut. The killer knew what they were doing. Owens was a trained soldier."

"Bobby Price was publicly humiliated by

Travis" Cryer pointed out. "From what his old teachers told uniform, Price had a liking for thuggery and an eggshell-thin ego. He could have stewed on it for a bit and then lain in wait…"

Blake shook his head. "They also said he wasn't exactly the sharpest tool in the box. Would he have the capacity for watching Travis and coldly calculating when was the best time to kill him?"

"Maybe Bobby just wanted to rough Travis up and got carried away," Kinnear said.

"The knife wound on Travis doesn't look like the work of someone who is carried away," Blake said. "That takes some knowledge and skill, Kath. While we're chasing these teenagers all over the place, we're not considering other options. I mean, how much money is going through that charity? Travis' death might indeed turn out to be an act of mindless violence, but doesn't it feel like more to you?"

"We could get a warrant to look at the books, sir," Kinnear said, with a grin. "Set Ian Ollerthwaite on the trail…"

Blake shuddered. DC Ian Ollerthwaite specialised in forensic accounting. The man was narcolepsy in human form and the moment he opened his mouth, Blake felt overwhelmed by drowsiness. But with his pedantic attention to detail and gift for numbers, Ollerthwaite was perfectly suited to the role. "Great," Blake said, rubbing his face. "Can I leave that with you to organise, Andrew?"

"Leave it with me, sir. I haven't caught up with Ian's latest acquisitions from the Chester Model Railway Mart," Kinnear said. "It'll be a blast."

"He's taking one for the team, there, boss," Kath said.

"Do it tomorrow, Andrew," Blake said, sipping the last of his tea. "No need to pop by his house and discuss it over his layout..."

"You're all heart, sir," Kinnear said, grimacing. "Isn't that tea cold?"

Blake looked into the mug as if the temperature of the drink hadn't occurred to him. "I suppose it was," he said, smacking his lips. "No waste with me. Right. Get off home you two. Hopefully tomorrow, we'll get some more intel on Bobby Price and bring him in. A lad like that can't stay hidden for long, surely."

Cryer lingered at the door as Kinnear left, then she muttered something to him, waved and returned to Blake's desk. "You not going home, sir?"

"Yeah, in a minute, Kath. Just a lot on my mind, right now."

"Is it Laura, sir?" Kath said, tentatively. "Only I heard a whisper today..."

"Yeah, she's back, apparently. It's all over the office, I suppose."

"Just gossip, sir, you know. So it's true then? Have you spoken to her?"

"I haven't Kath, no," Blake sighed. "The gospel according to Boredom McClague is that she came back and went straight to Kyle Quinlan, who was out for her blood last I heard. I don't know what she's up to. To top it off, Cavanagh is watching Quinlan and knew about her weeks ago. He's threatened me with the Super if I go anywhere near her."

Kath paused a second. "Can I speak candidly, sir?" she said.

"You don't normally ask for permission, Kath," Blake said with a tired smile. "Fire away, you generally talk sense, anyway."

"I don't know Laura Vexley as well as you, sir, but you know she had quite a chequered past. She was a criminal and was happy to associate with lawless and violent men for many years of her life. In my experience, sir, a leopard can't change her spots..."

"You're mixing spots and chequers there, Kath," Blake said, pinching the bridge of his nose. A killer headache was on the horizon, he could just feel it. "You think I should forget her and move on?"

"I dunno, sir. Not for me to say. But whatever life she's chosen for herself, you don't want to be part of it. Y-you're better than that. Smarter too."

The words were out of his mouth before he knew it. "But I love her Kath. She showed me how to move on. She brought me to life again after my mum disappeared…"

"I'm sorry, sir, I've over-stepped the mark," Kath said, blushing.

"No, Kath. Thanks. Really, I needed to talk to someone. Maybe you're right. Maybe I should start over. After all, that's what Laura's done…"

Kath looked pained. "She hasn't, sir. She's re-verted to type. I'm sorry, sir. Look, I'm going home, and you should too. Things always look better after a good night's sleep."

"Good night, Kath," Blake said, "and don't worry. I know what I'm going to do…"

"Sir?" Kath said, a concerned frown puckering her brow.

"Get some kip. Tomorrow's another day."

*****

Detective Constable Andrew Kinnear had a head full of thoughts as he drove home that night. It had been his husband Chris' idea to adopt ini-tially. Kinnear had agreed but part of him won-dered if he'd done that just to please Chris. The more he thought about it, the more he realised that he'd been quite happy with their life to-gether. He didn't feel like there was a huge void that needed to be filled by a child. They both had busy jobs.

Chris was a teacher and brought a lot of work home with him after the school day. There were parents' evenings and meetings that meant he wasn't always home. Kinnear's own job was a nightmare for anyone who needed routine hours and flexibility. Although he didn't need to, Kinnear was constantly apologising to Chris for meals burnt while waiting in the oven, missed anniversaries, cancelled parties and generally getting in late most nights. How would a child fit in with that?

Kath's comments about having a teenaged daughter had filled Kinnear with panic. She'd only been teasing him but it had really hit home. He didn't want to be an absentee father. His own childhood had been happy, idyllic even and he wanted that for any child of his own. Maybe now just wasn't the time to do it.

Chapter 18

Blake had taken something of a detour, on his way home, one that he suspected he would regret later. He had also come home to what looked like a dirty protest all over the kitchen by Charlie and Serafina. It looked like they'd been chasing around the house, too, judging by the broken vase, and torn curtains. Why they'd done that was beyond Blake. Ian Youde had left a note to say he'd called in to feed them and taken Charlie for a walk and Serafina had the cat flap to get in and out. Maybe the quiet house freaked them out. Blake glared at the cat who glared back. Maybe it was the antibiotics upsetting her and she, in turn, was upsetting Charlie.

"Or maybe you've got it in for me," Blake said to Serafina. After cleaning up, Blake dragged himself upstairs to bed.

All through breakfast the next morning, Serafina sat on the draining board and growled at Blake.

"Jeez, don't you start," Blake muttered. Charlie had constantly jumped up and down, burying his head in Blake's groin or under his arm. "I'm going mad, Charlie," he said, scratching the dog behind the ear. "Listen to me. I'm talking to a cat. I guess I could take you for a quick trot round the block myself, couldn't I?"

It was cold outside and still early. The river lay glassy and still, lights from the other side reflected in the grey mirror of water. At least it wasn't raining. Blake stood in the lane just listening to his breath. A few solitary birds sang in the trees that dotted the old gardens of the big houses. The general hum of traffic had begun already as commuters began their daily pilgrimage to offices, factories and shops. It was going to be another long day and he wondered if they'd get anywhere nearer the truth by the end of it. Charlie gave a yap and Blake paused, frowning.

A dark BMW sat at the side of the lane, just outside the house next door. Blake peered harder. Someone sat in the driving seat. As soon as he took a step towards the car, its engine grumbled into life and it began to pull off. It vanished up the lane in a haze of exhaust fumes. Blake didn't have his phone on him, but he memorised the registration number and made a promise to himself that he'd check it out as soon as he got to HQ.

*****

Standing in Superintendent Martin's office, Blake knew straight away that this was about his little diversion on his way home last night and that he was going to get cut off at the knees. Martin leaned back and looked hard at Blake. "Cavanagh has spoken to me about last night," Martin said, in a calm voice that was somehow more unnerving than when he was ranting. "Have you anything to add?"

"That depends on what he said, sir," Blake said, wondering if it was worth acting dumb or just confessing straight away.

"That you drove past the house of a person of interest, thus jeopardising his investigation."

"I wasn't thinking, sir, or rather, I was thinking. I lost track of where I was going while I was thinking, sir. I didn't mean to jeopardise anything. I'll apologise to DCI Cavanagh when I see him."

Martin grunted. "Thinking? What were you thinking about? Laura Vexley?"

"No, sir. The Port Sunlight killing, sir. Honestly, sir, as soon as I realised where I was, I got out of there. It was a genuine mistake."

"Cavanagh's officers said that you paused at the gate. Quinlan isn't an idiot, Blake. If he recognises your car or that Vexley woman does, then..."

"Then they'll just think it's just me, sir. Looking for Laura. It would be more suspicious if I didn't come looking for her. Nothing would tip Quinlan off more than my complete absence when it's common knowledge that she's back..."

"And is it common knowledge?"

"She walked into the Seraph a while back and told everyone to spread the news. It would have got to me eventually besides…" Blake hesitated.

"What?" Martin snapped, a dangerous look in his eye.

"I think Quinlan might be watching me. There was a car outside my house early this morning and the night before last. It drove away both times when I approached it. A black BMW."

"Did you get the registration?"

"It belongs to Quinlan, sir…"

Martin let out a hiss of disgust. "Nothing is ever simple with you, is it, Will?"

"I'm sorry, sir. I have no control over what Quinlan does. I…"

"Okay. Do you think Quinlan is a threat to you?"

"Not that I know of, sir. I've never met the man. He might be jealous or suspicious of me in some way but I've no immediate concerns about him wanting to harm me."

"I can authorise some surveillance on your house if you want me to."

"No, sir. Thank you. I think I'll be fine."

"Then, at the very least, you'll let us know if Quinlan's car appears outside your house again."

"Yes, sir," Blake said.

"And I have your word that you'll stay away from Laura Vexley?"

Blake took a breath. "Yes, sir."

"Good because if you break that promise, that's it, Blake, do you understand? It'll be a disciplinary matter. I'm tired of you grandstanding and running off with your own agenda. This is Cavanagh's case and, as far as I can see, Laura Vexley has thrown her hand in with Quinlan. That might be hard for you to stomach but I won't have you compromising the surveillance. The other case, *your* case is getting ticklish. Hannah Williams from Media and Communications has told me that it's getting a lot of attention on Twitter. All kinds of speculation going on. You can imagine; a veteran murdered on a war memorial. It's a powder keg just waiting to go off. All it takes is for someone to yell 'terrorist' loud enough and we'll have a major public order problem on our hands. Now go and find this teenager and don't come back until you've got some good news."

Blake hesitated for a second. He didn't mind being bollocked because of his behaviour last night but he objected to being accused of grandstanding. Martin looked up from his paperwork with a 'you still here?' look and Blake thought better of it.

The team were assembled in the Major Incident Room, but it was obvious word had got round judging by the lack of eye contact. "Okay people, what have we got? Good news, I hope."

"Bobby Price's new address has just come in, how's that, sir?" Alex Manikas said. "He still lives quite close to Port Sunlight. That's the good news."

"I assume from your tone that there's some bad news."

"His father is Lex Price."

"Lex? Were his parents Superman fans?"

Alex smiled. "He changed it by deed poll after seeing one of the Christopher Reeve films, apparently, sir. More importantly, he has form. The Niche database lists multiple incidents of assault and threatening behaviour. He did ten years for an armed robbery in the mid-Nineties. More recently, he's been accused of hate crimes…"

"Who against?"

"Everyone and anyone, it seems. But recently, he's had a go at some asylum seekers living in Birkenhead. He got off lightly – bound over. He can't go near the flats where the refugees are housed."

"Think we might need armed back-up, sir?" Kath Cryer said, rubbing her wrist. Kath had been caught in a shotgun blast over a year ago and was still recovering.

"I don't think so. It's his son we need to interview, after all," Blake said. "If we're heavy-handed, it might make things worse."

Kinnear put his hand up. "I've managed to get

a warrant to dig into the finances at Pro-Vet, sir. Ian Ollerthwaite will be reporting back as soon as he's been through them."

"Can't wait," Blake said.

"It'll take a while. Ian said not to get too excited…"

"Those were his exact words?"

"More or less, sir," Kinnear said, keeping a poker face.

"And Harley Vickers has turned up at Reception with his mum, sir," Kath added.

"Okay. So we've picked up some leads. Kath, can you talk to Harley Vickers and his mum and try to get to the bottom of why he ran away in the first place?"

Kath gave Blake a nod and a smile. He could see the relief on her face. "Can do."

"Right," Blake muttered. "Let's go and see if we can't bring in some glad tidings for Superintendent Martin."

Chapter 19

If Blake had been asked to plant a pin on a map of the world to show the most likely place for Lex Luthor to live, he would not have chosen Rock Ferry. Just North up the main road from Port Sunlight and not far from Blake's own home in Rock Park, Rock Ferry was a mix of houses, some large and grand, others split into bedsits. Most were spacious semi-detached houses built sometime after the ferry itself and the, then-famous, bath house attracted the large Victorian Villas of Rock Park. As the boundary of the settlement drew nearer the Cammell Laird shipyards, the houses became smaller, humble terraces. When the wealthy merchants moved out of the area and the railways rendered the ferries uneconomic, Rock Ferry began to decline. Many of the houses decayed or were split into flats. Many were demolished for a by-pass that cut the place in half.

Lex Price lived in a road of large semi-detached houses near the station. They were old but Lex's looked to be very well maintained with double glazing and modern cladding. A black Jaguar XE stood in the drive. Whatever Lex did for a living, he made plenty of money from it. Blake had brought along some uniformed officers but had requested that they wait at the end of the road rather than all piling in. With DC Alex Manikas and

DS Vikki Chinn, he knocked on the shiny black front door.

Blake was a tall man with a good physique but Lex Price towered over him. Even taking the height of the doorstep, the man must have been almost seven feet tall. He filled the grey sweatshirt he wore, his neck wider than his completely bald head if that was possible.

"Yeah?" he said, looking from Blake to Alex, to Vikki and back to Blake. "What d'you want?"

Blake showed Price his warrant card. "DCI Blake, Mr Price. We need to talk to your son, Bobby Price, if possible."

"Oh right," Price said, folding his arms. "What's that all about then?"

"I'm afraid we're not at liberty to discuss the details of the investigation, sir, but Bobby may be a key witness," Blake said. "We also need him to talk to us about assaulting a police officer outside Bebington High School yesterday…"

A look of annoyance spread across Lex price's face and Blake braced himself. "Dozy, little prick," he muttered. "Excuse me, one minute." The door closed and the sound of Lex running up the stairs shook the windows.

Muffled shouts and barked commands came from inside then a thumping and banging noise. Vikki Chinn winced and looked to Blake who raised his eyebrows. Something smashed and another yell ripped through the air. Blake was about to force his way in when the thunder of someone falling down the stairs ended in a thud against the back of the door. A second later it opened.

Bobby Price dangled in Lex's grasp, looking sorry for himself. He was a weedier, acne- ridden copy of his father only with a badly cut head of hair. "Sorry about that officer, he was a bit over eager to come and talk to you and fell down the stairs as he ran to the door. I'll be his appropriate adult. Can we follow you in our car?"

*****

Back at the station, Harley Vickers sat in the interview room staring at the tabletop while his mum scowled at him. Kath Cryer sat opposite them, wondering how best to start.

Mrs Vickers broke Kath's train of thought. "He came back this morning," she said, suddenly. "Thought I was out and was going to bunk off school for the day. Well, he didn't know I had a day off, did you?" she gave her son a poke. "I brought him in straight away."

"Harley, my name's Detective Inspector Kath Cryer. I wonder if I could ask you a few questions…"

"No comment," Harley said.

"Sorry, Harley, you aren't under caution or anything. It's just a chat, that's all."

"No Comment." Mrs Vickers gave him a shove with her elbow.

"It's okay, Jane. No need for that. I bet you're thirsty and hungry Harley, with you being out all night. Can we get you anything? Burger? Fries? Hot chocolate?"

Harley looked up and his stomach growled. As soon as his mum had set eyes on him, she'd freaked and grabbed hold of him. They'd argued so much that he hadn't had chance to get any breakfast. "Yeah…"

"Yes, please," Mrs Vickers said, jabbing her finger in his arm.

"Yes please," Harley said.

"Okay," Kath said. "I'll go and arrange that, you have a little rest and a think, there. Would you like a brew Mrs Vickers?"

Harley's mum looked slightly startled. "Oh, yes…"

"Yes please," Harley muttered. Kath smirked.

"Yes please," his mum said, giving him a side-long glance.

Kath nipped out of the office and phoned down to Madge to find someone to do the honours. Back in the interview room, Harley looked more relaxed already.

"Right, that's organised. You aren't in a hurry are you Mrs Vickers? Good. You gave your mum a fright, Harley, running off like that. Were you okay last night?"

"Yeah."

"I wouldn't know what to do if I didn't have my bed to go home to. Did you find somewhere dry to sleep?"

"Yeah. I… I found this pill box… you know like the concrete gun places."

"Wow," Kath said, glancing at mum. "And it was okay, was it? Nobody else there?"

Harley shook his head. "No, it was okay. A bit smelly, like a toilet but it was dry. There were no druggies in there or nothing."

Kath smiled. "Sorry, Harley. In my line of work, I come across all kinds of horror stories about kids running away from home. Sounds like you were lucky. Best not to put your mum through something like that again, though, eh?"

"You listen to the Inspector, Harley. You could've been killed," Harley's mum snapped.

Kath winced as Harley closed up again. "It's all right, Mrs Vickers, Harley strikes me as quite a streetwise young man. Is that true, Harley? You got a lot of common sense?"

Harley slouched in his seat. "I suppose so. Anyway, most people on the street are harmless.

They've got more problems than me."

"I knew you were a kind lad, Harley," Kath said, smiling. "I don't think you'd hurt anyone on purpose would you?"

Harley shook his head. "No way."

"Good lad," Kath said as the door opened and Madge came in with a tray of tea and biscuits. "The burger is on its way, Ma'am," she said, placing the tray on the table.

"Thanks Madge," Kath said, pleased at the cosy feeling Madge generated just by lifting the lid of the pot and giving it a stir. "Want a biscuit while you're waiting for the burger, Harley? Jammy Dodger, great choice."

Harley gave a fleeting smile, changing for a second to a little kid rather than a defensive teenager. "They're my fave."

"So, Harley, can I ask you, what happened in school yesterday? I promise you aren't in any trouble."

Harley glanced from right to left for a second as though he was searching for an escape route. He swallowed the biscuit. "I saw Bobby Price outside school, and someone said he was after me."

"Why would he be after you?"

Harley's face darkened and he stared at the tabletop again. Kath held her breath, fearing she might lose him and then the door swung open again and the smell of burgers and chips filled the room. They sat in silence watching the teenager demolish the burger in a matter of seconds.

"Blimey," Kath said. "You were hungry, weren't you?"

Harley nodded and took a huge slurp of coke. He looked up from his cup and caught Kath's eye. "He thinks I grassed him up, but it wasn't me it was Alfie Lewis."

Kath nodded. "And what did Alfie Lewis grass him up about?"

"About the old man..." Harley bit back on the next words, realising he'd said too much.

"Alfie has already grassed Bobby up, Harley. We'll pick him up. In fact I think another team may well have picked up Bobby Price already. You may as well tell us everything you know and get it off your chest. You'll feel better for it, I promise..."

Harley looked at his mum and then at Kath. "I stopped hanging round with them. Bobby's a psycho. He hit that old man with a baseball bat just cos he gave us some lip about litter." Harley paused. "And Bobby said he'd killed that other bloke. The one on the war memorial. Bobby said he'd done it..."

"He actually told you that?" Kath said.

"He kind of hinted at it. Said something about

the soldier fella getting what he deserved or something. Anyway, I ran away when he hurt that old man. I'd had enough." He looked up at Kath. "I never hurt anyone. Really, I didn't. Will I go to prison?"

"I very much doubt it, Harley," Kath said, catching Jane Vicker's eye. "Listen, you've been very helpful. Could you just wait outside while I have a chat with your mum?"

Harley looked puzzled. "What for?"

"Never you mind that," Jane Vickers said, giving him a gentle push. "Go and wait outside before Inspector Cryer changes her mind about prison."

Harley didn't need telling twice and hurried for the door. He sat on a plastic chair outside the interview room. He felt as though everyone who passed him was judging him. Even those who gave him a smile and a wink seemed as though they were laughing at him. Why was his mum in there with that policewoman? The sudden conviction that he should never have come along gripped Harley. His heart thumped as he thought about what they were saying in the room. He could imagine his mum begging the inspector to be kind and not send him to prison, but he'd been part of it, really hadn't he? He'd stood and watched while Bobby knocked that man down. What if the old man had died? It would be murder and he'd be part of it. Harley sprang to his feet. He wanted to run but he didn't want to upset his mum. He didn't want to wait until she came out, though.

And then, suddenly, Harley was flying across the corridor as Bobby Price appeared from no-where, howling abuse at him and slamming his fists into his stomach and face.

Chapter 20

To describe George Owens, the remaining director of Pro-Vets as angry would have been an understatement. Detective Constable Ian Ollerthwaite thought the man was going to explode. For a while, Owens opened and closed his mouth like a landed carp, then he made strange squeaking noises as he tried to formulate the words that would describe his rage. His red face bulged. "Isn't it enough that you lot have pried into my private life?" he said at last. "Now you want to disrupt the charitable work we're doing here. Who do I complain to?"

"There is a complaints procedure, sir," DC Ollerthwaite said, carefully. He liked to spell out things like this in great detail. Some people thought he was being pedantic, but he knew that when a complainant was all fired up, they didn't always take in the facts. "I can go through that with you before we begin our audit if that would help. I've just given you the warrant that allows us access to your accounts. You're holding it. If you could just pinpoint the particular area of the investigation that has contravened good practice or policy, I'd be happy to make amends for that…"

George Owens just blinked at him. "No… no… it's just very irregular and awkward."

"I understand that, sir. That's why I'll be as

unobtrusive and discreet as possible. Obviously, we're investigating a murder and want to leave no stone unturned. I'm sure you understand," Ian said, quite pleased with his measured pace. "Now, would it be acceptable to work here?" He pointed at Paul's desk.

"Oh, very well," Owens snapped. "I'll call Quentin, he's our IT guy. He can get you everything you need."

"Thank you, sir, this is my card should you need to get in touch out of hours. You'll see there's the main HQ number and my extension but also a mobile number and an email address you can contact me on, too. Otherwise, you'll be able to find me right here."

Owens seemed so keen to have the card that he snatched it and Ian congratulated himself on winning over another member of the public. He settled himself at Paul Travis' desk and watched with a satisfied smile as Owens hurried out of the office.

*****

The interview room felt packed with Bobby and Lex Price, his solicitor, Blake and Vikki Chinn all hunched around a table. As modern and clean as the room was, it wasn't built to accommodate five people, two of whom were particularly large. Blake had introduced everyone and explained Bobby's rights to him. The boy had to be peeled off Harley Vickers and Blake cursed himself for not checking if the interview room was free, he'd just assumed it was as he'd booked it in advance. He seemed to have calmed down now but Harley had ended up with a few bruises. He'd probably have a beautiful black eye later. Blake promised himself he'd have words with Kath later, but he suspected that it wasn't her fault. Harley and his mum had appeared out of the blue and she'd had to interview them in the first available room. He turned his attention to the young man in front of him.

"So, first of all, Bobby, you need to know that Harley Vickers is not the reason we picked you up. You can blame yourself for that after your actions outside Bebington High School. Some of your old teachers recognised you."

"Whatever," Bobby muttered.

"Let's start there, shall we? Yesterday, you were loitering outside Bebington High School when PC Mark Robertson approached you..."

Bobby glanced at his dad, who nodded. "I was just waiting for some friends when that copper came running at me. I was scared..."

"PC Robertson and a number of witnesses in the school office maintain that he approached you at walking pace when you ran straight at him. When he tried to defend himself, you head-butted him."

"I didn't know he just wanted to talk…"

"Okay. Why were you waiting outside the school?"

"Just waiting for a friend to come out…"

"It was barely afternoon, Bobby. Hours until school finished," Vikki Chinn said.

"So? It's a free country. I didn't have anything better to do."

"And who were you waiting for?" Blake said.

"Alfie Lewis and Harley."

"A bit young for you to be hanging around with, aren't they?"

Bobby gave a dismissive shrug.

"Were they the boys you hung around Port Sunlight Village with two days ago? The afternoon that Eric Smith was assaulted?"

Bobby glanced at his dad again. "Who's Eric Smith? I don't know any Eric Smith."

"He's the old man who was put in hospital by a young man with a baseball bat. Would that be you by any chance, Bobby?"

"No," Bobby said, looking disgusted. "I wouldn't do nothing like that."

Blake nodded. "Well a simple DNA test will clear that up, won't it?"

"What do you mean?" Lex Price said, suddenly.

"Whoever hit Mr Smith left their DNA all over the bat. It's just a simple case of taking a sample and comparing, really. Obviously, if it turns out that it's Bobby's then it'll look bad in court, won't it?"

Lex gave his son a murderous look and then nodded to the solicitor who nodded back. "Did you hurt the man, son?" Lex said at last.

Bobby Price lowered his head and nodded. "He was banging on about me dropping a can on the floor, slagging us off. I lost my temper. I didn't mean to hurt him, honest."

"So, just to clarify, you're saying you did assault Mr Smith," Blake said.

"No, I hit him with the baseball bat," Bobby said.

"And PC Robertson?"

"I thought he was going to arrest me for hurting the old man," Bobby said. "I just panicked, that's all."

"It's good that you've been honest with us about that, Bobby. We're going to charge you with those offences and your cooperation will be noted but it's also important that you continue to be honest with us," Blake said, leaning forward. "So tell me, where did you get the baseball bat from?"

*****

George Owens found Quentin Ufford hidden behind a stack of packing cases in the warehouse, munching on a large pack of kettle chips. The young man looked flustered as Owens advanced on him. "What the hell do you think you're doing, Quentin? I've been looking for you everywhere. And those crisps are for the punters, not staff!"

"Forry," Ufford said, spraying crisp crumbs between them. He cleared his throat. "I was starving, George. I forgot my lunch this morning in all the panic."

"You don't look like you're panicking now. Do I have to worry about Ollerthwaite finding anything he shouldn't?"

"I'm working on it…"

"No, you aren't. You're stuffing your face with crisps that aren't yours. Get back to your desk and sort this mess out. If that detective finds anything iffy, we're finished."

"Relax, have you spoken to him? He's a right dozy pillock. God, he nearly put me to sleep just asking me for the passwords."

George grabbed Ufford by the lapels of his brown suit. "He's dull, yes. Boring, obviously. How d'you think he gets his kicks? Jet skiing? Paragliding? No, his idea of a good time is picking through our accounts digit by dreary digit. He's *exactly* the kind of person who will pick us up on every fucking dot and every fucking dash.

So those accounts better be squeaky clean by the time he gets to them, or else!" He pushed Ufford back, sending him crashing into a pile of boxes and stormed off.

For a moment, Quentin Ufford lay there amongst the crushed boxes, shocked. There was no need for George to be like that, but he knew what would happen if Ollerthwaite found any irregularities. He clambered to his feet.

Terry White appeared, looming over him. "You okay, Quentin?" he said.

"Yeah, Terry, I'm fine," Quentin said, watching George stamping across the warehouse. "As you were Terry, as you were, mate."

*****

Looking at Lex Price, Blake wondered if there would even be any point in trying to restrain him if he kicked off. The man rippled with muscle. Blake had seen enough steroid merchants who looked like they had cushions stuffed up their sleeves but could barely make it up the stairs without getting breathless. Price exuded a rare kind of menace. There was just something about the way the man moved that told you he could snap you in half without breaking into a sweat. Blake really didn't want to find out, if he could help it. But Price's face was hardening and his foot was jigging.

"You spend a lot of time hanging round Port

Sunlight, Bobby. What is it you like about the place? The architecture?" Blake said. "You a fan of the Arts and Crafts Movement?"

"Dunno what you're talking about," Bobby said.

"Please don't take the piss out of my son, DCI Blake," Lex said. "He's not a genius but..."

"I could've joined the Army," Bobby said, scowling. "I'm not fucking stupid."

Lex's face twisted into a sneer. "You, a fucking toy soldier, lad? Get a grip. Anyway, answer DCI Blake what were you doing down the village?"

"Dunno. Just like it there. Lots of places to chill out, like in the Dell..."

"The baseball bat you had with you, Bobby, where did it come from?"

"What's with the interest in the baseball bat all of a sudden?" Lex Price said.

"We know that the bat was used in another assault the night before Bobby attacked Mr Smith," Blake said. "We need to know what Bobby was doing the night before..."

"You're talking about the murder, right? My son is not a fucking murderer!"

Blake raised his hands. "If that's the case, we need to know what Bobby was doing that night and where the bat came from. Can you tell us that Bobby?"

"No comment," Bobby said.

"Come on, son, you can tell them," Lex said. "There's no shame. You don't want to go down for something you didn't do."

"You told your mates that it was you who killed Paul Travis after the argument you had last week. Your DNA is all over the bat. Nobody else's. right now, you're our prime suspect for murder."

"For fuck's sake," Lex spat. "Just tell them the truth, Bobby. Now."

Bobby glanced at his dad. "I found it," Bobby said.

"Where did you find it, Bobby?"

"Go on, son…"

"I-I'm scared… they'll cut my head off…"

"What?" Blake gave Vikki a quizzical look, but she looked as puzzled as he did.

"Who will, Bobby?" she said.

Bobby stared at her. "Them… them… I can't say…"

"Bobby, you aren't making much sense. Can you explain where you found the baseball bat, first? If you're worried about your safety, we can protect you," Blake said, eyeing Lex Price and thinking that Bobby didn't really need much protection while his dad was around.

"I found it in Port Sunlight. I saw the men

beating up that Travis guy. When they'd finished with him, they walked off and threw the bat on the ground. I picked it up. Dunno what I was thinking of..."

"So you saw Paul Travis being attacked?"

Bobby nodded. "I-I was hanging out in the Hillsborough Gardens thing you know just behind the war memorial when I heard the noise. It was like hammers. Then I looked and saw them..."

"How many were there, Bobby?"

"Two men, all dressed in black, with face masks on."

Vikki raised her eyebrows. "You said you were scared they'd cut your head off, Bobby. Why say that?"

"They were terrorists, weren't they? Them muslamic terrorists!"

Chapter 21

Superintendent Martin had a good line in weary expressions, Blake had to admit. The current one needed no words but he gave them anyway. "Why can't anything be straight-forward, Blake? Why does it always have to get complicated? We've got the local community up in arms about the Travis murder and now you're telling me it's a possible terrorist attack?"

"I'm dubious, sir. Lex Price…"

"Lex? Who the hell calls their kid Lex?"

"He's actually Bobby Price's father. Changed it by deed poll…"

"Really? Good to know we're dealing with Wirral's crème-de-la-crème, Blake. Sorry, carry on," he said, massaging the bridge of his nose.

"Lex Price has previous for hate speech. He's been bound over for harassing some Syrian asylum seekers recently. I wouldn't be surprised if Bobby hasn't been put up to it by his father."

"Any evidence for that?"

"Bobby says that the men he saw were dressed in black and wearing face masks. So how could he know if they were white or black or any other ethnicity? There's nothing in his statement other than his own prejudice to suggest the men were politically motivated. Nobody has claimed responsibility for Paul Travis' death as far as I know," Blake said. "Price said they spoke to each other in a 'foreign language', but he couldn't identify what type of language."

"Marvellous. We're duty-bound to investigate this new angle, though. We can't just dismiss it. God, this'll crank up tensions, no end. If the press get hold of this, it'll go national."

"I know sir," Blake said. "I'm wary of making this public. You can imagine how some political groups would use this for their own ends. My only worry is Lex Price. With his record, I can't be certain he wouldn't blab to the press and try to make something of it, especially if we come down hard on his son."

"You've warned him, of course," Martin said.

"I was saving that conversation for just before he left, Bobby's being processed at the moment and his father's with him. Our only hope is that Lex Price wants to keep out of the spotlight, himself…"

"What do you mean?"

"I'm not certain, sir, but I suspect that Price isn't exactly squeaky clean himself and as such, he mightn't like any unwanted media attention."

"You think the man's a criminal?"

"It's just my suspicious mind, sir. He does have a record and for someone who did ten years for armed robbery, he seems very well set up."

"Let's hope he keeps his head down, then."

"Yes, sir. As you say, the fallout could be pretty dire."

"Can you imagine the headlines? 'War hero executed by terrorists on a war memorial,'" Martin groaned, scrubbing his face with his palms. "Lord above. So we tread carefully. Contact the Counter-terrorism Unit and see who we have locally who might pose any kind of threat. Take advice from them. We go softly on this. A gentle bit of asking around first. Please don't let this blow up in our faces, Blake."

*****

Lex Price filled a chair in the reception area with Bobby sat next to him. Blake watched Lex mutter some kind of advice to his son whilst simultaneously picking apart a plastic cup. It made sense, Blake supposed, the man had experience of courts and prison after all. What a thing to have to pass on to your kids, though. Bobby kept his eyes down, staring at the floor all the time. Something about the whole relationship made Blake's gut twist but he wasn't sure what it was or what he could do about it.

"Mr Price," he said, approaching them. "Hopefully, it's been explained to you that, although Bobby has been charged, we aren't going to detain him. We'll submit the DNA evidence and the interview recording to the CPS and we'll see what comes of it. Can you just ensure that Bobby stays close to home for now? It would be disastrous for him if he were to get into any more trouble..."

Lex Price nodded and extended his hand. "I understand. Thank you for your help, Inspector. I'm sorry he's caused all this bother, if you want an apology to the old man, I'm sure Bobby would be keen to make that."

Blake thought back to Smith's bitter comments about the leniency of the penal system these days. "Well, I'll feed that back to Mr Smith. Obviously, this will have to go further but, hopefully, Bobby has learnt his lesson."

"I've told him before, Inspector, you guys are just doing your job and lashing out at members of the public isn't acceptable."

"Could I ask one more thing. We need to verify Bobby's story and obviously, it's a sensitive area. It would probably do more harm than good if this were to become public knowledge..."

Lex's face hardened. "if some flippin' towel heads have done in a veteran, don't you think the public need warning?"

"If there has been some kind of terrorist atrocity, then yes, I agree we need to find and apprehend the people concerned quickly, Mr Price but if Bobby was mistaken, then we'll have caused a panic and that might hamper our investigation."

"Fair enough," Lex said, slightly mollified.

"Thanks, I knew you'd understand. We'll be in touch," Blake said, shaking Lex's hand. "If you don't mind me asking, what is it you do for a living, Mr Price?"

Lex Price levelled his gaze on Blake. "I'm in security, building sites, empty factory units, that kind of thing. Keeping things safe and secure. Not unlike you, Inspector."

Blake watched Lex guide his son out of the police station. "Totally unlike me, I suspect, Mr Price," he muttered to himself. "Totally unlike me."

*****

As soon as DS Vikki Chinn had finished interviewing with DCI Blake, she headed for the psychologists Nicola Norton's office in Heswall on the Deeside of the Wirral. Heswall was a small market town and wasn't immune to the damage online shopping had inflicted on high streets everywhere. But whereas many town centres succumbed to tattoo parlours and pound shops, Vikki noticed a large number of eateries and coffee shops.

Norton's office was above a shop selling second-hand mobile phones and other related technology near the bus depot in the centre of town. Vikki had trouble gaining access at first. She went into the shop and the woman behind the counter directed her round the back. A narrow staircase led up to a second floor and in the darkness above, Vikki could make out a door. As Vikki climbed the stairs, the door flew open and Nicola Norton loomed over her, coat on and bag over her shoulder. She gave a little yelp. "You scared me," Nicola said.

"Sorry, madam," Vikki said, showing her warrant card. "DS Vikki Chinn, we spoke on the phone the other day about Richard Ince. You were going to call me back."

Nicola Norton put a hand to her head. "I'm so sorry. With all that's going on, there's a lot of upset at Pro-Vets and I've been working flat out. It just slipped my mind."

Vikki nodded but didn't move. "I understand Ms Norton. Is there any chance you could look now?"

"Y-yes, of course" Norton said, glancing at her watch. She turned back to the office, unlocking the door. The room inside was neat and tidy. Vikki supposed it had to be if she used it for consulting. This was Norton's public face. Everything was painted a calming shade of pastel green. A couple of tall parlour palms stood in the corner, softening the sharp edges of a bookcase laden with volumes of books about psychology and self-improvement. There was a couch in the corner, and a leather armchair next to it. Norton sat behind her desk and Vikki noticed a number of framed certificates declaring the woman's professional accomplishments.

"I was hoping you would have got back to me sooner about Richard Ince's buddy, Ms Norton," Vikki said. "An investigation as complex as this takes time and I really didn't want to have to travel when I could be assessing evidence back at HQ."

"I'm so, so sorry. You should have phoned me …"

"I did several times and left voice messages but you never got back to me."

"Like I said, I've been busy," Norton said, smiling apologetically. "Honestly, it's been frantic at Pro-Vets. Everyone wants to talk and George has been surprisingly generous with my time."

"Well, we're here now, so, can you tell me who Richard Ince's buddy was?"

Nicola Norton looked as though she was weighing up what to say next. "Look, my experience of working with the police hasn't always been encouraging in the past," she said. "Two years ago, I helped on a case involving a troubled ex-serviceman. It was a total mess and the young man ended up dead. So forgive me but I'm concerned about just bandying names about without considering my patients."

Vikki pursed her lips for a moment. "Okay. I can understand that. What do you suggest? I really need to speak to this person."

Norton thought for a second. "The man works in the Pro-Vets warehouse. He has a number of problems due to an acquired brain injury. One of them is he finds it hard to process what people are saying, he also has poor executive function..."

"Executive function?"

"Imagine you want a drink of tea. You know that first you have to get the mug from the cupboard, then you know you need to fill the kettle with water, then you know you have to switch the kettle on. There's a whole chain of actions that lead to that drink being before you, right? He struggles with working out the steps needed to achieve the most basic tasks sometimes. It causes all kinds of problems for him."

"Then we'd have to plan what we were going to ask carefully so he could process and answer effectively," Vikki said. "You could help with that, couldn't you? I don't want to make this any more of an ordeal for him than it has to be."

Norton looked uncomfortable. "There's something else you should know. My client has always been... fragile. There had been concerns raised about him before he was injured."

"What kind of concerns?"

"Trauma can do all kinds of things to the mind, Sergeant. He was having bad dreams, making strange accusations against senior officers. Claiming they were spying on him or that other colleagues were going through his belongings. The injury only seemed to heighten this paranoia."

"Are you saying that this man is dangerous?"

"Not normally but he will be hard to interview. Have you ever heard of the Fregoli delusion, Sergeant? It's a very rare disorder that means the sufferer has trouble distinguishing between faces. Part of the delusional thought leads them to believe that certain individuals can change appearance or disguise themselves."

"So, as far as my client is concerned, I could be one of his friends…"

"Or enemies, out to get him. He had trouble with one particular NCO, a Corporal Graves. Witnesses suggest that Graves picked on my client when he was in the army. Graves was caught in the same IED explosion as him but didn't survive. In his worst moments, my client thinks Graves is still alive and out to get him, changing his appearance to get at him. He's on antipsychotics but, trust me, approach my client in the wrong way and you'll have big problems. His name is Terry White."

*****

As plans went, Blake knew it was foolhardy. Ian Youde, the voice of reason, sat in his kitchen and shook his head, Charlie curled at his feet. It was the end of another long day and Blake had treated himself to a chicken jalfrezi from the Wirral Tandoori in Bromborough. He'd phoned Ian in advance and got his order of fish and chips from the chippy. Blake could have predicted that he wouldn't be a fan of curries. Now they sat polishing off their respective meals, Blake sweating slightly and sipping a cold Cobra beer in an attempt to cool his mouth down.

"Is there someone in your department, anyone, you've really wanted to punch? Because you may as well do that before you launch into this stupid idea and lose your job, Will."

"There are a few people I wouldn't mind giving a good slap right now, Ian, but I need to talk to Laura and it seems like the safest way..."

"There isn't a safest way," Ian said. "If she's shacked up with her ex, you can't go muscling in, especially if the police are watching him. You shouldn't even have told me."

"What? You going to tell them all at your Bridge circle, Ian?" Blake said.

"I go down the Snooker club every now and then," Ian said, sounding hurt. "I like my own company, it's true but I do have friends other than you."

"I know but you're not a blabbermouth, are you? Anyway, it might just work and give me at least a chance to speak to her."

"You don't even know if she's still practising as an animal psychologist, Will..."

Blake showed Youde a website on his phone. It showed Laura holding a small black dog and smiling confidently out of the screen. A banner said: 'Paws for Thought' and a subtitle declared that Laura Vexley was an 'Animal Behaviour Saviour.'

"This is new," Blake said. "It can only have gone up since she came back. There's a number. All I need is an address she doesn't know and a bogus pet with a behavioural problem and she'll come round."

"It's creepy, Will," Ian said. "She won't be happy."

"I can't help that can I? Now all I need is for Jeff to let me use his house. Laura has never been there, so won't recognise the address."

"She'll recognise your voice, surely," Ian said.

"I have a secret weapon," Blake said. "Madge at work."

"I just hope you know what you're doing, Will," Ian said. "This could all go tits up in an instant and then where will you be?"

Chapter 22

Asking DC Alex Manikas for life advice was probably a bad idea, Kinnear thought almost the moment he opened his mouth. Not that Manikas wasn't experienced in some matters, just not the ones Kinnear was interested in. Alex would be the ideal mentor to someone who wanted to go out, get drunk and play the field but Kinnear was settled. So now, he felt foolish as he listened to Alex gush over all his excellent qualities.

"You'll make a great dad, mate," Alex said as they sat in the car before making their next call. "You're patient, sensible..."

"Sensible? Boring you mean..."

"Parents are meant to be boring, aren't they?"

"You aren't helping, Alex. I just don't know if I'm ready to take on such a responsibility yet. Chris and I are both so busy..."

"I thought you said he was going part time."

"Well, yeah but I'm not. I won't be there for her..."

Alex thought for a moment. "My dad built up a sign-writing and billboard business when I was growing up. He was mad busy and often came in after we'd gone to bed and was out before we woke up, but he was a good dad and he did his best for us. For what it's worth, I reckon that's all you can do, mate."

Kinnear smiled, surprised by Manikas' frankness. "Thanks. I need to think about it all."

"Right now, we need to focus on the job. Although why we're being sent to harass these poor people because some little racist scumbag points the finger to please his dad?" He looked at the stern front of the dilapidated house. It had once been a huge Victorian villa but had long been split into bedsits. "I can't imagine this is how these poor buggers thought they'd be living when they ran for their lives from wherever they were."

"There's one guy of marginal interest to Counter Terrorism who lives there," Kinnear said, glad to get back to talking about work. "We go wading in and we could push him over the edge. We could be recruiting sergeants for some nutjob terror group."

"And what if he turns out not to have an alibi?" Manikas said. "We've got to check. We'll just be polite, ask a few questions and then move on. If anything rouses our suspicions, we'll get back-up."

The front door of the house was open and they stepped into a hallway littered with flyers and unwanted post. As with many of these rented buildings owned by absentee landlords, it was unclear who was responsible for keeping communal areas clear. Similarly, the paintwork was battered by hundreds of people passing to and fro through the hall. "God, I'd hate to live in a place like this," Kinnear muttered.

The stairs creaked as they made their way to the second floor and a red door with a number twelve on it. "I bet you someone's raking money in off the council for housing these poor bastards," Manikas said and knocked on the door.

There was a pause and some shuffling behind the door, then it opened. A young man with dark hair and a long beard looked nervously through the crack he'd opened. "Y-yes?"

Kinnear flashed his warrant card. "DC Kinnear, DC Manikas, Merseyside Police. Are we speaking to Jamal Al Hadid?"

The young man's eyes hardened. "Yes. What do you want?

"No need to be alarmed, we just wanted to ask you a few questions. It'll only take a couple of minutes. Really, it's nothing."

Jamal looked them up and down. "Very well, take your shoes off."

Alex flashed Andrew a look of concern, but Kinnear slipped his shoes off without missing a beat. "Okay, Mr Al Hadid," he said. "Can we come in?"

Jamal backed away from the door. "You will have to forgive us. We have very little space and trying to keep everywhere tidy and clean with the damp in this house is almost impossible."

The room would have been a large bedroom at one time. Now it housed three beds, a sink had been plumbed in and next to that stood a small cooker. The smell of last night's cooking filled the air but there was that musty undertone of a room that hasn't been properly dry for many years. Clothes hung on a laundry rack, but Kinnear wondered if they ever dried. A few toys lay scattered on the floor. Kinnear and Manikas sat on a small sofa that filled one wall while Jamal perched on the end of his bed.

Manikas cleared his throat. "Can we ask Mr Al Hadid, where were you on the night of the 14th? Five days ago."

Jamal Al Hadid stroked his beard and looked troubled. "I was here with my wife and daughter."

"Can anyone else corroborate this?"

"I spoke to a number of residents here through the course of that evening. I also had to change a lightbulb for Mrs Kalil downstairs. That was around eleven fifteen. Where else would I be?"

"I don't know, sir," Kinnear said. "That's why we were asking. Does the name Paul Travis mean anything to you?"

Jamal's face fell. "Really? A man dies in Port

Sunlight and you come to me?"

"So you're aware of the investigation, sir?" Manikas said.

"I listen to the news and read the papers online. Why have you come to me of all the people in this house? You think I'm some kind of terrorist?"

"Not at all, Mr Al Hadid. We are just following up a lead..."

"I'm not stupid you know. Before I left Syria, I was a lawyer. This is because of Lex Price, isn't it?"

"I'm not sure what you're getting at, sir," Kinnear said, feeling himself flush red at the mention of Price's name.

"I had an altercation with the man in Birkenhead. He was screaming racist abuse at my wife and daughter, so I stood up to him..."

"I believe Mr Price was bound over for that incident..." Manikas cut in.

"And I am branded as a trouble-maker. You think I'm a murderer because I protected my wife and child from that... monster?"

"Having seen Mr Price, I think you're a very brave man, Mr Al Hadid," Kinnear said, standing up. "We're sorry to have troubled you."

Caught off guard, Jamal Al Hadid blinked. "Thank you," was all he could think to say. "You know, when I lived in Syria, I had a Mercedes, a wardrobe full of suits. My wife and daughter wanted for nothing. We fled in the clothes we were wearing. At the refugee camps we swapped our expensive, designer wear for warmer, secondhand things that didn't really fit us. By the time we reached England, we were in rags with nothing. Now look at us. I deliver takeaways and do some voluntary work in a local charity shop. I'm grateful for the shelter this country has given us in one way, but you aren't the first officers to visit me. I defend my family once and, whenever there is a hint of trouble, the police turn up. Sometimes I wonder if you bother people like Mr Price quite as much."

"I hope we treat all citizens of this country without fear or favour, sir," Kinnear said. "We'll leave you in peace."

Outside, Manikas blew out a long breath. "Do you get the feeling we've been led up a garden path?"

"How do you mean?"

"Well, do you honestly think Bobby Price saw two Islamic extremists at the war memorial or did he make that up? If he did, who put him up to it? His bloody father must have known that Al Hadid would end up getting quizzed over it."

Kinnear looked unconvinced. "He wouldn't know that Jamal would specifically get a visit, but he probably guessed someone would. And why go to all that bother if you aren't trying to hide something? Shall we go and report back to Blakey?"

*****

The counselling room at Pro-Vets was a small office really but instead of desks, it had comfy chairs, beanbags and walls painted in the same cool green as Nicola Norton's office. Norton had offered to sit in with DS Vikki Chinn as a support to Terry White and Vikki could see no reason why not, as long as White was happy with the arrangement.

Terry White filled the armchair opposite Vikki, he was clearly a strong man but had lost a lot of his fitness and muscle tone. He wore a blue Pro-Vets overall, black boots and a baseball cap. His round face looked calm and serene as he stared at Vikki. She could see the puckered skin at the side of his neck that grew into a large scar at the back of his head. Nicola Norton, sat in another of the chairs, dressed in a tailored black trouser suit.

"Terry, thank you for agreeing to talk to me today. My name is DS Vikki Chinn and I want to ask you a few questions about Richard Ince."

Nicola put her hand up to stop Vikki saying anything else and they waited.

Finally, Terry nodded. "That's okay. Ritchy's gone. Taken from us."

"I know, Terry. I'm sorry about that. Can you remember when you last saw him?"

Another long pause. "Yes."

"When was that, Terry?"

"When was what?"

Vikki exchanged glances with Nicola who scribbled something down on a small white board. "This might help, Terry," she said, showing him the board.

"We went to the pub the night before he was taken."

"What do mean when you say he was taken?"

Terry looked up. "He killed himself because Graves took his body. He looked like Ritchy but he was Graves really. I could tell."

Vikki bit her lip. "And how did that make you feel, Terry?"

"Scared. A bit angry. Graves shouldn't do that. It's not right. He needs stopping."

"You do know that Graves is dead, Terry?" Vikki said.

A strange, tight smile spread across Terry White's face and he shook his head. "How come I see him everywhere, then?"

"Where do you see him, Terry? Is he here right now?"

Terry looked closely at Vikki and then at Nicola Norton. "No. But I do see him. In the crowd, laughing at me..."

An awkward silence fell across the room. Vikki finally broke it with a cough. "On the night Richard Ince died. You said you went for a drink with him. What happened then? Where did you go?"

The seconds ticked away as Terry White frowned into the past, trying to fit together pieces of his fragmented memory. "We went to the pub and had a few drinks. I shouldn't really. It messes with my medication. Then I went home," he said at last. "Ritchy went up to his flat and Graves made him take heroin."

"Made him? Didn't Richard take heroin normally?"

"Ritchy never took smack. I told the police that before. They didn't believe me about Graves, either. Nobody does."

"What kind of mood was Richard in when he left you?"

"He wasn't in a mood," Terry said. "He was happy. Drunk happy. Told me he was coming into some money or something. It was like he'd won the lottery. Then Graves killed him."

"Why would Graves want to kill him?"

"Ritchy was my friend. Graves hates my friends. He kills them all. Paul was my friend. He killed

Paul, too."

Vikki looked over to Nicola who shook her head. "Well, thank you for your time, Mr White," Vikki said, starting to stand.

"It won't be long, though. Graves is weak. I've trapped his soul…"

"I see," Vikki said, glancing again at Nicola in despair. "How have you done that?"

White grinned and tapped the side of his nose. "A special kind of voodoo. Soon he'll be finished and I won't have to worry about him ever again. Nobody will."

Vikki nodded. "Thank you again, Mr White. I'll let you get back to your work. They must be missing you by now."

Terry White nodded but the smile still clung to his face and he opened the door with trembling hands. "I hope I haven't over-excited him or anything," Vikki said, once he'd gone. "Did you see how animated he became?"

Nicola nodded. "Yes. His answers became less monosyllabic, too. I might check and see that his medication is all up to date and that he's taking it. I haven't seen him like that for some time."

"What was all that voodoo stuff?"

"I told you that Terry had a lot of difficulties," Nicola said with a sigh. "He's quite paranoid and had a phase of burning little effigies of people he thought were out to get him. Look, I'm not sure I can go further into it without completely breaking confidentiality. I've compromised it enough."

"Do you think we should take him seriously when he says that Richard Ince never took heroin before?"

"I don't know. I suppose it's possible that he was a first-time user. As I said when we spoke on the phone, it wasn't something we were aware of initially. Maybe he'd chosen heroin as an easy means of ending it all. He did leave a suicide note."

"Yes, he did," Vikki muttered, looking at the door and making a mental note to check out the note carefully. Something wasn't quite right here and frankly, Terry White gave her the creeps.

Chapter 23

The first ripples of the media storm arrived in the form of Deirdre Lanham, reporter from the Wirral Argus, a local paper. She was a short, middle-aged woman with a round face, framed by long, blonde hair. Blake had run into her on a number of occasions and knew her to be hard-nosed but fair. She sat waiting in HQ reception as he entered to start the day which he didn't take as a great omen.

"DCI Blake," she called as he passed her. "Is it true you're investigating a possible terrorist link to the murder over in Port Sunlight?"

Blake winced. "No comment," he said.

"I take it from the expression on your face that we weren't meant to know," she said, with a mischievous grin. "You should know, it's all over Twitter."

"What are you asking me for then?" Blake said. "Isn't that what you journalists do these days? Look on social media and regurgitate unfounded comments and opinions?"

Deirdre bridled a little. "I came here, hoping to get some kind of helpful information, DCI Blake. There was a time when you didn't object to the media helping you fight crime. You revelled in it in fact." She hummed the opening bars of the Searchlight theme. "So, what are you looking at?"

Blake leaned on the reception counter and folded his arms. "I'm looking at you and wondering why you're clogging up reception, to be honest."

"Look, Blake," Deirdre Lanham snapped. "This is going to be a shit show and you know it. You'll need all the help you can get in a few days. I can go and mine social media for information and print that or you can give me a few morsels that I can use and print the truth. Or maybe you want Tommy Robinson holding a rally in Port Sunlight..."

"Jeez," Blake muttered. He turned to Madge at the counter. "Is there an interview room available Madge? Just for ten minutes."

*****

Superintendent Martin sat blinking at Blake as though he'd just pinched his cheek, ruffled his hair and called him 'darling'. "You did what?"

"It was a snap decision, sir. What Deirdre Lanham said was true. There's a huge scope for misinformation here..."

"Which is why we have a Media and Communications Manager whose job it is to handle... the media, funny that isn't it, Will? Fancy that eh? Hannah Williams gets paid a wage for dealing with journalists. She's a qualified professional."

"All I said was that we had interviewed some

teenagers in connection with the murder and we were sceptical about reports of it being a terrorist incident..."

"And that's enough, is it? In your professional opinion? Oh no, wait I forgot, you used to be on the telly, didn't you, Will, so you know better than Hannah." Martin threw his hands up.

"Sir, why would terrorists kill someone wandering home from the pub in the middle of the night? Hardly a huge spectacle, is it?"

"You're an expert on terrorism now, too. Christ on a bike! Why don't we just sack half the force and use your incredible, wide-ranging talents, Will? Did it ever occur to you that Travis might have been targeted? Personally, I can't think of anything more terrifying than hit squads selecting ex-squaddies to kill."

"It's not that, sir..."

"You better make sure it isn't," Martin said. "We are going to look complacent and incompetent at the least. What other leads are you looking at?"

"I think it's connected to the charity in some way. I've got Ian Ollerthwaite looking into their accounts..."

Martin went as white as his shirt. Blake was genuinely worried that the man would pass out. "You're poking around the accounts of a veterans' charity? How about running over a few grannies while you're at it? The optics of this are terrible!"

"Optics, sir?"

"Yes, Will, optics! You know, the way things look to the public."

"With respect, sir, I'm not just 'poking around.' Paul Travis wasn't randomly killed. He had his throat cut. It was premeditated..."

"Terrorists!"

"I don't think so, sir. I haven't got to the bottom of it yet but..."

"You better bloody had. The clock's ticking, Blake," Martin said, snatching up the phone. "I'm going to contact Hannah to arrange a press conference and see if we can't sort this mess out before we have protestors of all persuasion descending on Port Sunlight." He waved his hand at Blake. "Go on, get this sorted!"

*****

Numbers had fascinated DC Ian Ollerthwaite ever since he was a child at school. Maths had been his best subject and he had always been a compulsive collector of train and bus numbers. He like the order it brought to the world. His parents had been surprised when, in a rare spark of independent thought, he'd told them he wanted to be a police officer rather than go to university and study Pure Mathematics. But he was a big and solid young man with a good store of common sense and totally committed to anything he joined. He knew he wasn't the most dynamic or flashy of people and he rarely took up invitations to the pub or on social nights out. Somehow, though, over the years, he had ploughed his own furrow at work, and he liked to think people respected him for it. They certainly respected his head for figures.

Ian leaned back in his chair and looked at his surroundings. He could easily have ended up being an accountant in an office like this one at Pro-Vets. He might do yet, if his plan to retire from the force at 55 and take up a new role came to fruition. There was a demand for a forensic mind like his in auditing and inspection. His general calm and unflappable nature would be an asset when having to ask awkward questions.

This had served him well yesterday when George Owens had kicked off. He made a mental note to let DCI Blake know about Owens' reaction. It seemed more than irritated, Ollerthwaite detected a note of fear in the man's look. Looking at the computer screen and the file open on his desk, he could see something was amiss.

A gentle knock brought Ian's attention to the door. Quentin Ufford's shaggy, round head poked round it. "Fancy a cuppa, Ian?" he said, smiling.

"No thank you, Mr Ufford," Ian said. "I've

brought my own flask and I'd prefer you to call me DC Ollerthwaite, if you don't mind. It keeps things on a more professional footing I find." He turned the screen slightly, inviting Ufford to look over his shoulder. "Can you explain where this amount comes from? I'm having trouble locating its source."

Ufford reddened slightly. "Dunno. That's odd. It must be a glitch…"

"What kind of glitch?"

"I'd have to look into it," Ufford said, vaguely.

"Well could you do that for me as a matter of urgency, Mr Ufford?" Ollerthwaite said, raising his eyebrows. "I'd hate to think anyone was obstructing an investigation."

"Yeah, sure. I'll schedule it into my workflow…"

Ollerthwaite fixed Ufford with his sternest gaze. "I'm afraid that I'm going to have to insist that you make it a priority, Mr Ufford. This is part of a murder investigation. I don't want to spend any more time here than I have to. It's not efficient and will hamper proceedings."

"Is there a problem, detective?" George Owens appeared from behind Ufford and Ollerthwaite suspected he'd been listening.

"It's okay, George," Ufford said, reddening. "DC Ollerthwaite is just querying some missing information. I'm going to sort it for him as soon as

I can..."

"Right away," Ollerthwaite said.

Owens scowled. "Look detective, we have a charity to run, here. Quentin has to make sure that everything runs smoothly. We're one missed bid away from bankruptcy. If he gets distracted..."

"I have been looking at your accounts for the best part of eighteen hours, Mr Owens, so I do know the financial situation. It doesn't seem that precarious to me, quite the opposite. There's money in your accounts. I'm just not sure where all of it is coming from or going to. The sooner Mr Ufford provides me with the appropriate information and files, the sooner I can go back to HQ and let you get on with your work here. If there's some kind of 'glitch' in the system, then I'm sure you'll be as eager as I am to see it remedied." Ollerthwaite allowed himself a brief smile.

George Owens smoothed his beard down and glanced at Ufford. "Well? What are you waiting for? Go and sort it, Quentin!"

Quentin Ufford glared back at Owens for a second and then pushed past him out of the room.

"I'm sure it's nothing," Owens said, backing out of the room.

"And I'm sure it's not," Ollerthwaite muttered to himself when the door had shut behind

George Owens.

*****

It felt almost like a formality, given that Bobby Price had confessed to the assault on the old man and partially explained where he got the baseball bat from, but DI Kath Cryer had agreed to go and interview Alfie Lewis, the third of the boys in Price's little trio. As she drove through the tunnel, she thought it odd that Lewis hadn't been spoken to earlier. There had been some talk of awkward parents and difficulty finding an appropriate adult to accompany him to an interview room in Hamilton Square Station in Birkenhead.

Alfie Lewis lived in a flat above a derelict shop on the A41, the main road that ran alongside Port Sunlight and separated it from New Ferry. It was hard to tell what kind of shop it had been as the signs above the boarded-up windows had peeled away to the bare plywood. Stepping over a rather large dog turd, Kath went around the side of the shop and knocked on the flaking side door. She looked up at the blinded windows and the cracked guttering. Inside a small dog yapped and someone screamed at it to shut up. Then a baby started crying. Kath knocked again.

"Okay, okay, fucksake, I'm..." the woman who opened the door stopped dead and stared at Kath's warrant card. She was a skinny woman with dyed blonde hair growing out at the roots. It was all tied up above her head in a messy bunch. She wore a vest and pyjama trousers and clutched a grumbling baby in her arms.

"Detective Inspector Kath Cryer, Merseyside Police."

"Yeah? Is this about Alfie? I'm his mum. What do you want?"

"I'd like to speak to him if I may. He's not in any trouble. We just want to get a statement from him about an incident he might have witnessed."

"Alfie's not a grass, you know. That Bobby Price was looking for him. I told him fuck off. You should go and arrest him. He's a fuckin' psycho..." The baby gave a warning growl and began to squirm.

"I just need to speak to Alfie," Kath said, holding up her hand. "Can I come in?"

Reluctantly, the woman stepped back and led Kath up a flight of stairs to the flat above and into a small living room. The place looked as though it had just been burgled. Clothes lay strewn all over the floor and furniture, along with packets of nappies and ashtrays. "I'd have tidied up if I'd known you were coming. ALFIE! GET HERE NOW." A small chihuahua yapped at Kath, baring its needle teeth but the woman shoved it away with her foot. "ALFIE!"

A small red-headed boy, who didn't look fourteen peered sullenly into the living room. "What?"

"Hi Alfie, I'm DI Kath Cryer. I need to ask you a few questions."

For a second, Kath thought the lad was going to run for it but then his shoulders slumped and he dragged himself into the room, collapsing onto the split cover of the old leather sofa. "I didn't hurt nobody. It wasn't me…"

"We know that, Alfie. Bobby Price told us what he did and Mr Smith, the man who was hurt…"

"Well, what do you wanna know then?"

"The baseball bat, Alfie. Where did that come from?"

"Bobby said it was his. He said…" The boy paused and bit his lip.

"Go on. Look, Alfie, Bobby told us everything. There's nothing new here, so you needn't worry about 'grassing' anyone up, okay?"

"Really? What everything? Even about his sister and that Travis bloke?"

Chapter 24

Back at HQ, DS Vikki Chinn stared intently at a piece of paper sealed in an evidence bag. She looked troubled.

"You okay Vikki?" Blake said, perching on the edge of her desk.

"It's this Richard Ince case, sir. It's a bit ropey if you ask me."

"Really? In what way?"

Vikki paused, choosing her words carefully. "Well, on the face of it, you could say it was an open and shut case. Ince took a heroin overdose after suffering from PTSD for so long. He even left a note."

"But?"

"Ince was reportedly with a drinking buddy the night he died and yet that wasn't explored. I managed to track the buddy down. He's another ex-soldier who works at Pro-Vets, Terry White…"

"Yeah, I met him the other day. Bit of an un-usual drinking partner. Can't imagine he'd be the kind to take your mind off things. How come the original investigation team didn't pick up on that?"

"I don't know, sir," Vikki said. "Also, Terry White insists that Ince never took heroin and that he seemed really happy on the night he died.

The trouble is, White wrapped it up in his own paranoid fantasy, so I imagine the original team would have disregarded it."

"An unreliable witness, then?"

"White believes that the ghost of an old corporal of his is able to take on the identities of other people and is stalking him, killing his friends."

"Do you think there's a nugget of truth in there somewhere? I mean someone stalking White and his friends?"

"I don't know, sir, but I decided to approach the manager at the Asda store where Ince worked up to the time of his death. He provided me with Ince's personnel file. It had his letter of application in it. Look..." Vikki placed the letter of application alongside the suicide note.

"Jeez, you don't have to be a handwriting analyst to see that they are written by two different people," Blake muttered.

"Even if we accept that he was stressed and suicidal, that wouldn't account for the difference in the script, sir."

"Who was the original Senior Investigating Officer?"

"DCI Cavanagh, sir," Vikki said, her expression saying everything that she couldn't say out loud.

Blake chewed his lip for a second. "Have another word with Jack Kenning and see if he thinks a second post-mortem would be appropriate. I'll have a word with Matty Cavanagh."

"There was something else, sir," Vikki said. "I feel a bit daft mentioning it, really but Nicola Norton told me that White went through a phase of burning little effigies of people who he thought were out to get him." She paused, reddening. "It just reminded me of the toy soldiers, sir, that's all."

"Why did White burn them?"

"I don't know. He described it as voodoo. Apparently, he believed it trapped part of Corporal Graves' soul. Maybe when he burns them, he destroys that little bit of Graves. I don't know. It all sounds ridiculous, sir, I know but…"

"White was the last person to see Richard Ince alive," Blake said, finishing her thought for her. "And if he could kill Ince, maybe he'd be capable of killing Travis."

"He mentioned Travis as one of the people whose identity Graves had taken over."

"But the toy soldiers found in the men's hands weren't burnt, were they?"

"No, sir. It could be that it's nothing and I'm getting carried away. The counter argument to all this is that White has an acquired brain injury. He struggles to make links with anything. I find it hard to imagine him planning a murder."

"And yet Ince's suicide note looks to have been forged," Blake said. "Keep it quiet for now, Vikki but ask a few discreet questions around Pro-Vets. See if you can build up more of a picture of Terry White. Is his counsellor helpful?"

"She's disclosed quite a lot, sir but she's rightly worried about confidentiality. I can try and push her on giving us more information, sir, if you want me to."

"See what you can do, Vikki," Blake said, looking down at the file on Ince. "If push comes to shove, we'll get a warrant. Meanwhile, I'll go and have a word with Cavanagh."

*****

How anyone could work in such a tip of an office, George Owens didn't know but Quentin Ufford almost made the mess a point of pride. Owens seemed to recall a poster on the wall that read: 'A Tidy Office is the Sign of a Diseased Mind,' but it had long been hidden behind the piles of books and files that seemed to cover every inch of desk surface, seat or even floor. Some of them weren't even anything to do with work. There was a whole filing cabinet top dedicated to fantasy paperbacks, so dogeared and yellowed that George wondered if anyone had read them in decades. At the centre of this maze of paper towers sat Ufford at his desk, the surface of which had disappeared long ago. There was room for the screen, keyboard and mouse, nothing more. Several cups perched on top of books and files, indicating the man's total disregard for the importance of what he was doing.

Ufford slouched in his seat, his rounded shoulders and large belly giving Owens the impression that he'd been poured into the seat rather than sat in it. "Well?" Owens snapped.

"Well what?" Ufford snapped back. "Okay, so you were right. He's more thorough than I expected him to be. Listen, I think it might be too late..."

"What?"

"It's not like I can just delete accounts. That'll be as obvious as a signed confession..."

"Look, right now, our partners and supporters are sympathetic. Our CEO is a victim of some cruel, random act of violence. Murder is one thing but the moment they get wind of any financial irregularity, this charity is sunk. Right now, you're that close to dismissal. And in case you're thinking you could pick up another role easily, forget it; this shit sticks and the smell follows you around, Quentin. Get it sorted."

"It isn't that easy, George. There's a half-covered trail of money going in and out of Pro-Vets and Ollerthwaite is onto it. It might be too late."

"It's never too late, Quentin. Do something. Make a call."

*****

On reflection, Blake thought, he should have realised that someone as thin-skinned as Cavanagh would take any question about one of his past cases as a criticism. Going into his office holding the file and launching into a series of questions might have been a bit over the top. But Cavanagh was sitting there with his feet on the desk again and it wound Blake up no end.

"I know what this is about, really. It's your bit of stuff, isn't it?" he said, his cheeks reddening.

"If you're talking about Laura, then, no, it isn't about her. I'm trying to find out who killed Paul Travis..."

"Then what the hell are you looking at one of my past cases for, if not to trip me up and make me look bad."

"Okay, Matty, two things: one, I'm investigating the death of Richard Ince because it has a number of connections with that of Paul Travis. Two, if you're so touchy about this case, then you must know it was a ropey one from the start."

"There's nothing ropey about it. Richard Ince took a heroin overdose deliberately. He left a note..."

"Not written in his handwriting. He didn't even

have a history of drug abuse…"

"First timers often get the amount wrong…"

"Then how would he even know the right amount to kill himself with unless he had help from someone with experience or medical knowledge?"

Cavanagh pursed his lips, stuck for words for a moment. "Anyway," he said at last. "What's it got to do with the Travis case?"

"Travis was found with a plastic toy soldier in his hand."

"Shit," Cavanagh hissed. "Look I didn't know. It all looked nice and tidy to me. There were no objections raised at the time…"

"Terry White had something to say."

"That head the ball? He's a nutter. Can you imagine me going to the Super, 'erm, sorry boss, we've just looked into an obvious suicide, but a brain injured friend of the deceased reckons he was done in by the ghost of his dead corporal?' Do me a favour."

"There could be a nugget of truth in what he says…"

Cavanagh gave a bitter snort. "The only nugget there would be the nugget who tried to launch an investigation based on the testimony of Terry White. He's a fruit loop! If anything, his insane conspiracy theory convinced me there was nothing suspicious at all."

"And you didn't think to assess whether or not White was dangerous?"

"No. You've met him, I take it? He may be a big fella but he wouldn't harm a fly," Cavanagh snapped. He shook his head. "Nah. This is all about you, this is, Will. Your piss is boiling because I warned you off the Quinlan case and you're trying to make some kind of point. Take it higher for all I care. Just do your job and let me do mine."

"I intend to, Matty. I intend to."

*****

Nobody had mentioned a drill and so when the fire alarm began to scream at Pro-Vets, DC Ian Ollerthwaite stood up to investigate. It was at that same moment that the door exploded inwards, sending books and files flying from the shelves on the wall beside it. A giant of a man filled the room and stared blankly at Ian.

"Graves," he said, picking Ollerthwaite up before he could register what was happening. The room whirled around him and then he was weightless, flying through the air. A sudden stab of pain shot up his back as he crashed into the desk, sending his laptop spinning away. He tumbled over behind the desk and tried to scramble to his feet, but the man was on him again, punching and punching him in the face.

Ian heard a crack, but it was inside his head and he felt warm, wet blood smear his cheek. Something had broken. In desperation, he swung his fist down on the side of the man's head, sending him staggering back. But he launched forward with renewed ferocity, snatching up a landline phone and cracking Ian with it hard. Stars exploded in front of him, and he couldn't see but once again he was being thrown through the air. He landed heavily on his side, the breath punched from his body by the hard ground and his arm burned with pain. He tried to stand but couldn't. The man stood over him, he could see his boots, smeared with blood and Ian wondered if this was the last thing Paul Travis saw.

He suddenly felt calm but a little sad. Was this how he ended his life? He thought of his wife, Theresa and his son Joey who loved watching the trains with him. If he had the strength, he'd get up. But DC Ian Ollerthwaite could do little other than let darkness take him.

Chapter 25

It was an adventure, Blake supposed, that was the reason Madge looked so excited at being asked to make the call. Or maybe it was the romance. The gossip about Blake and Laura seemed to have leached down to reception and he was left wondering just how far beyond the building it had gone.

"Don't forget, Madge, you mustn't tell a soul about this," Blake said, the words sounding pathetic the minute they left his lips. Of course, everyone would be hearing about this eventually. Madge wouldn't let a good bit of 'goss' go to waste.

"You know me, Will," she said, winking.

"Okay, so here's the number. Can you remember what you're going to say?"

Madge looked hurt. "Will, I'm a professional. I do this for a living. What do you take me for?"

Blake just smiled and watched as she dialled the number. He knew that Superintendent Martin would skin him alive if he found out that he was trying to contact Laura but, as Blake had pointed out, it would look downright odd if he didn't make some kind of attempt. This seemed the best way without rousing any suspicions. But deep down, Blake just had to know what Laura was thinking. The idea she could just ditch him for Quinlan was torture. He needed to know why.

"Hello? Is that… Laura?" Madge said. Blake had to admit, she was brilliant. "Yes, it's my dog, he keeps barking incessantly and I'm at my wits' end." The conversation went on. Blake could just about hear Laura's voice and he felt a weight in his chest. He just wanted to snatch the phone and speak to her but there was always the danger she'd hang up. He needed to see her in person and find out what the hell was going on. Madge continued talking. "I'm at work at the moment, would you be able to come around seven tonight? You would? Lovely…" She left Laura with the address Blake had given her and hung up.

"Perfect," Blake said. "I owe you a bottle of fizz, Madge, thank you."

Madge coloured a little. "Oh, give over. You just tell me how you get on."

"I will," Blake said but he didn't think he'd have any good news for Madge in the short term. His phone rang. "Kath? Where are you?"

"I'm at Arrowe Park Hospital sir," Kath Cryer said. "It's Ian…"

*****

In the busy hospital with nurses and doctors hurrying back and forth, the side ward felt like another world, silent and shaded. Although DC Ian Ollerthwaite sat upright in bed, he was unconscious, his arm plastered and bandages wrapped around most of his head. Theresa, his wife, sat at his side, holding the tips of his fingers. She was a short woman with ringlets of mousey brown hair and sharp blue eyes. Blake would have said that she was a few years younger than Ian but then, Ian always seemed a hundred years older than everyone else. Although her face was lined with worry now, there was a softness and kindness about it. Blake could tell she was used to laughter and smiles. He felt a tug of guilt that he knew nothing about Ollerthwaite's personal life and had never asked. And now he was meeting Theresa for the first time over the drips and monitors attached to her husband. Ian's face was purple with bruises.

"Theresa, I'm DCI Will Blake. Ian's on my team. I'm so sorry this has happened. Believe me, we'll get whoever did this. How is he?"

Theresa Ollerthwaite gave a brief smile. Her voice was subdued. "Broken arm and ribs. He punctured a lung, too. And then..." she waved her hand around the bruised face. "There's quite a lot of trauma around his head. Hopefully there's no permanent damage." Her face creased briefly and she scrubbed a tear from her cheek.

"If there's anything we can do, anything at all," Blake said, feeling powerless. What could he do? Heal her husband?

"Is this to do with the case he was working on?" Theresa said. "Was it the murder in Port Sunlight?"

"It was. I'd asked Ian to go through the books at the Pro-Vets charity. Given that he was attacked by a member of the Pro-Vets staff, I'd say it's a strong possibility that there's a link. Did he say anything to you about it?"

She shook her head. "Ian never tells me anything confidential about his work but I piece things together from what he does say. All I gathered was that the staff weren't being very cooperative."

"That's useful in itself. We can look into that, too." Blake paused, uncertain whether to reveal any more detail. "The man who we think attacked Ian wasn't very well. He had mental health issues and an acquired brain injury. I'm not certain it was malicious, Theresa..."

"Malicious or not, he needs catching, doesn't he?"

"We'll do that, I promise."

*****

Cars blared their horns as Terry White staggered across the road. There was blood again, everywhere. It seemed like he was leaving a trail of bloody footprints behind him. The sky above was red with it, spinning round as though he was on a merry-go-round. Seagulls screamed at him and swooped. When he threw his hands up to defend himself, he bumped into people who yelled or screeched wordless abuse. His heart thumped in his chest and sweat soaked the back of his shirt under his overalls.

Graves had agents who could pick him up at any moment. He needed to get away from the town and under cover of trees or bushes but where? Terry ran his fingers through his hair and tried to gather his thoughts. Bidston Hill, that would do for a start. If he could get there, he could hide out for a while and decide what to do. He'd disabled Graves for the moment but he didn't think he'd finished him. It would mean living rough for a while, keeping his head down but he could do that. Survival. That's what he did best.

*****

Although the fire alarms had stopped and people had been allowed to go back inside, all work had stopped at the Pro-Vets offices and work-shops. George Owens' office where Ollerthwaite had been working was taped off and crime scene investigators were photographing and picking through the mess. DC Alex Manikas sat in the office next door with Quentin Ufford who looked visibly shaken.

"I spoke to Terry just before the alarm went off. He seemed agitated," Ufford said. "He was pacing back and forth and muttering about George. He said something else I couldn't quite understand. Something to do with graves."

"Would you normally talk to Terry White?"

"No but like I said, he seemed wound up about something. I don't know what it was, though."

"What did he say about George Owens?"

Ufford looked as though he was trying to make sense of a complex puzzle. "He said something like Owens knows what to do or Owens knows what he wants me to do. I'm not sure what he meant but he walked away before I could reason with him. I went to talk to George because I was concerned but then the alarm went off."

Alex looked up from his notes. He didn't know what it was, but he felt as though Ufford wanted to say more but was holding back. "Had White had any interaction with DC Ollerthwaite before the attack to your knowledge?"

"I wouldn't know. I spend most of my time with computers, not people. I hardly knew Terry, really."

"And yet you stopped to talk to him..."

"I was worried. He didn't look right. Anyone would, yes," Ufford said and glanced out through the office window for a second and then leaned forward. "Look, I'm no psychiatrist but, I couldn't help noticing his strange behaviour, especially recently."

"How recently, Mr Ufford?"

"I've said too much, already. The poor guy is probably…"

"That 'poor guy' just put one of my friends in hospital, sir. What did you mean, behaving strangely and when did you first notice it?"

"Just the muttering and stuff. He'd point at people but a weird kind of pointing with two middle fingers or his two index fingers pressed together. He'd say things under his breath as though he was… I dunno… casting a spell or something. I know it sounds ridiculous."

"No, it might be useful, Mr Ufford. Thank you. How long had you noticed this happening?"

"A good few weeks ago, but it escalated and then…"

"Go on."

Ufford rubbed his face. "He used to do the pointing thing at Paul Travis a lot, that's all. And then he was off the day after Paul, you know… was killed, it all just seemed a bit odd to me…"

"Are you suggesting that Terry White might have killed Paul Travis?"

"God, I feel terrible when you say it out loud like that. I dunno, do I? I'm just saying what I observed, that's all."

"How come you didn't mention this before now?"

"Because you don't do you? You never think someone you work with might be a killer. Or point at someone with a brain injury and say, I bet it was him. You just don't. I'm sorry." Ufford put his head down and steadied his breathing.

"That's all right, Mr Ufford. It's not easy for any of us."

Ufford looked up. "It was George he listened to the most. Not that head shrinker, what's her name? Nicola. George was the one who could persuade him to do anything. If George had been there, he would have stopped it, believe me. Your mate wouldn't be hurt so badly, now."

Chapter 26

Given that they were so close, Blake had gathered his team in a meeting room at Birkenhead police station just behind the Town Hall and Magistrates Court on Hamilton Square. DI Kath Cryer sat next to DC Andrew Kinnear as usual and DC Alex Manikas sat with DS Vikki Chinn. A number of uniformed officers joined them too. It was a long, echoey room with a large window covered by old strip blinds that didn't keep the Spring sunshine out very well. Blake felt like he was back in a school classroom.

"I know you'll be as worried as me about Ian Ollerthwaite. I 've been to see him and his wife at Arrowe Park and he's stable at the moment. He took quite a beating. What's the update on Terry White, Kath?"

"We've got officers searching for him, sir. Last sightings had him heading out of town towards Bidston. We suspect he might be trying to hide out around the hill."

"We followed up the leads that Counter terrorism gave us, sir. There was no way Paul Travis's murder was a terrorist attack."

Alex raised a hand. "I had an interesting conversation with Quentin Ufford. He said White had been acting suspiciously for some time now and a lot of his strange behaviour was targeted at

Paul Travis."

Blake looked over to Vikki. "You have your concerns about White, don't you Vikki?"

DS Chinn nodded. "Yes, sir. White has an acquired brain injury but, whether because of that or the trauma, he also suffers from Fregoli Delusion. It's a condition that leaves the sufferer thinking that a particular person can take on many identities. White's particular take on this is that an old corporal who used to bully him, a guy called Graves, has returned from the dead and is possessing people he knows, trying to ruin his life..."

"Did you say Graves?" Alex asked, flicking through his notebook. "Ufford said something about White going on about... ah, here we are: 'Something to do with graves' were his exact words."

"Do you think White thought Ian was..." Kinnear struggled to find the right word, "possessed by this Corporal Graves and attacked him? Same with Travis?"

"It's a possibility, I guess," Vikki said.

"Just to throw a spanner in the works, sir," Kath said. "There could still be a more rational motive for Travis' murder. I was talking to Alfie Lewis earlier today and he told me that Bobby Price had it in for Paul Travis because Travis was knocking off Layla Price, Bobby's sister."

"Jeez," Blake muttered. "Maybe Travis wasn't so perfect after all."

"We've unlocked Travis' mobile, sir," Manikas said. "There might be evidence there."

"But Bobby Price is a streak of the proverbial, Ma'am," Kinnear said. "There's no way he could take out Paul Travis..."

"Maybe Lex Price could though," Blake cut in. "I can imagine he wouldn't take too kindly to the news that his daughter was seeing an older, married man. Okay, it may be that Terry White just lost it and poor Ian was in the way, but we need to bring him in as a matter of urgency."

"We've put an alert out on social media and all radio stations advising the public to look out for White but not to approach him."

"Great Kath, thanks. Can you and Andrew check Travis' mobile and have another word with Lex Price? We need to talk to his daughter, too. Talk to Tasha Cook, the FLO, as well, see if she's picked up on anything that might corroborate the story."

Kath's phone rang and she hurried to the back of the room while she answered it.

"Sir," Vikki said. "White lives just round the corner from Port Sunlight Village in a flat run by a housing association. It's a ten-minute walk from the war memorial."

Kath came back, her face pale. "That was CSI, they found a plastic soldier on the floor next to where Ian lay. They've also sent a team to White's place and want you to go and see what they've found there."

*****

Youth was such a powerful aphrodisiac for some men, DI Kath Cryer thought as she strode up to the counter at the Superdrug store in Birkenhead's Grange Precinct. Layla Price was a good example of that. Beneath the false eyelashes, make-up and bottle-blonde hair, Kath reckoned she'd be a pretty ordinary-looking girl, but she was only twenty and that was all some blokes needed.

Kath had experienced similar advances from older men herself when she was younger and it always puzzled her what, beyond the physical, they got out of it. The idea of having a toyboy, a phrase she hated, left her cold. There would be no shared experience or culture, no common memories of pop songs or events from a certain year. Of course, she was fully aware that people of wildly different ages did fall in love for a whole host of reasons but she doubted that this was the case for Paul Travis.

Layla's face dropped when she saw Kath's warrant card. With a resigned look, she called a colleague over to take her place at the counter. "I haven't got long, so you better have your questions ready. This is about Paul Travis, yeah?" She led Kath to the back of the shop and through a door into a small staff room.

"You seem very relaxed, Layla," Kath said. "Have you had dealings with the police before?"

Layla gave a humourless grin. "With a dad like mine, they're regular visitors, Inspector Cryer. All through my childhood, I've been told to be polite to coppers and give away as little as possible."

"Right," Kath said. "That might come under giving away too much information, Layla…"

"Are you here to ask about my relationship with Paul or my interview technique?"

"Fair comment," Kath said, pulling out her notebook. "You don't deny having had a relationship with Paul Travis, then?"

"No. I met him in the Bridge Inn a few months ago and my dad works with his charity so…"

"Really? In what capacity?"

"He does the security on their buildings I suppose. Guard dogs, watchmen that kind of thing…"

"Your dad knew Paul Travis quite well?"

"Not really. There was someone else who he dealt with, I think. Why are you asking about my dad?"

"Just building a picture, Layla, that's all. Carry on."

"Like I said, I met Paul in the pub. He bought me a drink, made me laugh and we hit it off. I liked him."

"I see. Did anyone else know about this relationship?"

Layla rolled her eyes. "You mean Bobby, don't you? Yeah, he knew. He wasn't very happy about it for some reason. He called Paul a paedo for seeing someone so young. He threatened to tell my dad…"

"Threatened? I take it your dad wouldn't be very happy, then."

"What do you think? Most dads would go mad at the idea of their daughters getting off with an older man."

"And how did you think *your* dad would react?"

Layla Price pursed her lips and Kathy saw something of her father's steel in her eyes. "He might have had a quiet word with Paul."

"'Had a quiet word?' What do you mean by that?"

"Exactly what I said. Dad wouldn't do anything that might damage his business prospects and he had a security contract with Pro-Vets, didn't he?"

"Your dad has a history of violence, though.

He's been locked up for armed robbery in the past."

"D'you honestly think I'm going to stand here and say, 'Oh, God, yeah, maybe he murdered Paul?' My dad wouldn't do anything like that. Besides, Bobby never said anything to him, did he?"

"I don't know, Layla. Did your dad ever speak to you about it?"

"No, because he never knew about it. Now, look, I've got to go back to work or I'll get into trouble with my boss."

"When did you last see Paul Travis?"

Layla looked at the ceiling. "God, when was it? About two weeks ago. He told his wife he was working late and we went out for a meal. Posh restaurant over in town. It was a nice meal but he finished with me that night. I really must…"

"Finished with you?"

"Yeah. Not very original reasons, really. He felt guilty cheating on his wife, he had a little kid, it was all getting too much. It had been fun but we didn't have much in common apart from the sex…"

"You don't seem very cut up about any of this, Layla, the fact that he broke up with you, the fact that he's *dead*."

Layla price shrugged. "We had a laugh. I liked him but I wasn't in love with him. Yeah, I'm sorry he got killed, it's horrible but I've shed my tears, thanks and I don't have to cry for your benefit, do I? Anyway, I've got to get back to the counter."

Chapter 27

Terry White's flat was small, with one bedroom, bathroom, kitchen and a living room. It felt claustrophobic even with just two other crime scene investigators. Mallachy O'Hare leaned over, frowning at a small green, mound that lay on the draining board in the kitchen.

"What is it?" Blake said.

"Looks like melted plastic, Will. It's a wonder it didn't set the smoke alarms off."

"What melted it?"

Malachy kept his steady gaze focused on the mound. "Something hot, Will. Yep, definitely something hot..." He looked up and grinned.

"Hilarious," Blake said. "You competing with Kenning for the crime scene comedy awards or something?"

"I'd win hands down, mate," Malachy said, with a twinkle in his eye.

"Green plastic. Could it be a toy soldier?"

"I'd say so. Can you see there, at the base?"

"They look like boots. Yes, and there's a leg..."

"The lab will be able to compare the composition of the plastic with that of the soldier found on Travis and at the scene of the assault earlier today. How is Ian?"

"Stable, last I heard. Have you found anything else?"

"You might say that. Nothing else that would put White anywhere near Paul Travis on the night of the murder, no. There are no blood-stained clothes or anything like that, more's the pity. Have a look in the bedroom, though."

Blake walked into the tiny bedroom. The curtains were still drawn, giving the place a subterranean feel. His legs grazed the double bed that dominated the room. A small chest of drawers and a wardrobe took care of the rest of the floor space meaning Blake had to sidle in to get to the end of the bed.

The wall was covered with pictures. There were cuttings from recent news coverage of the Travis murder and two large photographs sat in the middle of it all. The first was of Paul Travis himself. It looked like a corporate shot, Travis half turning as if greeting a friend. A blurry picture of an older, bald man with a hawk like nose and a mouthful of tombstone teeth set in a mirthless grin sat next to the one of Travis. The picture had been blown up so there was little background but Blake could see the collar of a sandy brown uniform. He wondered if this was Corporal Graves. One thing was certain, they had to find Terry White as soon as possible.

Blake went back to Malachy in the kitchen.

"Anything else?"

Malachy raised his bushy, white eyebrows. "What d'you want, a signed confession? If those pictures and these little melted fellas aren't enough for you, I dunno what is."

"I suppose so. Thanks, Malachy. Let me know if anything more turns up, okay?" He hurried out of the door, leaving his car in the flats car-park and heading out into the road. He looked at his watch. It was six forty-five. He needed to be at Jeff's five minutes ago but, thankfully, his brother only lived just down the road. His heart thumped and his stomach squirmed. If Laura stayed long enough for him to talk to her, he could be a little while but he had a terrible feeling that she would take one look at him and leave.

Jeff had been house-sitting the semi-detached for almost a year now and banking the rent from his swish London flat. The house was in stark contrast to Jeff's metropolitan writerly image; it was homely, with flowery curtains and a neatly trimmed front garden. Blake assumed whoever owned the house paid for a gardener because he couldn't imagine Jeff getting his hands dirty. It still rankled with Blake that Jeff managed to land on his feet so many times despite being hopeless with money. So many things rankled with Blake about his younger brother, though. Maybe that was why he found Jeff's discomfort at this plan so satisfying.

His little brother answered the door looking like he was sucking a wasp. People said that he and Jeff looked alike. They were both tall and square-jawed. Jeff was slim without the bulk of muscle that Will carried.

"I'm not happy about this, Will." Jeff said as he let Will in.

"You could have said no."

Jeff gave Will a mutinous look. "And how would you have reacted to that?"

"Fair enough," Will said, with a sigh. "Look Jeff, I just need to talk to her. I can't phone her; she'll just hang up on me. At least this way, I can try and talk to her."

"It's borderline creepy, Will. And what if she has one of Kyle Quinlan's heavies with her? Or Quinlan himself? If this place gets damaged in any way, you're paying for it."

"Relax. It'll be fine," Will said. "When she calls, just pretend you can't open the front door and ask her to go round the back to the garden…"

"What?"

"If she sees you, she'll know it's all a plan for me to talk to her. You could disguise your voice, perhaps…"

Jeff looked horrified. "Seriously? Who do you want me to sound like? Kenneth Williams perhaps? Or maybe Sylvester Stallone."

Will opened his mouth to answer but the sound of a car pulling up cut him short. He looked through the net curtains. A black BMW idled in the road outside.

"She's here. Remember what I said. Get her to come round the back. I'll be waiting."

There was an old wooden shed in the garden, and Blake decided to hide behind it. He felt ridiculous but he didn't want Laura to bolt at the first sight of him. He heard the back door open and then footsteps on the patio. They sounded heavy.

"You can come out now, Mr Blake," a male voice said.

Blake peered round the edge of the shed and saw a tall, dark man dressed in jeans, a cream shirt and a bomber jacket standing with Jeff. He had a mane of black hair and a beard with a few flecks of silver in it. He smiled but his dark eyes smouldered with a suppressed anger.

"Laura couldn't make it I'm afraid, or rather, didn't want to." He extended a hand. "My name's Kyle Quinlan. You've probably heard of me."

Blake narrowed his eyes, ignoring the hand. "What have you done with her?"

Kyle raised his eyebrows in a pantomime of surprise. "I haven't done anything with her. She sent me to give you a message." He pulled out a phone.

"If you don't believe me, you can call her if you like."

Blake hesitated, not wanting to be part of Quinlan's game but eventually, he took the phone and pressed the call button.

"Will, what the fuck are you playing at?" Laura's voice was loud and Blake found himself colouring at the exasperation in it. It was like being told off by his mum.

"Hi Laura," Will said. "More to the point, what the hell is going on?"

"Don't try and wriggle off the hook like that. You tried to trick me into meeting you. Isn't that stalking?"

"I'm worried about you. You could have called and told me you were around. What are you doing going back to him?" Blake had turned his back on Quinlan and paced down the garden.

"I could have called you but I didn't. That's my choice, Will. You know, I did a lot of thinking while I was away and it struck me that I was running away from the wrong person..."

"The man who beat you up? A criminal? He hasn't changed, Laura, you wouldn't have fled the Wirral when he arrived otherwise."

"Maybe, but *I've* changed and he knows it."

"But if you've changed then why be with him?"

"You'll never understand, Will. Never. It wasn't him I was running from, it was you."

"Me? What? I never..."

"When we first met, you said you were like a ghost trapped in your mother's house, remember? And I watched you break free, but you trapped me in your place. I'd hang around waiting for you to come home, prop you up when things got tough and slowly, I was being smothered and locked in that airless house. One thing the last six months has taught me is how to be myself."

"I'm sorry. I never meant to..."

"No, Will you didn't, but look at yourself now. You were trying to trick me into meeting you. Trying to force your agenda on me again. And think back to how you judged me when you discovered just a little of my past. Don't try and deny it, I could see it in your eyes. The shame."

"Laura I..."

"At least with Kyle, I can be myself and don't have to keep apologising for my past and who I am now. So please stay away from me, Will. Goodbye." The phone went dead.

Quinlan stood with his hands in his pockets, with an apologetic smile. "She's a feisty woman," he said, taking the phone back from Blake.

"What have you got over her Quinlan?" Blake

snapped.

Quinlan held his hands up like a footballer accused of a foul. "Nothing," he said, his voice rising an octave. "Listen, I didn't want to come, she sent me. And if you hadn't pulled such a dozy stunt in the first place, maybe she would have let you down a bit easier."

"What are you up to?"

"Me? Nothing. I'm just a businessman, making my way in life, Mr Blake. As far as Laura goes, I'm just lucky I guess. Some you win, some you lose. You lost her. Get over it."

Blake took a step forward. "I'm warning you, Quinlan, if you so much as put a foot wrong, I'll be down on you like a ton of bricks…"

"Did you hear that, Jeffrey? DCI Blake here threatened me because his girlfriend left him for me. I'd call that a conflict of interest, wouldn't you?"

Jeff looked pale and said nothing.

"And what makes you think you can trust her, Quinlan?"

"I can't, Mr Blake. That's the beauty of it as she explained to me in great detail. You see, life is great until you start to take it for granted. You get complacent and you lower your guard. Then it rushes up and bites you on the arse. Hard. Laura keeps me on my toes. And if I'm on my toes, then

I'm playing my 'A' game. She could have come here tonight without me knowing but she told me that this would be a perfect chance for her to betray me. She's straight with me. I can trust her because I can't trust her, if that makes any sense..."

"No," Blake said. "Not to me."

"Yeah. Laura explained it better." Quinlan gave Jeff a thoughtful look. "You're writing that biography of Joshy Gambles, aren't you?"

Jeff nodded. "I am."

"He's a funny fish, he is. The stories I could tell you. Maybe you should pop by my house some time and I'll give you an inside scoop."

"That would be great..." Jeff said, his voice dry and raspy as he glanced at Will.

"Good," Quinlan said. "In the meantime, tell him Kyle says hi."

"You can tell him yourself after I've arrested you and put you away," Blake muttered.

"Is that so? And what are you going to arrest me for, exactly? I'm a legit businessman, straight as an arrow. Besides, like I said, you better not come within a mile of me, Mr Blake, it wouldn't be professional, what with your... association with my ex-wife, would it? It might seem like sour grapes or even a vendetta. Wouldn't look good in a court of law, would it? I've already had to come here to ask you not to pester my ex-wife. Besides, imagine poor Laura standing in a court of law because you made some wild accusations. I reckon that'd break your heart Mr Blake. If it isn't broken already." Kyle Quinlan gave a little shrug and strolled out of the garden, gently closing the gate behind him.

*****

Darkness pressed in around Terry White as he crouched in a thicket of bushes and young saplings. There wasn't really enough cover here for daylight but now it was late and Terry could relax a little. He had to think straight. Where should he go now? He pulled out the mobile phone from his pocket and dialled the usual number. It was answered but nobody said anything. "My mission failed. I need evac, quickly. They'll find me by morning. I've got to get out of here."

The phone trembled in his hands but there was no reply. "Please. I need help."

"I'll text you the address," the voice said. "Stand by." The phone buzzed again and Terry stared closely at the phone. "Come at midnight. Don't let them follow you."

"Okay," Terry whispered. "Okay, okay, okay." He lowered himself back and stared into the sky through the canopy of leaves. Soon he'd be safe.

Chapter 28

The beeping of Blake's mobile phone confused him. He was driving along a featureless highway in the dark and somewhere ahead, Laura was trying to get away from him. He wanted to reach out to her except he couldn't move his left arm and his right cheek felt wet. The beeping of his phone became more insistent. He couldn't answer it, though, not while he was driving. Louder, it drilled into his aching head, dragging him to wakefulness until he realised he was lying slumped on his sofa in the living room, Serafina perched on his back and Charlie curled up at his feet. The phone lay on the floor alongside several beer bottles and had stopped buzzing before he could pick it up.

He groaned and slowly eased himself upright, allowing Serafina to slide onto the sofa with an indignant growl. It was light and, outside, a few rowdy seagulls had flown in from the river to perch on Blake's roof and squabble with each other. His head pulsed. Alcohol wasn't really Blake's chosen method of drowning sorrows. Usually, he dived headlong into work but the phone call with Laura had been a punch in the gut, one he didn't quite understand. Part of him wanted to believe she was doing all this under duress. But maybe he was judging her by his own standards, he realised that now. Her upbringing had been totally different from his. He had a safe childhood; he'd been nurtured and encouraged. She had a tough time and now she believed she didn't deserve any better. Maybe he should just move on; it wasn't his job to fix everything in Laura's life. He had no right to either. And yet the one truth Blake had learnt from Laura was that you can change and leave the past behind. It puzzled him why she couldn't practise what she preached.

The phone bleeped again and Blake looked at the text message. A voicemail from Theresa Ollerthwaite. Blake sat up and, without listening to the voice message, phoned Theresa back. A tearful voice answered the phone. "Will, it's Ian he's..."

Blake groaned. "Theresa, I... I'm sorry... I don't know what to say..."

"No! He's awake. He's fine," she gave a sobbing laugh. "He wants to talk to you. Won't settle until he has. He's threatening to discharge himself if I don't put you on the phone. Here..."

There was a rustling and some muttered conversation, then Ian's voice rang out.

"Quentin Ufford, sir," Ollerthwaite said.

"You okay Ian?"

"Sorry, yes sir, they've got me on some kind of opiate-based painkillers and they're clouding my thought processes, somewhat. I had a strange dream that I saw the Flying Scot at Crewe Station only it was painted with dazzle camouflage rather like the Mersey Ferry boat. It was most disconcerting and I forgot to note down that I'd seen it..."

Blake smiled. He was glad the man was alive but even Ian's psychedelic experiences were somewhat dull. "Ian, it's so good to hear you're okay. Theresa said you had something important on your mind..."

"Yes, it was Ufford. Quentin Ufford, sir, you know the man who does the accounts and maintains all the computers? I wonder why he was on the train. It was a model train too... tiny, tiny train..."

"Ian..."

"Sorry, sir. I need to concentrate. Con-cen-trate. Right, when I was looking at the accounts, Ufford was very evasive. Evading me all over the place he was. Evasive. It's a funny word that, isn't it, sir?" Ian's speech slurred a little and Blake wondered how he was going to extricate himself from this conversation until Ollerthwaite was a little more coherent.

"Maybe I should call back later when your head has cleared."

"That's it you see. It *is* clear. Clear as a brass bell. Ding, ding! Ufford was withholding information from me. He seems to be claiming thousands of pounds for equipment and travel..." Ollerthwaite began humming 'Come Fly with Me.'

"Ian..."

"Yes! An excessive amount in my estimation. There's a lot of money sloshing around, too, sir. Donations from offshore companies, and local small businesses. Lots of cash is going out too. In and out. Shake it all..."

"Are you thinking the charity is being used to launder money or something?"

"Could be, sir. They spent lots on Lex Price's security company. Even a payment to a pet psychologist, would you believe it? I mean who sends their dog to a shrink?" Ollerthwaite chuckled to himself for a moment. "Mad dog!"

Blake caught his breath. "Really? Can you remember the name of the psychologist?"

"Sorry, sir," Ollerthwaite said, obviously stifling a yawn. "It just stuck in my head. Don't know why. I think I've overdone it, sir...I'm cream crackered as Kath Cryer would say. Cream crackered! I mean spending a small fortune on a human psychologist but putting your dog on the couch? Madness!"

"Ian, you've been a godsend, get a good rest now." When he'd said his goodbyes and spoken briefly to Theresa, Blake lowered the phone and stared across his living room. He didn't want to jump to conclusions but if Laura was involved in this, then, in all likelihood, Kyle Quinlan was too. He tapped the phone against his stubbly chin as he thought. If Quinlan was laundering money through the charity, maybe Paul Travis found out. He couldn't imagine Ufford being able to take Travis down but it was possible if he took him by surprise. Or what if he'd just alerted Quinlan to the fact that Travis knew and let Quinlan do the rest? Maybe Lex Price was involved somehow. He was a big lad and could probably handle Travis. Either way, Quentin Ufford had a few questions to answer.

Blake turned on his laptop and checked Ufford's address. He smiled. The man only lived fifteen minutes' drive away and it was still early. He could call in on Ufford and catch him before he went to work. He hurried upstairs, pausing only to let Charlie out for a toilet stop and then got washed and dressed. The pulsing pain behind his eye had subsided a little and Blake tried to wash it away with a couple of mugs of strong coffee, vowing to lay off drinking on a school night. Charlie and Serafina played the essential role of trip hazards until he fed them. Leaving a note for Ian, he locked the house and jumped into the car.

Raby, where Ufford lived was a pleasant little village in South Wirral. Blake's journey took him along the M53 and off at the Clatterbridge hospital exit. He knew this area quite well having cycled around it a lot as a boy. This side of the motorway was more rural, with narrow, hedge-lined lanes and cottages dotted along them. This part of the Wirral seemed more like rural Cheshire and many who lived there often expressed a wish to return to the county rather than be in Merseyside. Raby comprised of a couple of farms, a few houses and a rather nice pub known locally as The Thatch, renowned for its good food and real ales. There were apocryphal tales from older Wirral residents of being snowed-in at this pub and having to spend the night, but Blake struggled to remember a time when the snow could fall so heavily and suddenly to take punters by surprise.

Quince Cottage was a tiny, thatched, one-storey bungalow on the edge of a field. Blake reckoned there could only be a couple of rooms inside, and maybe a tiny kitchen. It surprised Blake that a young man like Ufford would choose to live out here but then, he hadn't really got the measure of the man when he first met him. The curtains were drawn and a black Mini sat in the small, gravelled car port at the front of the house. Blake knocked on the front door, hard. If Ufford was asleep, he wanted to startle him and put him off guard. The house lay still, so Blake hammered his fist on the door again.

Cautiously, he eased open the garden gate and

went around the back of the house. The garden at the back was tiny, a postage stamp lawn, a couple of borders and two planters. The back door was locked too. He could see a narrow kitchen area inside that lay in shadow. A mug sat on the side by the sink. The house was still.

There were any number of reasons why Ufford might not answer the door. Maybe he went out last night and was staying with friends. He could have dropped his car off first and taken a taxi, easily. Or he could have seen Blake arrive and have decided to lie low. But something gnawed at Blake's gut. Something was wrong.

Pressing his nose against the back door window and cupping his hands around his eyes to blot out the light, Blake peered in. On the floor, Blake could just see a hand poking from behind a leather sofa. And it held something green.

Blake pulled out his phone but a sudden click made him look up. The back door had been unlocked and a huge shadow filled the door. Then it burst open, smacking Blake full in the face and sending him staggering backwards. The figure loomed over him, gripping his lapels and hurling him like a ragdoll across the small garden. Blake felt weightless and held his breath for the impact.

Chapter 29

Everything had gone wrong.

Even as he crept across the Wirral, making his way to the rendezvous point, Terry had felt his mind clearing. The medication started to wear off and everything had clicked into place. His mind wasn't as foggy. He was on a mission and he had a job to do. He wasn't certain that the policeman at Pro-Vets had died but if nothing else, Terry had slowed Graves down. He'd have to find another host and Terry reckoned he knew who it would be. A cold fury burned in his gut. Ufford had been a friend but that's what Graves did. He took your friends from you. It was deliberate and the sooner he was stopped, the better. Sadly, there was only one way to stop Graves.

Terry hadn't liked seeing Ufford lying dead in a pool of blood but that was Graves' fault. Take it up with him. Soon, Graves' spirit would be trapped in these little plastic soldiers, fragmented and incinerated. It would be over.

Melting the plastic figure had been tricky but Terry hit upon the idea of using the electric stove. He stood the figure on the ring and switched it on. Watching the little man subside into a puddle of green, bubbling goo had made him laugh a little because it meant a little bit more of Corporal Graves was gone. He couldn't hurt anyone else. Then Terry remembered who the dead man was, and he felt his heart burst.

Tears scalded his cheeks and he had slumped into an armchair next to the body. His body shook with grief and once more he lay in that Foxhound armoured car. Thunder roared in his ears and hot metal burnt in his head. Corporal Graves snarled and gripped him as they tumbled over and over into blackness.

The next thing he knew, it was light and someone was hammering on the door. The policeman was trying to get in. Terry panicked and charged at him, knocking him down but he knew he had to run, so vaulted the fence into the fields behind the cottage.

Now Terry's legs burnt with the effort of running on the rough ground. He'd taken a tumble once or twice when his foot went into a rabbit hole but fear spurred him on. He didn't know where he was going and he didn't know who he could trust. They were meant to evacuate him but there was nobody there to save him. Now he was in deep trouble. All he could do was get away from here, lie low and try and work things out.

*****

Gasping for breath, Blake staggered to his feet and looked around for the man who had attacked him. The garden was empty and, staring across the fields behind the house, Blake could just about see a distant figure running for the woodland on the other side. It was tempting to set off after him but he knew he needed to secure the scene of the crime first and check inside. Pulling on his gloves and mask, he inched his way into the house. He didn't want to disturb the crime scene but he had to verify that whoever was lying in the room was: a) dead and b) Quentin Ufford.

The smell of blood filled what would have otherwise been an unremarkable living room. There was another stink, too, smoky and plastic. Blake backed into the kitchen and looked down at the cooker. A melted pool of plastic covered the hob. Ufford lay on the blood-soaked carpet staring at Blake with empty eyes. He'd been dead for a while as far as Blake could tell. A ragged gash across his throat told Blake all he needed to know.

He pulled out his phone and called DI Kath Cryer. She sounded as though she was just getting up. "Wow, you're early, sir, are you okay?"

"I'm fine, Kath, listen get a Crime Scene Investigation team down to Quentin Ufford's house in Raby as soon as possible. He's been murdered."

There was a pause as a thousand questions ran through Kath's head before she realised that now wasn't the time for questions. "Will do, sir. I'll get some uniform over to you right away, too."

"Thanks, Kath and get a team to search the

fields behind here up towards Thornton Hough. I was attacked by someone who might be the killer..."

"Was it Terry White?"

"I think so. We need to warn the public, too. He's dangerous." Blake hung up and went outside into the fresh air. His cheek and eye still ached from the impact of the door and his ribs throbbed. He rummaged around in his pockets for the painkillers he'd become accustomed to carrying but was rewarded with an empty blister pack.

Was that it then? Had all the death and bloodshed been down to Terry White's psychosis? Somehow Blake wasn't convinced. All the victims were connected with Pro-Vets, even Richard Ince, who Blake felt convinced was murdered now. Ollerthwaite was actively investigating the charity's accounts. Paul Travis, given he was the CEO, would have been ultimately responsible for the charity's finances. It was the attack on Ollerthwaite that struck Blake as odd. It was easy to see how White could become fixated on people he encountered every day at work. Ollerthwaite was a new face, someone different. Why suddenly single him out? There was something not quite right here, as though Blake had two final pieces of the puzzle but they didn't quite fit together.

Sirens wailed in the distance and Blake went round to the front of the house to flag them down. One thing was certain, he had to pass the information Ollerthwaite had given him to Cavanagh, along with his suspicions. Quinlan had been right when they met, any involvement by Blake could compromise an investigation. But Blake wasn't going to stop trying to bring the murderer to justice.

*****

DI Kath Cryer wanted to be at Ufford's cottage helping Blake with the investigation there but she'd managed to get Lex Price to agree to an interview at his house.

"If Ufford was killed by Terry White, why are we grilling Price again, Ma'am?" Andrew Kinnear said, a little wearily as they climbed out the car.

Kath grinned. "Leave no stone unturned, Andrew," she said in a pantomime impression of DCI Blake. She reverted to her own voice. "To be fair, mate, we don't know for certain that White killed Ufford and I reckon Lex Price is about as shifty as they get. I wouldn't be surprised to find out he was mixed up in all of this."

"How did he take it when you said you wanted to talk to him and not Bobby?"

"He sounded surprised but like the kind of surprised you are when you find your glasses aren't where you left them or you're half an hour early for an appointment. Price is spookily calm for a man of his background. He's exercising a lot of self-control and the only reason he'd do that is because he's covering something up."

"God, let's just hope he doesn't lose it while we're interviewing him," Kinnear said, his eyes wide and his face pale. There was another reason not to adopt. Imagine Chris breaking the news of Kinnear's injury or even death to Niamh, their daughter. Imagine turning up at home with cuts and bruises and trying to explain them to the child. He shook himself.

"Don't worry, Andy, I reckon he's on a tight leash. I just wonder who's holding the other end," Kath said, ringing the doorbell.

If Lex Price had murdered Quentin Ufford last night, it wasn't apparent to Kath. He stood at the door dressed in jeans and a sweater as though he was just heading off for an evening with mates at the pub.

"Come on in," he said, once Kath and Andrew had identified themselves. "I've put the dogs out the back so they don't make a big fuss of you. I can't stop them jumping up to save my life." He led them through a tastefully decorated hallway and into an immaculate lounge with leather furniture and a white carpet. Kath resisted the urge to check the soles of her feet before stepping on it. The words 'forensically clean' popped into her head unbidden. She glanced at Kinnear and saw her thoughts reflected in his eyes. This house screamed 'control.' Kath doubted Price tidied the house personally but she imagined an army of cleaners came in on a very regular basis.

"You'll have to forgive the mess," Lex Price said, without a hint of humour.

"I was just thinking how incredibly tidy your house is," Kath replied, "compared to mine, anyway."

"Yeah, it looks... very tidy," Kinnear added, glancing round.

"Take a seat," Lex said, lowering himself into a huge armchair. "What is it you want to talk to me about?"

Kath sat down next to Kinnear on the sofa. "There's no easy way to say it, Mr Price, so I'll come out with the question. Were you aware that your daughter, Layla, had been in a relationship with Paul Travis?"

Lex's jaw clenched and the bald skin on the side of his head rippled and he fought with his emotions. "Yeah," he said, quietly, "I knew."

"You can see how that might colour our investigation into his death. Your son had possession of the murder weapon and knew Layla was seeing Travis..."

"Bobby didn't kill Paul Travis. He tried to use

the information to blackmail his sister. When she told him to sling his hook, he came whining to me, didn't he?"

"And what was your reaction?"

Price paused for a beat. "Well I wasn't best pleased, was I?"

"You were angry about Layla, then?"

"No, don't be daft. She's a big girl. Travis was a bit of a big head but I knew he'd get tired of her. What really pissed me off was Bobby being such a weasel. I dunno where I went wrong with that lad, honestly. Imagine grassing up your own sister."

"You held no ill-will towards Travis?"

"He wouldn't be on my Christmas card list, but his charity is a client. I'm not going to balls that up because my daughter is a poor judge of men."

"But there's quite an age difference. Didn't you think Travis was taking advantage?" Kinnear said.

"My wife's younger than me. What are you trying to say? That I should have wanted to kill Travis? Is that it? You want me to throw my hands up and say, yeah, I did it. You got me. He was shagging my little girl and I couldn't bear it? Is that what you want?"

"I'm sorry, Mr Price. We didn't mean to upset you, but we have to explore all possibilities,"

Kath said. Price was reddening and she wondered if they hadn't made a mistake coming here after all. An interview at the station might have been safer.

"Yeah, well, the one possibility you don't seem to be exploring is the obvious one. The one you have a witness to. Paul Travis was killed by jihadis but you lot don't want to know, do you? It all gets swept under the carpet, doesn't it? You'd rather pin this on me or my son than go upsetting some immigrant ISIS freaks, wouldn't you?" He jumped to his feet. "I tell you what. I reckon we're done here. It's always the same, isn't it? Bloody liberal elites trying to do down the hardworking man. Paul Travis was just an ordinary bloke trying to do some good. Yeah, he was no angel but he's gone and now you're coming after us. It makes me sick."

"Mr Price, we aren't…"

"Just leave, please before I lose my temper. Go on go. I tell you what, though, I'm not keeping quiet about this. People have a right to know what's going on here."

Chapter 30

The van squealed to a halt on the Clatterbridge Road and Terry White couldn't believe his luck. He hurried towards it. It was a plain, faded blue Ford Transit, grimy with miles of travel. A scruffy-looking man in a black donkey jacket and a woolly hat looked out at Terry from the driving seat. Silver stubble covered his chin and lank grey hair dangled out of the hat and down his neck. He looked scrawny and as in need of a wash as Terry.

"Need a lift, mate?"

Terry nodded.

"Where to?"

"Just away from here."

The man grinned again. "Fair enough. I've been there before, myself, mate. Hop in."

Terry glanced around and then looked at the man hard. He didn't look like Graves and besides, he'd only recently trapped another part of the man's black soul in an effigy and melted it, so he'd be weak. He might even be dead. Properly dead.

"Are you coming? I haven't got all day," the man said, revving the engine and still grinning.

Terry hopped in and slammed the door shut.

*****

Malachy O'Hare sniffed at the green puddle on the hob in Ufford's kitchen. "Looks like the same thing again. A melted plastic soldier. Was it Terry White who attacked you then?"

Blake nodded from the kitchen door. "I think so. I've had a brief look around, Malachy but only to ensure that Ufford was beyond help. If you find anything else let me know, right?"

"Of course I will. When's that gobshite Kenning going to be here?"

Blake smiled, stepping aside to let more crime scene investigators in. "He won't be long, but it's pretty obvious how Ufford died."

"Aye well, the big hole in his neck would present him with problems for a kick-off," O'Hare said, smiling through his mask, "but we better wait for the experts to confirm that."

"You'd make a great pathologist, Malachy," Blake said. He stepped into the garden and scanned across the fields behind the house where a line of officers followed the deep footprints through the dark soil. Overhead a helicopter tracked back and forth, searching for any sign of the fugitive. Under any other circumstances, Blake would have loved to be out on this glorious Spring day, enjoying the birdsong and the blue sky. Right now, however, he felt a sense of foreboding. Everything pointed to Terry White being responsible for the deaths but there was the added complication of Quinlan's possible involvement in a money laundering enterprise. And then there was Laura being paid out of the charity's coffers for some reason. Blake shook his head and jumped into his car. He needed to see Cavanagh.

*****

A scrum of reporters hung around the entrance to police HQ in Liverpool. Blake had been so deep in thought that he'd forgotten all about the media interest the case would generate. Deirdre Lanham, the terrier from the Wirral Argus had elbowed her way to the front of the pack. "DCI Blake, is it true a second victim has been found?"

Blake waved a dismissive hand at her. "I can't help you at the moment, I'm afraid. Our investigations are on-going and we will give a press conference in due course."

"Why are your team so dismissive about a terrorist connection, DCI Blake?"

"What do you think about the proposed rally at the war memorial in Port Sunlight? Should that be allowed to go ahead?"

Blake flinched at the last question. He hated getting tangled up in politics and mass gatherings. They always ended up in a mess. He barged his way through the crowd and got inside. Marge stood smiling expectantly at him. "Well?" she said.

"Well, what, Marge?"

Her face fell. "Laura," she said, lowering her voice. "How did it go?"

Blake gave her an apologetic smile. "Sorry, Marge. Not your fault but it didn't work. She sent her boyfriend to put me straight."

"Oh, you poor boy," Marge said, pouting. She sounded so heartfelt that Blake feared she was going to come from behind the counter and give him a hug.

"Don't worry, Marge, I'm over it. Plenty of work to keep my mind off things and like I said, it wasn't your fault. I'm sorry I got you involved. It was a daft thing for me to do." Blake hurried up the stairs to the Major Incident Room.

DI Kath Cryer and DC Kinnear were waiting for Blake at his desk. Kinnear stared at Blake's face. "You okay, sir?"

"Yeah, a gift from Terry White, I think. How did you get on with Price? Why's everybody yelling terrorist?"

"It didn't go very well, boss," Kath said. "He didn't seem that bothered by the fact that his daughter was seeing Travis. He was more uppity that we didn't seem to take Bobby's statement about the so-called terrorists seriously. He's kicking up a stink about it on social media already. Hence the call for a rally."

"Jeez," Blake murmured. "That's all we need. Okay, then, let's call his bluff and get Bobby in for a second time and get more detail, shall we?"

"Lex is going to want to be there as an appropriate adult, sir," Kinnear said.

"More the merrier," Blake said. "Maybe we can find out where this baseball bat really came from. What about Paul Travis' mobile records?"

"Oh, yeah," Kath said, opening a file. "Looks like plenty of communication, very lovey-dovey between them up until a couple of weeks ago then it ends abruptly. It backs up Layla Price's version of things that Travis had ended their relationship. Other calls were to immediate friends and family, no real surprises." Kath pursed her lips for a second, clearly bracing herself to say something. "Do you think we're complicating this too much sir?"

"How do you mean?"

"I mean, the obvious suspect here is Terry White. Bobby just happened to be there and saw him dump the baseball bat and picked it up. He wouldn't be too upset to see Travis get a good hiding, would he? Maybe there is no sane motive, just Terry White's paranoia."

"I'm not so sure. There's something else going on and I can't believe they are not connected Ollerthwaite noticed unusually large sums of money flowing through that charity, he suspects that it's being used to launder money. Maybe Travis noticed unusual transactions. Ollerthwaite also claimed that Quentin Ufford was being obstructive. Now Ufford's dead..."

"Or those things could just be coincidences, sir. If Quentin Ufford was trying to stop Ian Ollerthwaite from investigating, why would someone kill him?"

"Because he knew too much?" Kinnear said, with a shrug. "Or because he failed to cover someone's tracks?"

Kath gave Kinnear a look of disgust. "Behave, Andrew, this isn't Dr No, people don't get dropped into a shark tank for failing..."

"I dunno, Ma'am. If there's a lot of money at stake, maybe Ufford had to be silenced before we put the screws on him..."

"But how does Terry White fit in with that, Andy?" Kath said. "If White was at Ufford's cottage when the boss arrived, then why was he hanging around for so long after killing Ufford? Hardly the hallmark of a professional hit. I'm not saying there isn't something going on at Pro-Vets but I'm just saying that it just might be separate to what Terry White is up to, that's all."

Before Blake could answer, DCI Matty Cavanagh appeared at their side. He looked sleek and well-groomed as ever. He reminded Blake of a fox, cunning and hunting for any weakness. Cavanagh might be vain and a bit of a corner-cutter but he wasn't stupid. "Hi, Kath, Andrew. Erm, Will, have you got a minute? I want to discuss a development with you."

"Sure," Blake said, following Cavanagh to his office. "I wanted to talk to you about something, anyway."

Once they were inside, Cavanagh shut the door and turned to Blake. "Please tell me that my team didn't see Kyle Quinlan enter a house in Bebington last night…"

"How would I know, Matty? I live in Rock Park…"

"Yeah, but this house is occupied by your little brother, Will, remember him? The author who hangs out with psychopaths?"

"Research, maybe?"

"Oh, yeah. Thanks, Will, I hadn't thought of that. Research. Of course. Were you helping him with his research? Because you were there too."

Blake sighed. "Okay, I admit it. I tried to trick Laura into seeing me. I pretended I was a client and had a rogue pet that needed her attention. She sent Quinlan along… I honestly didn't expect that…"

"Bloody hell, Will. What the fuck were you thinking? Quinlan's going to be spooked now. My team are going to have to be extra careful because of you."

"If it's any consolation, Matty, Quinlan seemed anything but spooked. Like I said, I think he'd have been more suspicious if I hadn't tried to contact Laura."

"I've got to tell the Super, Will, you were warned…"

"Wait, listen, I know it was a stupid thing to do but I had to find out what was going on. If anything, Quinlan's strutting about like cock of the walk now. He thinks he's got one over on me…"

"Well he has hasn't he?"

Blake gave a wry smile. "I suppose so, yeah, but I know, now, Matty. Laura has no interest in me. It's over. What I mean is that Quinlan saw me as his Achilles' heel. If Laura still had feelings for me, then he could never be sure I wouldn't get her to turn him in. She pretty much denounced me in front of him. So now he feels secure, which is always dangerous. Far from rattling him, I think it will have made him complacent."

"I dunno, Will, what else did you get from him?"

"He said that I couldn't touch him because the moment I came for him for anything, it would appear like some kind of vendetta. He thinks he's bulletproof."

"I can see his point. That it?"

"From that encounter, yes but it might be useful for you to talk to Ian Ollerthwaite…"

Matty looked pained. "God, do I have to?"

"You know he's in hospital, right? Attacked by this Terry White character we're chasing," Blake said. "He was investigating the Pro-Vets accounts and there's a lot of money going through their coffers, an awful lot. Some of it to an animal psychologist, apparently."

"Laura? You think Quinlan is using the charity to launder money?"

"It's a strong possibility," Blake said. "Have a chat with Ollerthwaite. Again, having a conflict of interest, it would be hard for me to investigate impartially but you could look into it as part of your investigation into Quinlan."

Matty Cavanagh looked at Blake warily. "Okay, Will but if this jumps up and bites me, then I'm going straight to the Super, understand? He'll give me a rap on the knuckles but it you who'll get your arse kicked."

Chapter 31

Despite his history with the media, and maybe because of it, Blake hated press conferences. He knew they were a good way of getting the public on your side. There were times, though, when he thought he may as well go into the street with a sign on his back that said: I'm a copper please kick me. That's how it felt sometimes. Three people had died and a tortured soul was on the loose but Blake had to waste time listening to inane questions and speculation that did nothing to inform the public.

Sitting next to Martin, Blake did his best to keep a poker face while the Superintendent rambled through the basic details of the case and expressed his great concern over the whereabouts of Terry White. On the other side of Martin sat Hannah Williams, Media and Communications Manager. She was a slim, black woman in her forties, with strong cheek bones and a pointed chin. She scanned the press pack with stern, glittering eyes like a security guard watching for the first sign of trouble. Blake had not had many dealings with her before. It was a measure of how seriously Martin took this case that she was sitting in on the conference.

An earnest young man with a goatee beard and a tweed jacket put his hand up. "There have been accusations that a witness to the Travis murder was ignored when he claimed to have seen two men of Middle-Eastern descent fleeing from the body. Is it true that you're dismissing the terrorist angle on this case?"

"Angle?" Blake muttered under his breath. He looked up at the journalist. "We're looking at this case from every 'angle' possible, including the one you have just alluded to."

"Then you don't rule out a possible terrorist atrocity?"

Blake winced. "Given that a second body has been found, we are confident that Paul Travis was not the victim of a random attack with terrorist motives…"

"Something more orchestrated and premeditated then?" the young man said.

Hannah Williams leaned forward, giving Blake a quick, sidelong glance. "What DCI Blake means is that other than the one witness, we have no other evidence that there are any connections with terrorist activity in this case. We do have other evidence that points strongly in another direction. Next question please."

Deirdre Lanham raised her hand. "Given that you're investigating the Pro-Vets charity quite closely, is there an implication that they didn't do enough to help Terry White?"

Blake opened his mouth to speak but Hannah

got there first.

"Our role is purely to investigate the circumstances around the crimes and present the evidence to the CPS, we do not make judgements about anything…"

"But you have to admit that they've failed this man," Deirdre Lanham insisted. "I mean he is obviously troubled…"

"Which is why we need the public's help to find him as a matter of urgency," Blake said.

"But we must remind the public not to approach him as he is extremely dangerous. Call 999 if you spot him," Hannah said before Blake could continue. "Next question."

"What support did this young man have before he went off the rails, though?" Deirdre Lanham said, not backing down.

"I believe he had access to a counsellor who was working closely with his GP, but nobody could have…" Blake began to say.

"I don't feel it's appropriate to discuss Mr White's medical history. That's well out of our remit, I'm afraid. Next question." Hannah Williams' eyes slid away from Deirdre Lanham and towards another journalist.

"What are your views on the planned rally at the Port Sunlight war memorial this weekend?"

Hannah's expression was deadpan, unreadable.

"People have a right to protest and we hope that any marches or vigils will proceed peacefully."

Blake ground his teeth as the Media and Communications Manager fielded almost every question, butting in when he tried to answer. Finally, she wrapped up the conference by standing up. "Thank you, ladies and gentlemen, I think the take-home message here is that we aren't looking at this as a terrorist attack but we are looking for Terry White, a troubled and dangerous young man who needs urgent help. We'd be grateful to the public for their assistance."

Murmured conversation filled the room as everyone began to pack up and compare notes. Some journalists hurried out to prepare their stories. Blake followed Martin and Hannah out of the room and into the corridor at the back.

"Well, that could have been a lot worse," Martin said, breathing a sigh of relief. "Thank you, Hannah, sterling work there. Wouldn't you say so, Will?"

"I wondered what I was doing there, to be honest, sir…"

Hannah suppressed a smile. "You aren't sulking are you, Will Blake?"

"No. It's just that I would have happily missed the conference altogether and spent the time on the investigation if I'd known I wasn't required to speak…"

"What's up Blake? Someone stealing your lime-light?" Martin said. "Talk about bruised egos. I'm sorry, Hannah..."

"It's not that I just wondered what I was doing there, that's all."

Hannah Williams' eyes narrowed. "So did I, DCI Blake, so did I. I had to pull your fat out of the fire a number of times back there, as it happens but, hey, you're welcome." She gave Martin a curt nod and stalked off down the corridor.

"What is it with you, Blake?" Superintendent Martin said, putting his hands on his hips. "How do you manage to make any situation worse?"

"I'm sorry, sir, but what do the public think when they see us sitting there like a couple of stuffed shirts, hardly saying a word? They want to see us in control of the situation..."

"And are you, Will? We have a homicidal maniac running around Wirral, what looks to be a far-right rally assembling in one of our most picturesque villages and no arrests. We need a resolution as quickly as possible."

Blake watched Martin disappear after Hannah Williams and sighed. But something had been said in that conference that made him think and it was worth exploring.

*****

It would have been next to impossible for Lex

Price to object to bringing his son to Birkenhead Station for a second interview after he'd made such a fuss about the police not taking Bobby's statement seriously enough, but Kath felt nervous all the same. "Price knows he's been cornered," she said to DC Kinnear as they stood waiting in the foyer and watched Lex sign in with Bobby. "That can only wind him up more after our conversation this morning about his daughter."

Kinnear nodded. "On top of that Lex Price's got an obvious agenda, now. It'll be hard to get Bobby to tell the truth with his father breathing down his neck."

"We'll have to tread carefully. The last thing we need is Lex standing on a platform on Saturday claiming we tried to make his son change his story. That would play right into his hands."

"So, what are we going to do?"

"Details, Andrew, details. That's where the devil is. That's where we'll trip him up. I hope. Otherwise, we're stuffed." She walked across the foyer and shook Lex's hand, noticing the clamminess of his palm and the tight grip. "Mr Price, Bobby. Thanks for coming in again. I thought it important to give you another chance to give us your evidence."

"Don't be trying to get him to change his story, now, DI Cryer. I know what you lot can be like."

"Trust me, Mr Price," Kath said, "nobody here's trying to get Bobby to say anything but the truth. Would you come this way?"

Kath and Kinnear led them down a corridor and into an interview room. Once they'd settled, Kath reached over to a recorder. "You aren't under caution or anything, Bobby, we're talking to you as a witness, but it would help us if we had it on tape. Do you mind?"

Bobby looked at his father who shrugged. "Nah, it's okay," Bobby said at last. "Go ahead."

"Okay, Bobby. Think back to the night Paul Travis died and then tell me in your own words what you remember."

Bobby glanced over at his dad. "Go on son," Lex said. "In your own words."

"I was hanging around the Hillsborough Memorial Garden when I heard voices from the war memorial. So I sneaked up and hid behind the bushes..."

"Could you show me where you were hiding, on this map, Bobby?" Kinnear said, sliding a paper street map across the table.

"So, you were hiding behind a hedge on the edge of the pavement, just by the war memorial, here, yeah?" Kinnear said.

"Yeah."

Kath leaned forward. "What kind of hedge,

Bobby?"

"Eh?"

"What kind of hedge was it?"

"Oh, come on, Inspector, he's not a fucking gardener," Lex snapped.

Kath flashed Lex a cold smile. "Please Mr Price, if you think I've confused your son or need to clarify something or I'm not following proper procedure, then do shout out. Otherwise, interruptions aren't very helpful."

Kinnear continued. "What kind of leaves did it have? Small? Large? Was it a thick bush, or just twigs?"

Bobby glanced over at his father who nodded. "A thick bush with small leaves."

"And you crouched behind this, right?"

"Yeah."

"Okay. What did you see?"

"Two guys dressed in black. They had hoodies on and scarves over their faces so I couldn't really see them. I could hear them, though and they were shouting that 'Ally Akbat' thing they shout, you know."

"I see," Kath said, grimacing. "Do you mean 'Allahu Akbar' Bobby? What were they doing while they shouted this?"

"They were hitting him with baseball bats..."

"How many baseball bats? Did they have one each?"

"Yeah. That Travis guy was on the steps. I mean he must have been dead already, but they kept on hitting him and shouting…"

"Then what happened?"

"I kept hidden and they ran off but they left the bats behind…"

"Both bats were on the ground?" Kath said, scribbling a note. She noticed Lex's leg bouncing up and down, he was getting agitated. He could see she was going to tie Bobby in knots any minute.

"Yeah."

"Which way did they go, Bobby?" Kinnear said, pulling Bobby's focus from Kath.

"Up the road past the garden centre. I think they might have been going to the station."

"It's possible, I suppose," Kinnear said with a smile. "What did you do then?"

"When they'd gone, I sneaked out and went to have a look."

"And what did you see?"

Bobby paled. "Loads of blood," he whispered. "Loads. It was horrible. Anyway, I picked up the baseball bat and ran."

"Why did you pick up the bat? Bobby?"

"I dunno," Bobby said. "It was just kind of… cool, you know? Like it had been used for a murder." He lowered his head. "That sounds a bit sick, doesn't it? Sorry."

"See?" Lex said, his voice a threatening rumble. "He's telling the truth."

"Oh I believe some of it, Mr Price," Kath said. "Have you got the tablet, Andrew?"

Kinnear produced an iPad with Google maps already loaded up. "So you say you were here Bobby, yeah?" Kinnear pointed at the spot on the map.

"He's already said that," Lex muttered.

"Yeah," Bobby said.

"The trouble is, Bobby, look," Kinnear said, holding up the streetview of the memorial area. "There're no bushes on the side of the road. In fact, the wall that hems in the gardens there is so low, you'd have had a real job hiding behind it at all."

"Maybe he was mistaken," Lex said.

"Bobby was very clear about the type of hedge, Mr Price and I'll say it again, if you think I'm overstepping the mark, just say but otherwise, could you let Bobby answer? So, where were you hiding, Bobby?"

Bobby looked down. "I dunno, do I?"

"Okay, mate. Don't worry," Kinnear said in a soothing voice. "We're just trying to get a full picture of what actually happened that night."

"So, the other problem I have is that from where you say you were hiding, Bobby, you wouldn't have been able to see a thing."

"What?" Bobby looked like a rabbit caught in the headlights of an oncoming juggernaut.

"Paul Travis was found dead on the opposite side of the memorial to your alleged hiding place. If you'd been there, you wouldn't have seen anything, would you?"

"That's it, let's go," Lex Price said. "I knew this would happen. You lot just don't want to face the truth. This country's under attack and you're letting it happen…"

Bobby didn't move. "I didn't see nothing," he muttered.

"What, Bobby?" Kinnear said.

"I said I didn't see nothing. I was pissed, wasn't I? I'd been sitting by the Art Gallery and walked down to the memorial. I found Travis lying there already dead. I took the baseball bat. I dunno why. I'd had a skinful."

"Bloody hell, son!" Lex hissed and stormed out of the room.

"I-I'm sorry," Bobby said. "Dad said it was probably Muslims or something and I went along with him. I didn't mean it. I just wanted to say the right thing for him."

Kath rubbed her forehead. "You know what perverting the course of justice means, don't you, Bobby?"

Bobby's eyes widened. "I'm not a pervert, honest!"

"No, but you're in big trouble, now."

"Wait, I do remember something and I'm not making this up. When I was walking down from the Art Gallery and there was a woman running towards me. She bashed into me, like. Sent me flying but didn't stop."

"What time was this, Bobby?"

"Dunno. Maybe round midnight, something like that. I didn't get a good look at her, but she was in a real hurry."

Chapter 32

A sense of quiet desperation gripped the Major Incident Room. Some people were tapping away at computers, other staring at screens as though willpower alone could force the solution to the case to appear before them.

DI Kath Cryer, DS Vikki Chinn, DC Kinnear and DC Manikas all sat around Blake's desk, updating him on the scant progress they'd made. "It looks like Terry White managed to get away from the search teams around the crime scene, sir," Alex Manikas said. "It's like he's vanished. The only thing I can think is that he was given a lift."

"He could be anywhere, then," Blake murmured. "What about Bobby Price's ISIS invasion?"

"Popped that particular balloon, boss," Kath said, "but Bobby reckons he encountered a woman running away from the scene about midnight. I believe him. Thing is, she'd have been running in the direction of Travis's house."

"D'you think it could be his wife, Ma'am?" Kinnear said.

"He described her as being tall. Rachel Travis is short," Kath said.

"Plus, I can't see how she'd be involved in the murder of Ufford or Ince. It keeps coming back to Terry White. We've just got to find him," Blake said, tapping his pen on the desk. "But it might be worth getting Tasha Cook to check with Rachel, discreetly. This woman might have witnessed something. Put a request out to the public and reassure anyone who might be afraid of coming forward, especially if they think it's terror related."

"Do you think he's likely to strike again, sir?" Alex Manikas said.

"I don't know, Alex," Blake replied. "We need to get some kind of handle on White. A profile of him. With the exception of Ian Ollerthwaite, all of his victims have been known to him. That means any of his workmates at Pro-Vets could be in danger."

Vikki raised a hand. "What about Nicola Norton, the psychologist, sir? She could give us a good idea of White's frame of mind."

"Yes, good idea, Vikki, at the same time, let's get a warrant to look at his medical and personal records, so we can see what kind of medication he's on and how effective it is. It might be useful. It's getting late. Let's do what we can but don't forget to get some rest, too."

"That includes you, boss," Kath said, with a smile.

"That includes me, Kath, yes," Blake said, grinning back. "I'll go and talk to Martin first and see if he'll let us bring Norton on board."

It struck Blake as he regarded Superintendent Martin's scowl that he probably should have been more conciliatory with Hannah Williams the Media Manager.

"Ah, I see. Now you're all in favour of having the right person for the job when it suits you, Will," Martin said. "Do you know how long it took me to calm Hannah down? She was that close to putting in a complaint about you."

"I'm sorry, sir. I didn't mean to offend anyone. I just wasn't sure what our role was once she took over, that's all."

"Her role was to spot the traps that crusty old-timers like you and I can't see and steer us around them. Which she did. You never win a debate with a journalist, Will, you know that. Even if you do, they go away and write something entirely different and make you look wrong. Hannah's good at her job."

"Yes, sir. I'll make a point of apologising to her next time I see her," Blake mumbled. "Anyway, you'll be pleased to hear that Bobby Price has retracted his statement about the two jihadis. He made it all up. It means we can focus on Terry White…"

"I thought you were dubious about White's guilt, Will?"

"Possibly, sir," Blake said, feeling his cheeks flush. "But I suspect there might be money laundering going on at Pro-Vets…"

"Well why aren't you digging into that?"

"There's a possible connection with the Quinlan case, so I've passed the information over to Matty Cavanagh, sir. I know my past connection to Laura Vexley might compromise things."

Martin nodded his approval. "Good thinking, Will. That's one less thing to worry about, anyway. Go ahead then, bring this Norton woman in for advice if you think it'll help us pick up Terry White sooner rather than later."

"Thank you, sir," Blake said, turning to go.

"And Will," Martin said as Blake reached the door. "Don't forget to speak to Hannah."

Blake winced. "I won't forget, sir."

*****

The smell of oil and petrol filled the air. Cold nipped at Terry White's face and cheeks but a heavy blanket kept the rest of him warm. For a moment he lay, luxuriating in the cosiness. He couldn't feel anything because he hadn't moved and he didn't want to. He wondered where he was. Thinking back, Terry remembered a dead body and lots of blood. It was Quentin. Quentin was dead. Then a big man came banging on the door. Terry had escaped. In a van. And now he was here.

Someone shifted and coughed to his left. Terry sat up, the blanket slipping down his body.

"Woah, big fella, you're fine. You're safe," said a soothing voice. The scrawny old man who had offered Terry a lift yesterday. He still had his black donkey jacket and woolly hat on. He smiled at Terry, showing a crooked line of small, yellowed teeth. "I'm making a brew. You want one?"

"Yes please." Terry put a hand to his forehead, which throbbed fiercely.

"You had a funny turn yesterday," the old man said, stirring a spoon in a mug. "A seizure or something. I damn nearly called an ambulance but then you stopped and fell asleep. Does that happen a lot?"

"If I don't take my tablets," Terry said, frowning. "It's cos of my injury."

"I guessed that," the old man said. "My name's Noel, by the way." He handed Terry the mug.

Terry took it in trembling hands and looked around. They were in a wooden garage of some kind. Cobwebbed ropes, hoses and chains dangled from low beams above him. Shelving filled with old cardboard boxes, cables and bits of angle iron covered one wall. A cold, grey light bled in through the grimy windows that comprised the top third of the doors. The table on the other side of the garage housed an electric hob, a kettle and some chipped plates and battered pans. "Do you live here?" Terry said.

"Sometimes," Noel replied. "When I'm not travelling. The owner lets me stay. I do a few jobs for him now and again. You're safe here."

Terry looked into his mug. "What do you mean?"

"I'm not daft, mate. You were running away from something when I picked you up, weren't you? I don't wanna know who from or what for. You're welcome to stay 'til you feel better. No pressure. You look like you've been in the wars."

"I have," Terry said. "I need orders. I need to know what to do next." Suddenly, hot tears began to scald his cheeks and he scrubbed at his face. "I don't know what to do. I need orders."

"Who from?"

Terry shook his head slowly. "I dunno." He pulled a phone from his pocket. "They call me on this, but it's stopped working."

"Let me see," Noel said, taking the phone. "Just needs charging, mate. I've got a charger somewhere." He pulled open a drawer and rummaged through a tangle of wires and cables. "Here we go." He plugged the phone in.

"Thank you." Terry pulled his knees up to his

chest and stared ahead. His stomach grumbled loudly.

"Sounds like you need some food, fella. Are you hungry?"

"I dunno," Terry said. "I suppose so."

The phone beeped and Terry leapt up. A text read:

You are in danger. Lay low for a while.

He looked at Noel. The old man had his back to him while he fussed over some tins. Terry didn't think Noel was a threat. Graves hadn't taken over the old man. He was pretty sure. He'd met him at random on the road. The old man was being kind. He'd do as he was told and lay low for a while. When it was dark, he could decide what to do next.

Chapter 33

Although she had a swish office in Heswall, Nicola Norton lived in a small, terraced house to the north of Port Sunlight at the Bebington end. Blake had phoned her and agreed that he would call in to discuss her involvement in the case. Standing outside the house now, he found himself wondering if the original occupants looked over the road and envied the Port Sunlight employees living in the bigger houses or was that something they aspired to?

She answered the door almost as soon as Blake knocked. She wore black leggings and her long, golden hair spilled down over a baggy sweater. "DCI Blake, come on in," she said. "You look surprised about something."

The house had kept many of its original features, with high skirtings and ornate ceiling cornicing. But Norton had put her own stamp on the place, too with subtle pastel paints and soft furnishings. "To be honest, Ms Norton, I had expected you to live over by your office rather than on this side of the Wirral."

"Call me Nicola. This was my mother's house, DCI Blake. I grew up here. When she passed away, I inherited it. My business seems to haemorrhage cash and the Heswall office is so expensive to run. It's cheap, but full of memories, not all of them happy."

Blake nodded. "I know what you mean, I live in my parents' old house too. I keep meaning to get organised enough to sell it and move on but..."

"Life's too busy. Things get in the way. Yeah, tell me about it," Nicola said. "Would you like a coffee?"

Blake followed her into the kitchen. "You worked quite closely with Terry White, then."

"I did, Inspector. He was a troubled soul. Full of guilt for surviving, full of anger at what happened to his friends and so confused."

"This condition that he has, the delusion. Can you explain that to me?"

"Fregoli delusion," Nicola said, stirring the coffee. "Terry sustained a serious brain injury when he was caught in an explosion. He'd had psychological problems before but doctors think that the injury exacerbated an already existing condition. Put simply, Terry had trouble recognising faces and so would attribute the same identity to different people."

"This Corporal Graves character for instance," Blake said.

"Exactly. For whatever reason, Terry had a thing about Graves. He believed that Graves bullied him and had it in for him. There's no written evidence to support this but it was certainly how Terry felt. When Graves died in the explosion, somehow, Terry convinced himself that he wasn't actually dead and that somehow, he was possessing the bodies of people close to Terry."

"To what end?"

"To ruin Terry's life and ultimately kill him."

"It seems incredible that anyone could believe this..."

"That's why he was on anti-psychotics, Inspector. It's hard for us to understand or empathise because it seems so bizarre but for Terry, it's cold logic. He believes that each time he kills and leaves an effigy, part of Graves' soul is trapped in it. Terry has a twin for that effigy which he destroys, thereby wiping out part of Graves' being."

"Then eventually, he'll have finished Graves off, surely?"

"You'd like to think so, wouldn't you, Inspector? But it doesn't work like that. I'm pretty sure Terry will convince himself that somehow Graves escaped the trap and someone else will have to go."

Blake sipped his drink. "I can't understand where he's gone. Do you think he might leave the Wirral? Just run away?"

"I think that's unlikely. Terry is still fighting Graves and he sees it as a mission. I don't think he'd run. It would be like deserting his post. Besides, his problem is in his head. Even if he were to run, then Graves would just pop up wherever he was."

"Jeez, it's not like the Wirral is a big place. Where can he be?"

"Someone might be sheltering him. It might be worth re-emphasising how dangerous he can be. Of course, there is the other possibility…"

"Which is?"

"Terry's brain injury left him with epilepsy, too. Normally, his medication would control it, but he hasn't got any of that with him. He might have had a seizure somewhere and be injured, disorientated or worse."

"If you can think of anywhere he might be drawn to, anywhere he might go. Because, to be honest, we're stumped and from what you say, it looks like it's only a matter of time before he kills again."

Nicola Norton bit her lip and looked thoughtful. "One thing that does come to mind. Terry's focus has certainly been Pro-Vets and that's partly because he works there but his paranoia seems to be focused on the charity staff. Or the more senior ones. Should there be another victim, I would be most concerned about one of Paul Travis's drinking buddies, Barry and Dave but mainly on George Owens. He was Paul's best friend and in Terry's mind, most susceptible to control by Graves. If I were you, I'd keep a close watch on George Owens.

*****

George Owens stood in the middle of his untidy living room, looking at his phone. The police had just called. In one way, it had been a stroke of luck that White had attacked that tiresome DC Ollerthwaite but he had to think what to do now. Things were getting more complicated.

Ufford had got what was coming to him, that was certain. The twisting little runt should never have gone on the fiddle like that. He was always taking things that weren't his. A few bags of crisps here, a few printer cartridges there. Pretty soon, you just think anything is up for grabs and start syphoning off actual money.

Well, that was all over. Pretty soon, it would all be over. He'd make sure of that.

*****

Rock Park, where Blake lived was only a ten-minute drive from Nicola Norton's house but Blake drove deep in thought. Something nagged him about this whole business. He'd handed over the financial investigation side of things but part of him still wondered if there was something connecting the murders to financial impropriety at the charity.

Wearily, he pushed the door open, bracing himself for the onslaught from Charlie but nothing happened. "Charlie?" he called. The little dog never failed to greet him. In fact, Serafina usually sauntered after him and neither of them were present. "Serafina?"

With a mounting sense of dread, Blake crept into the kitchen but found nothing. "Where are you?" he whispered as he entered the living room.

Blake's stomach lurched. Serafina lay still on the sofa. Very still. Charlie whimpered, softly and licked at her ear. "Serafina?" Blake gasped hurrying over. The cat felt cold and she stared at Blake with glazed eyes. "No, no, no, no," Blake hissed as he felt her flank. Her breathing was weak. Charlie whined and Blake scratched his ear fleetingly. "Don't worry, don't worry, boy." He pulled his phone out quickly and called the vet. It went to answerphone and gave another number for emergency calls. Hissing with frustration, Blake hung up and rummaged in his pocket for a pen and paper. With trembling fingers Blake called the vet again, scribbling the new number frantically. "Don't worry, girl, we'll get you help," Blake said. Serafina gave a pathetic rumbling growl and tried to scratch Blake, then slumped back onto the sofa.

Chapter 34

Chopper blades cut the air, sending sand and exhaust fumes spiralling outwards towards Terry. The constant whup, whup, whup sliced into his brain and made him scream for mercy. Graves sat in the cockpit grinning and beckoning for Terry to jump aboard but he knew that if he did, then the chopper would fly off with him dangling from the landing skids. He'd fall to his death. And all the while, Graves's face closed in on him, laughing with that mouth filled with tombstone teeth that looked yellow and cracked against the leathery, suntanned skin.

Terry's eyes flicked open.

Noel leaned over him. "Are you okay son?"

Terry scrambled back across the floor, pressing himself against an old cupboard. "Leave me alone."

"Okay, okay," Noel said, holding his hands up and stepping away. "You must've been having a bad dream or something. Yelling out like that."

"I- I'm sorry," Terry panted. He shivered, dragging the blanket up around him. Sweat beaded his forehead. He looked up at Noel. Maybe Graves could reach them, after all. Maybe Graves was in this very building with him now, seeping into Noel's body, infecting his blood and nervous system. Terry shook his head. "Mustn't think like that."

"Like what, son?" Noel said, squatting down. "Are you ill?"

"I-I'm fine. I just need my tablets. Can't think straight without them."

"And where are they?"

"At my flat but I can't go there."

Noel shook his head. "There must be some heavy-duty lads after you, mate. What if I went?" Noel said. "If you give me your keys, I could get your medication for you."

Terry tried to read his face. Once he could just look at people and know if they were joking or lying. It had never been easy but he had learnt to be pretty good at it but now, he had to think. Noel's eyes were wide and he had a slight smile on his face but not a broad grin. "Okay," Terry said at last and fished his keys out of his overall pocket. "I'll give you the address. Thanks."

*****

Serafina had just appeared one day as far as Blake could remember. He'd come home from a late shift and the cat had been there on the sofa, growling at him. "She's had a tough life, Will," his mother had said at the time. "She needs a little TLC."

"But where did you get her from?"

After all this time, he'd forgotten the answer his mother had given him. It was lost in the distress of her subsequent disappearance. Now he remembered it clearly, she'd looked up at him with twinkling eyes. "I rescued her," she said. Blake just assumed she meant that she'd got her from a cats' home or something but now, it hit him like a thunderbolt. The way his mum had looked, the proud defiance on her face, all told him that she had got Serafina from somewhere else. Why he suddenly realised that, he didn't know. Mum had been at the beginning of her slide into dementia. It wasn't apparent when Serafina appeared on the scene but, looking back, there were little signs; bouts of forgetfulness or slightly odd behaviour. What if stealing someone's cat had been part of it?

By the time Blake's mother wandered out of the house one dark night, Serafina had become part of the furniture and Blake never questioned where she came from again. He sat up and stretched, trying to get comfortable on the plastic chair that had tortured his big frame all night. The vet had tried to get him to go home but Blake couldn't leave. He wouldn't have slept anyway. So he twisted and turned on the seat, jumping up occasionally to read posters about ticks, canine flu and vitamins then settling down again.

"It looks like the infection from the abscess on her tooth has spread," she had said. "We've put her on intravenous antibiotics and some drugs to stabilise her blood pressure. We'll keep her sedated and comfortable but all we can do now is wait and hope."

Serafina had become so important to him because she was a link with his mother, despite the cat having a seemingly psychotic hatred of Blake to begin with. When Laura came along, she'd helped them come to an understanding of sorts. The monster cat had even taken Charlie under her wing, the two becoming partners in crime. Blake had to admit that he wasn't sure what he'd do if he lost her now. He'd lost his beloved Opel Manta up in Scotland, but that merely had sentimental value, being his father's old car. Serafina was family.

It was getting light outside now and Blake's mouth felt furry and rough. He needed food, drink and a shower. A change of clothes would probably be in order too. The vet stepped out into the waiting room and Blake leapt to his feet. "Any news?"

She shook her head. "I'm sorry Mr Blake. It's still touch and go but we can call you if there's any development. You can't sit here all day…"

"I know, I know. Look. Here's my card. If you need to make any sudden decisions and can't get hold of me, just do them anyway. Whatever it costs. I don't care. Okay? Just do it. I don't want to lose her."

The vet nodded and rubbed Blake's arm. "We'll do everything we can."

*****

Even though he'd gone home to wash, change and look after Charlie before heading to HQ, Blake felt haggard and stiff as he stood in the Major Incident Room. It was clear that his team had noticed, too. "Are you okay, sir? You look as rough as a robber's dog," Kath said, peering at him.

"Thanks, Kath, your concern is duly noted," Blake said with as much good humour as he could muster. "Just a bit of cat trouble. Spent all night at the vets."

"Serafina, boss? Is she okay?"

"We'll see. She's sedated at the vets." He shook himself. "What have we got? Any developments?"

"Still no sign of Terry White, sir," Vikki Chinn said. "But a punter did come forward yesterday saying he saw a big man in overalls getting into a blue Ford Transit van just by the Thornton Hough Roundabout. The timing would fit with Terry White fleeing the area. We're checking CCTV."

"Good work. It might lead somewhere. I just hope that whoever picked him up is safe, that's all."

Kath raised her hand. "Nicola Norton sent us a list of haunts that Terry talked about. Places he went as a child, favourite pubs he talked about. Uniform are looking around them just in case."

Alex Manikas gave an embarrassed cough. "I don't know if it affects the case, sir but there's a lot of noise on social media about this rally tomorrow. Far-right groups are talking about coming to Port Sunlight tomorrow and there's chatter at the other end of the political spectrum about stopping them. It could end up in trouble."

"It's going to pull numbers away from searching for Terry White," Blake muttered. "If uniform are having to focus on crowd control, there won't be as many people to help us. I've put a guard on Barry Davies, Dave Jones and George Owens on Nicola Norton's advice."

Kath looked puzzled. "Why just them, sir?"

"Norton thinks they're particularly vulnerable because they're prominent members of Pro-Vets and were good friends with Travis..."

"But Norton had a lot of contact with Terry White, sir," Kath said. "She could be at risk, too, surely."

"Apparently, Terry White's problem is rooted in a problem with facial recognition, especially amongst men. She doesn't think she's in any danger. What about White's family?"

"His mum lives in Wallasey but doesn't have much to do with him, sir. We've got a car outside her house but I get the impression she'd call us if he showed up," Vikki said. "Sad really. Imagine your own mother being afraid of you."

"Sad? The man's killed three people, Vikki," Kath Cryer said.

"Yeah, Ma'am," Vikki said, "I know that but when he joined the army, he didn't imagine it would change him so much. And to be trapped in a paranoid world like that. It must be awful."

"You're right, Vikki," Blake said. "I think it's fair to remind ourselves that whilst White has committed some serious crimes, and as dangerous as he is, he's a sick man. He needs our help. Which makes finding him doubly urgent."

*****

The blue and white police tape crisscrossed over the doorway of Terry's flat gave Noel pause for thought. What had Terry done? Not for the first time, Noel wished he listened to the news a bit more closely. He spent most of his time stoned, reliving his wild youth and listening to seventies rock bands. Whatever they wanted the lad for, he'd promised Terry he'd get the medication for him and the poor lad was suffering. He had to act fast, though, that tape hadn't been up long, maybe a couple of days at the most. This place could be crawling with coppers at any minute.

He approached the door and inspected it closely. If the police had been in, it could have been forced and a new lock put on, so the keys Terry had given him might be useless. On the other hand, if the police had the cooperation of the landlord, then they wouldn't have had to crash the door. It was a housing association property, so Noel reckoned they'd cooperate fully.

The old man had a lifetime's experience of breaking and entering but he was glad just to use the keys. Rummaging in his pockets, Noel was rewarded with the smoothness of a pair of latex gloves. Although he wasn't very active these days, he always kept a pair in case the opportunity to nick something presented itself on a plate. He pulled the gloves on with a theatrical snap and pushed the key into the lock. The door swung open and, smiling, he ducked under the tape.

Noel's heart thumped as he scanned the small flat. He was getting too old for this and turning over a crime scene wasn't a clever idea at any age. There was a good chance that the tablets would have been removed, especially if they were needed for evidence of some kind. Terry had said that he kept them in a kitchen cupboard. There was a faint whiff of burnt plastic in the flat and a few number markers dotted around but Noel couldn't see anything else that told him what Terry might have been up to.

"Bingo," Noel muttered, opening the cupboard. Two paper pharmacy bags stood on a shelf inside. He grabbed them then froze. Voices drifted in from the corridor. A key rattled in the door. Noel scanned the room frantically searching for an escape route.

Chapter 35

There were days that PC Mark Robertson wished he could retire tomorrow. No, make that today, right now. He'd been sent to George Owens' house to keep an eye on him but the moment Owens' spotted Mark's patrol car pulling up, the man was out of his house and standing by his front gate with his arms folded. Babysitting ungrateful members of the public wasn't his favourite task.

"I told the woman at your office that I didn't want police protection," Owens said. "So you can get back in your Batmobile and go and search for Terry White rather than drinking coffee outside my house."

"That's news to me, sir," Mark said. "We have intelligence that suggests White may target you. Doesn't that worry you?"

"Terry White wouldn't harm me, I'm a friend of his…"

"So was Quentin Ufford by all accounts, sir."

"I have to go to work…"

"Look, Mr Owens, you don't have to have a police guard, it's your right to choose, obviously. And, frankly, I'd be happier hunting for White but I was asked to come here. I don't have to sit at your side, I can be around outside your work if that suits you. As for coffee, I do have a flask in the car but then I'm facing a long weekend what with the rally tomorrow…"

"Honestly, I'm fine, officer," Owens snapped. "Now call in and tell them that I don't want you hanging around me all day."

"As you wish, sir," Mark said, climbing back into his car. He pulled away, glancing in his rear-view mirror every now and then. Owens didn't move but watched him, arms folded until Mark rounded the corner of the road and lost sight of him. Owens was up to something, Mark felt sure of it.

*****

Although the drugs had worn off, DC Ian Ollerthwaite still looked very frail, sitting up in his hospital bed. DCI Matty Cavanagh didn't mind visiting hospitals, there were plenty of pretty nurses to chat up and there were always grapes or chocolates to be had. The idea of being a patient filled him with dread, though. Matty was a fit young man and had managed to avoid spending even one night in a hospital ward. He imagined shuffling round in one of those smocks that tied up at the back, his arse hanging out as he dragged a drip stand about and shuddered. In some ways, visiting someone else in hospital cheered him up. At least it wasn't him wedged in a metal bed surrounded by kidney bowls.

"It's good of you to come and see me, sir,"

Ollerthwaite said. "I must confess, I've had a few visitors but the painkillers they gave me were so strong that I'm not sure I can remember who were real and who weren't." He paused and thought for a moment. "Casey Jones wasn't real. Or rather Alan Hale Junior, the actor who played him in the TV series. He came to see me. So did Elly May Clampett, sir…"

"You've lost me Ian," Matty said, snatching a grape from the bedside cabinet and popping it in his mouth. "Anyway, it's not a social call, I wanted to check with you about Pro-Vets before I go charging in."

"I thought DCI Blake was investigating Pro-Vets, sir."

"Nope. He handed it over to me once he realised his ex was mixed up in it. Good thing too, I reckon."

"His ex, sir?"

"Don't you ever listen to office gossip, Ian?" Cavanagh said, his eyes tracking the progress of a nurse on the other side of the ward.

"No, sir."

"Well, you should. Listen when you spoke to Blakey, you said something about Pro-Vets having a lot of money going through its accounts from and to all kinds of companies, right?"

"At first glance, it seems to me that Pro-Vets is

being used to launder money. I could be wrong of course but I think a deeper dive into the accounts might raise some questions. I bet you'll find a lot of them are shell companies... with crabs in them..."

Cavanagh peered hard at Ollerthwaite. "You sure the drugs have completely worn off, Ian?"

"Yes, sir. Mostly."

"You also told Blakey that Pro-Vets was paying an animal psychologist," Cavanagh said, grabbing another grape, throwing it in the air and catching it in his mouth. "Can you remember a name?"

Ollerthwaite looked thoughtful. "Yes, it rhymed, 'behaviour saviour' or something like that. Why would a veterans charity hire a pet psychologist? I mean, I can see why they'd pay their main counsellor so much but this other woman? Seems odd to me."

"I'll remember to ask that question," Cavanagh said. "How about the name Quinlan? Kyle Quinlan. Did that come up anywhere?"

"Yes. He was an executive director, nice little earner that one is, from what I remember. There may be a way to link Quinlan with some of these shell companies but it'll take months, sir."

"We've got all the time in the world as Barry White used to sing..."

"Louis Armstrong, sir," Ollerthwaite said. "He sang 'We Have All the Time in the World, not Barry White. It was from a James Bond film, On Her Majesty's Secret Service. The one with George Lazenby..."

"All right, all right, Ian, I don't need a lecture. The point is we're in no hurry."

"Right, sir. Have they caught him, yet, sir?"

"Who?"

"Terry White, sir. The man who attacked me."

"Sorry, mate, not my case. I think they're still looking."

"I hope they find him soon, sir. All that money spent on psychologists and it still couldn't help him. He must have serious problems."

*****

"One step behind him all the time," Blake muttered, standing in the middle of Terry White's flat. "What do you think brought him here?"

The uniformed police officer standing next to him reddened a little. "We think he came to get his medication, sir," she said.

"Hadn't it been logged and taken in as evidence? Jeez, at the very least, it's hazardous stuff. They aren't smarties, those tablets, are they?"

"No, sir," the officer said.

"And you're certain it was him?"

"He jumped out of the window as we came in. We only caught a glimpse of his back in the distance but there's no sign of forced entry into the flat, so whoever it was had keys. We were assuming…"

"It doesn't pay to assume anything, constable," Blake said, staring out of the window. "It could have been someone acting for him or it may have been someone who stole the keys from him."

"Yes, sir. Sorry, sir."

"I'm assuming you called for back-up to come and search the area, he can't have got far if it is him.

"We've got people out there now, sir but it's like he just vanished…"

"Or jumped into a car and drove away."

"But, I thought he wasn't able to drive, sir because of his condition."

"It seems to me more and more likely that he has some kind of accomplice, constable," Blake sighed. "How could he stay hidden for so long without any assistance and how is he getting around?"

"It would explain why we couldn't locate him, sir."

"Check with all the residents of the flat and with the houses over the road. Someone might have seen something." Blake said. He wandered into White's bedroom and sat on the bed. The killer was wandering free and Blake didn't have a clue where he was. If there was an accomplice, perhaps they were connected with Pro-Vets too, all of White's contacts seemed to have some kind of link to the charity. The pictures on the wall of Paul and Quentin had been photographed and taken down for further inspection and analysis. There had been some files and documents but they revealed little about the inner workings of Terry White's mind and more about his inability to choose an affordable energy provider. In fact Blake wondered how a man who barely knew how to pay his gas bill could murder three people and avoid arrest for so long. That in itself was something of a conundrum for Blake and the accomplice theory helped solve it. But who in their right mind would help him?

His phone buzzed and he answered it immediately. "Mr Blake," the vet said. "I'm sorry but I need you to come to the surgery immediately. It's an emergency."

Chapter 36

Taking the long route back to the garage cost a bit more in petrol but Noel had plenty of time to check he wasn't being followed. His ankle throbbed as he pushed down on the clutch and, not for the first time, he declared himself too old for this game. He'd managed to jump out of the window at Terry White's flat, but he'd landed awkwardly and twisted his ankle. It was a wonder his knees hadn't given out as well. He was glad he'd parked the van nearby because he was able to hobble up to it and jump in. There was a woman over the road going into her house who glanced over at him but hopefully, she wouldn't remember much about him, if anything. She didn't look like her suspicions had been aroused.

Once he was satisfied that he wasn't being followed, Noel headed for Heswall and the old garage. It sat at the bottom of a long back garden down a narrow, unadopted lane. Feral plum trees and brambles more or less blocked it off from the main house which was in a similar state of neglect. Noel's mate, Clifford, had made good betting on the horses and bought the house years ago but old age and slow horses had taken their toll on him too. Clifford didn't mind Noel coming and going. Every now and then, Noel would drop in on Clifford with a few quid or some bottles of ale by way of rent, but Clifford seemed just grateful for the company these days.

Noel drove the van up the overgrown lane and grunted as he got out of the car. Most of Heswall had been smart and suburban for as long as he could remember but there were pockets like this one where neighbours didn't watch each other or tut at the weeds growing in each other's gardens, both literally and metaphorically. This was a great hideaway and Noel had stored some pretty hot goods here over the years before selling them on. Not that he needed much privacy, these days. He was more prone to the odd spot of shoplifting food when he was short of cash or had forgotten his card. Wincing, he limped over to the old wooden gate that marked the entrance to the rear of Clifford's property. It scraped across the gravelly earth as he pushed it open.

Terry was still in the garage, standing at the back as Noel came in. He rocked back and forth nervously.

"Only me, Terry," Noel said, setting down the pack of medication on an upturned box. "I got your tablets and I picked up some food along the way." He set himself down in an old camping chair with a groan.

"Are you hurt?" Terry said, nodding at Noel's foot.

"Bizzies came to your flat while I was there. I had to jump out of the window," Noel said, pulling his boot and sock off. His ankle was purple already. "What did you do, that they're so keen to catch up with you?"

Terry sat down and buried his face in his hands. "I don't know," he said. "I hit a copper but yesterday, Quentin died. There was blood everywhere…"

"Who's Quentin, Terry?"

"My friend."

"And did you do it?"

"No. I don't know. I can't remember properly. Everything gets mixed up with the past. Sometimes I'm not sure what's real anymore."

"So where was this Quentin when he died?" Noel said.

"In his house. Near where you stopped and picked me up."

"And do you remember how you got there?"

"I walked. I'd been told to go there."

"Who by, Terry?"

"The orders on the phone. I got orders to go there and wait for help," Terry looked up as though a penny had dropped. "They sent there and I found Quentin's body."

"Then you didn't kill him?" Noel said. His heart thumped. He'd met a few psychos in his time, but he'd always been able to outrun them. Now at his age, stuck in this garage with a gammy ankle, he was a sitting duck. Terry didn't seem like a killer, but what if he just lost control? Noel wasn't a psychiatrist. He didn't know if Terry was sane or not. "Who calls you and gives you orders, Terry?"

"They never say," Terry muttered. "They just tell me to be somewhere and then someone dies..."

"This has happened before, mate?"

Terry nodded. "With Paul. I wasn't there when Richard died. I tried to tell the police that Richard had been murdered but they didn't believe me."

"So let me get this straight in my old head, mate. You get a call telling you to go somewhere and when you get there, someone's dead. Why do you go?"

"It's Corporal Graves, see. He hates me. He can get into anyone's body and control them. But every time a body he's in dies, he gets weakened and if I burn an effigy, a bit of his soul dies too. They place the effigy for me, I melt a replica..."

"If you don't kind me saying, Terry, that sounds a bit... crazy," Noel said, easing himself into a standing position and putting the kettle on.

"I know. It is but it makes so much sense to me."

"Does it make less sense when you take your tablets?"

Terry nodded and sighed. "Yes. No. I don't

know. I need help, Noel. I had a counsellor, she was good. I could talk to her, a bit like I'm talking to you now and everything made sense then for a while. She understood me."

"Maybe we should find this counsellor then. See if she can help you," Noel said. "Do you know where she lives?"

"I'm not meant to but I do. She lives by me. I saw her on the train and followed her home once. She's called Nicola. Nicola Norton."

*****

The Veterinary Surgery was only a couple of miles up the road and Blake employed the blue lights to get there in a matter of minutes. His mind raced, fatalism stumbling over panic as he imagined worse and worse scenarios. He couldn't lose Serafina, not now, not ever. If she was gone, then he was cut loose from his past. Lost.

Abandoning the car by the roadside, he ran in, banging the door open. The receptionist gave a little squeal of fright. A woman sat hugging a dachshund and stared at him in horror.

"W-Will Blake... I'm Serafina's... the cat... big Persian one..."

The receptionist's eyes widened even more at the mention of the cat and she pointed mutely at the door through to the actual examination rooms. "Can I go through?"

The receptionist nodded once, still looking as though Blake was levelling a sawn-off shotgun at her. Blake nodded back and rushed for the door, bracing himself for the worst. He remembered all the times he'd accompanied bereaved relatives when they were required to identify a body. This wasn't that bad. Not by a long chalk. "It's only a cat," he muttered to himself, grabbing the handle. But it was Serafina!

"It's only a…" The low growl he heard as he opened the door was the most welcome sound he'd ever heard. Then things got strange.

"Please, no. Good pussy cat…" The vet stood on the examination table, holding a clipboard to her face.

Serafina, a ball of mad, exploded blue fur stalked around the base of the table like a tigress on the hunt. Her tail lashed from side to side.

In the corner of the room, a young girl huddled on top of a filing cabinet, desperately ensuring that no part of her dangled over the edge. It was quite a feat. Thin scratches lined her hands. She looked at Blake. "Please help us…" she said, weakly.

"Serafina," Blake whispered, squatting down and rubbing his finger and thumb together as though he had a treat for her.

"Mr Blake, I wouldn't advise…" the vet began to say.

"It's okay, she knows me…" Serafina padded up to him and gave a plaintive meow, rubbing her head against his knuckles. Then she bit him, drawing blood before scrambling up onto his shoulder. "I missed you, too, old girl," he muttered. He looked up at the staring veterinarian who hadn't come down from the table yet. "Could I borrow a crate to take her home?"

"Absolutely," the vet said, making no attempt to hide the relief in her voice. "I think we can assume she's made a full recovery."

*****

It was only two storeys but it was a fall that could easily kill. George Owens had been sitting on top of the Pro-Vets building most of the afternoon holding a bottle of vodka and a knife. PC Mark Robertson had spotted him from the carpark and called in assistance as well as phoning Blake.

"I'm sorry, sir. He was so insistent on not having any protection and now I can see why," Robertson had said.

Blake had been at home just settling Serafina into her basket. The cat had become drowsy after giving him a few more scratches and bites. "Keep him talking, Mark. I'm on my way over."

Owens had accessed the roof through a service

door on the second floor. The office part of the building was a brick tower in the corner of the warehouse and the door opened onto a small flat roof. Owens had climbed off the roof and onto the corrugated metal that formed the warehouse part of the premises. The surface was smooth and slippery as Blake inched his way across it towards Owens.

"George?" Blake called when he got close enough. "Are you okay?"

"Don't come near me," Owens said, waving the knife in Blake's direction. "Leave me alone. I'm ending this. It's over for me."

"I can't leave you, George, you know that," Blake said. "What's happened?"

Owens threw Blake a disgusted stare. "What's happened? My best friend has been murdered and now another member of staff too. That's what's happened."

"I know that, George but what good is killing yourself going to do?"

"I deserve to die, Blake. It's all my fault."

Chapter 37

Kinnear's house lay on a small, modern estate just on the edge of Knowsley by the M57. It was a detached, three-bedroomed property and they kept it spotless. Or rather, Chris did. A typical teacher, Chris was ruthlessly organised. Every activity was mapped out on year planners, things were stored in labelled boxes and woe betide a fleck of dirt that landed on the polished floor. Having said that, the mere presence of Kinnear meant that Chris was fighting a constant battle against entropy, so the house was always homely.

Right now, Kinnear sat in the car, not wanting to get out. He had come home early to go through some adoption papers with Chris. How could he go prancing in there and pretend he was all for this when he had so many reservations? He should have spoken earlier but that was no reason to be dishonest now. Chris deserved the truth. With a sigh, Kinnear climbed out of the car.

Chris had set out all the papers on the table so that Kinnear could look over them. He gave Kinnear a hug and settled him down.

"Okay, so these are declarations about convictions and health," Chris said, leaning over Kinnear's shoulder. "I've managed to cover up your drug cartel years, but they found out about your fungal infection…"

Kinnear smiled, wearily. Chris sounded so excited. "Listen, Chris," Kinnear said, resting his hand on top of his husband's. "I've been thinking…"

Chris hugged him. "I've told you about that, Andrew. It does you no good. You'll start wondering about the role of the police in a modern society and the effectiveness of prisons and then where will you be?"

"Just listen. I-I'm not sure we should do this. We're both so busy and my hours are so unpredictable. How can we bring up a child?"

Chris settled into the chair next to him. "What brought this on, love?"

"It all happened so fast. And there's work. We've been chasing these feral kids all week and it just made me think what kind of family life they might have. Honestly, if you saw some of the depravation and squalor and the useless parents…"

"But they aren't us, are they, love? What we're doing is lifting someone, a small child, out of that situation and giving them a chance."

"And how are we going to do that with the hours we work?"

"I'm going part time, aren't I? And your mum and dad are dying to help out. Mine too. Blimey, Andy, I thought we discussed this so many times.

Were you just smiling and nodding while I went through it all with you months ago? Why didn't you say sooner?"

"I was listening, but it just didn't seem real. Now we're a few weeks away from actual adoption and I don't know. Is that so wrong?"

Chris pursed his lips for a second. "No. It's not wrong. I just wish you'd got your head straight before we went so far down this road. I thought we were committed to Niamh. We were going to do so much for her..."

"But what if I get injured or even worse?"

"I don't know, Andy. What if you do? What if I do?"

"I'm more likely to get..."

"I know that but it's a risk I'm happy to take. And make no mistake, if you were killed, it would be me who would be left behind to cope and help Niamh. But that won't happen and you can't go through life expecting it to, can you?"

"No but..."

"Listen Andy, I work with some kids who have been dealt a really shit hand from the start. You know that. I see them too, every day and I know how hard life is for them. I work with kids who have busy, hard-working parents who love them, too. Those kids are safe and secure. It's not being busy or taking a risk that changes a child's life.

It's how much they're loved."

Kinnear smiled and hugged Chris tight. "I face angry bruisers and criminals all the time, but this scares me witless."

"If you really don't think you can go ahead, then that's fine. It'll break my heart but I love you. But we aren't doing this alone and you don't have to be frightened.

Chapter 38

It struck Blake that George Owens' current predicament summed up the man's life so far. Dutch courage to help him do something he probably wasn't going to, a knife he wouldn't use and a drop that might kill him but, in reality, he didn't want it to. Owens had been told what to do all his life. He was a half-measures kind of man. Blake didn't think he'd actually kill himself but people were full of surprises, so he had to be careful.

"What do you mean, this is all your fault?" Blake said, sitting down a few feet away from Owens. "All what?"

"The deaths, the state of Pro-Vets. I should have stood up to Paul. I should have said, 'no,' a few more times when he went on about expanding the charity all the time."

"I'm sorry, George, you've lost me. How are those things connected?"

"Shut up! I know what you're doing. You're just trying to confuse me."

Blake could smell the alcohol even from this distance. "I'm just trying to work out who killed Paul and Quentin, that's all and you said it was your fault. So, before you throw yourself off the roof, would you mind explaining what the hell is going on?"

"You're not meant to talk to me like that,"

Owens slurred.

"Probably not but I've had a bad week. I don't like seeing people dead, and I don't like chasing homicidal maniacs around the Wirral. So why would you not having the balls to stand up to Travis cause his murder? I'm at a loss, please explain it."

"It was Ufford. I don't know quite where Paul found him but it was him who filled his head with all these ideas, put him in touch with all these faceless companies that slosh money around the charity. 'Nothing succeeds like success,' Paul always said, and if you can show potential donors that you're drowning in cash, then they're drawn to it."

"Really?" Blake looked dubious.

"Yes, think about it. Who are you going to invest in: some poor little one-man band working out of a wooden hut that's likely to go under when you're late with a donation, or a big, swish organisation with good connections and plenty of resources? Which one is likely to give you the best PR boost?"

"The big one, I suppose," Blake said. "But it doesn't make it any more or less deserving. It depends on what good you do, the help you give." Owens got to his feet, swaying slightly and making Blake wince. For all his talk, the last thing he wanted to see was Owens disappearing over the side.

"Not according to Ufford. He reckoned that as long as companies can donate, set it against their tax, get a bit of good press, they're happy. Paul would spout this crap all the time and you could tell where he got it from. Quentin Ufford."

"So you're saying that Ufford introduced Paul to some shady customers."

"Damn right that's what I'm saying and then Ufford started taking money out of the charity. Stealing from us. Paul wanted to sack him. I said that we couldn't. Imagine the scandal and the embarrassment when you lot looked at the accounts. But Paul was adamant he was going to report Ufford to the police. So they cut his throat," Owens said. "And when Ufford couldn't cover his tracks, he got it too."

"You said, 'they' killed Paul. Who do you mean, George?"

Owens waved his arms around, making Blake's stomach lurch. "I don't know. Whoever runs those shell companies that pour their money into the charity and then syphon it out through cleaners and security. Them. Pro-Vets is ruined. Everything we built up, gone. Donors will pull out the minute they hear about the scandal. All those people let down badly."

"So where do you fit into it all, George?"

"Me? I knew, didn't I? I never stood up to Paul and then when I did, it was to protect Ufford because I was scared of what would happen to the charity." Owens waved his arms again and staggered a little.

"And what about Terry White?"

Owens looked genuinely puzzled. "What about him?"

"What's his connection to all of this?"

"Dunno," George opened his arms. "None as far as I know. Why are you talking about poor Terry?" He stumbled again and this time, Blake threw himself forward, dragging Owens down. His feet slid on the smooth metal and he landed with a loud thud. Blake's stomach lurched as they began to slip towards the edge. He pressed his heels against the roof surface, producing a loud groaning sound. The lip of the roof came closer and Blake could see cars below and a crowd of people. They slowed and he pushed himself back, still gripping Owens tightly.

"If you so much as twitch, I swear I'll make sure I land on top of you. I don't intend to fall off this roof and I'm not going to let you go either. Got it?" Owens' nodded and sirens sounded in the distance. "If you want to make things right, you'll make a statement and help us sort this mess out. Now keep absolutely still until the fire brigade get us down."

It was late and, being Friday evening, quiet in the Major Incident Room. A few small groups huddled around computers or shared files. A feeling of expectant tension filled the air as officers prepared for what was likely to be a stressful day tomorrow. The rally was going ahead despite a news conference held by Martin and Hannah Williams announcing that there was no terrorist attack. Some protestors had come to Liverpool a day early and hit the pubs. Already news of scuffles and arrests were beginning to filter back. It seemed like the madness could only get worse as the weekend progressed.

George Owens had been taken to hospital for observation. Blake sat at his desk with DI Kath Cryer and DS Vikki Chinn. Vikki held a photograph and a file. "It seems that a blue Ford Transit van was spotted outside Terry White's flat this morning. CCTV picked up a vehicle matching this description passing the Three Stags pub later on. It's close enough to probably be the same van."

"Anyone we know?" Blake said.

Vikki passed him the open file. "Noel Roscoe, 65, numerous petty offences, theft, shoplifting, drugs, burglary but not recently. I tried the address in his file but he hadn't been there in a couple of years. A woman said she saw an old man limping out of the gateway to the flats and getting into a blue van. The description she gave matches Roscoe."

Kath looked over Blake's shoulder at the file. "Wasn't it a blue Transit that was seen picking Terry White up in Raby, sir?"

"It was, Kath. So we can assume Roscoe picked up Terry White and then, what? Did he steal the keys? He'd have to have been given the address."

Vikki nodded. "The officers at the scene said that medication was missing from the flat, didn't they sir? Anti-psychotics, anti-epilepsy tablets, that kind of thing."

"D'you think he went to get the medication for White, sir?" Kath said.

"Possibly. Or maybe he thought he could nick them and sell them on. There's a market for that kind of stuff, after all."

"But, like you said, White would have to give Roscoe his address," Vikki added.

"Could Roscoe be manipulating him, sir?"

"It's possible. But I can't see any obvious link between Roscoe and Ufford or Pro-Vets. That doesn't mean it isn't there. One thing is certain, if we can pin down Roscoe, we might be able to catch up with White. Check with ANPR and see if we get any hits on Roscoe's van."

*****

The events of Wednesday afternoon had left Jeff Blake jittery to say the least. He'd been used to talking to Josh Gambles in prison and that unnerved him enough. But to have Kyle Quinlan roaming free around his back garden, that was like opening the door on the shark cage as a Great White swims past. He knew Gambles was vicious and dangerous but he was confined, with help close at hand. Jeff knew that Quinlan could be just as vicious, Gambles had described some of his escapades with Quinlan. Even worse, because of Will's rather selfish use of Jeff's garden as a rendezvous, Quinlan knew where he lived now. People used that phrase in a jokey kind of way, 'I know where you live.' Everyone laughs because it means nothing. But the idea of Quinlan actually knowing where he lived was another thing altogether.

On the other hand, part of him, the impulsive, 'seize an opportunity' part, realised that this was a chance to get a unique perspective on Gambles. Quinlan and Gambles had been in prison together since they were young, on and off. According to Gambles, they'd been like brothers but that could well be typical Gambles hyperbole, Jeff was sure of it. He could see the life slipping out of the story as he tried to work with Gambles' self-aggrandising tales. Getting this unique perspective would bring more energy to the book, Jeff was sure of it.

He'd contacted Laura on the night Will and Quinlan had their confrontation. Partly because he was pumped up by the idea of capturing Quinlan's voice in the book and partly out of spite. Will had no right to include him in his ridiculous schemes. Laura hadn't sounded very happy to hear Jeff."

"Just hear me out. It's not about Will at all. It's about me."

"You? And what on earth can I do for you Jeffrey?"

"Kyle Quinlan said that if I wanted the low-down on Josh Gambles, then I should have a chat with him some time. I'd really like to do that..."

Laura had laughed, then. "Bloody hell, Jeffrey, do you enjoy winding Will up? He's going to love that."

"Will isn't writing the book, Laura," Jeff had said, through clenched teeth. He hated the way his brother crept into any conversation about the book. "Look all you have to do is give him my number. You can do that, can't you?"

"All right then."

Jeff had paused, leaving the unasked question floating between them.

"What else do you want, Jeffrey?" Laura said. "You want to know why I split with Will? Why I'm here now? I think you know."

"He can be a thoughtless bastard, Laura, I know that. So wrapped up in his work and quick to judge people. So I don't blame you..."

"But?" It was almost as if she was testing him.

"He's not as bad as Kyle Quinlan, is he?"

"You'd never understand, Jeffrey. You haven't come from where I came from. You haven't lived the kind of life I did. I'd never fit into Will's world. Never." There was a moment's pause and Jeff could sense the regret in her voice.

"You don't have to be in either of them, Laura," he said, before he could stop himself.

"Look, I'll pass your number onto Kyle. Maybe he'll enjoy regaling you with tales of prison life and violence. And I'm sure you'll lap it up. Goodbye, Jeffrey."

Quinlan had phoned him and suggested the Seraph on Friday night and so now he stood outside the pub, steeling himself to enter. He'd been here once before and ended up being bundled into the back of a car with a bag over his head. It was only the fact that Will was his brother that had saved him on that occasion. He hoped Quinlan would just buy him a pint and give him some dirt for the book on Josh Gambles. But you could never tell. The last character who had kidnapped Jeff was Harry Thorpe, a local criminal who had a grudge against Quinlan. Jeff knew the potential for this to get messy.

Boredom McClague's face worked through a range of muted emotions when Jeff entered the tiny pub. Jeff recognised a moment of shock, then a little resentment followed by pity which was rather disturbing. The murmur of conversation stopped and the huddled groups and couples all looked at the unlikely figure standing before them in red chinos and a corduroy jacket.

"He's in the back room," Boredom said. "Do you not learn?"

"Seems not, Mr McClague," Jeff said with a smile.

As he passed the bar towards the back door, McClague grabbed his arm over the counter. "Not a word about this pub, do you understand? If any mention of this premises or my name crops up in your book, then you won't live to enjoy the royalties. Do I make myself clear?"

"Are you threatening me, Mr McClague?"

"Too right I am. I don't care if you are Will Blake's brother. He won't see you again if you even hint at the existence of this establishment. Got it?"

"Yes," Jeff said, trying to keep his voice steady and failing. "I understand, Mr McClague. You and the Seraph will not be singled out. I can keep it vague."

"Very vague, please. Mr Quinlan's waiting for

you. Take this pint in for him. You can pay for it later."

Chapter 39

Serafina lay purring in her basket with Charlie curled up almost on top of her. Blake wondered if he'd given her too much sedative because she seemed remarkably calm after her rampage at the surgery. Still, he was relieved to see she had recovered. It had been a frustrating day and the weekend looked to be no more promising, with the pointless protest and still no prospect of finding Terry White.

The knock on the door took Blake by surprise. It was late and he wasn't expecting anyone. There was something about the knock itself, too. It was tentative and cautious. Charlie's ears pricked up but instead of barking, he wagged his tail. Serafina gave a sleepy meow and curled up again.

Picking up a poker from beside the hearth, Blake edged into the hall. He could see a figure silhouetted against the frosted glass. "Who's there?"

"Just open the door, Will, it's cold out here," Laura said from the other side of the door.

"What the hell are you doing here?" Will said, as he pulled the door open.

"Nice to see you too," she replied, sweeping past him into the hall. "Where's Serafina? Is she okay?"

"She's fine. How do you know about...?"

"Hello, Charlie boy!" Laura said, squatting down and scratching the little dog behind his ear as he tried to leap all over her. "How are you? Has he been looking after you?" She stood up, cradling Charlie in her arms as she did. "One of my clients mentioned a ruckus at the emergency vets involving a big Persian cat. It didn't take a huge leap of the imagination?"

"You came to see the cat?" Blake said, unable to disguise the hurt in his voice. "Does Quinlan know you're here?"

"He does but he's not my keeper, Will and he's learning not to be jealous."

"I can't believe the change in you, Laura..."

"You preferred me terrified? Was it better when I was running scared, frightened of my own shadow?"

"No, of course not, but I thought you had some kind of moral compass..."

"Me? Tell me Will, what would you have said if I'd turned up on your doorstep? Would you have welcomed me with open arms?"

"Yes, of course."

"You'd have ignored the fact that I'd been involved in stealing money and was living off the proceeds?"

"Well, no," Blake said, crestfallen. "I thought you'd face up to that. Do your time and then..."

"Then come back to you penitent and chastened, right? I thought so. Hopefully, that answers your question about why I went back to my own people. You want a humbled, rescued version of me, Will. Can you imagine how I'd be received by your colleagues? This is Laura, she was a criminal once but now she's seen the error of her ways. I'd never have fitted into your world or at least, I would but it would have been as a dirty little secret, kept at home and never talked about. Would you want to live like that?"

"But you changed my life. *You* saved *me*. Not the other way round," Blake said. He threw his hands up. "Anyway. You've made your choice and I've no right to try and stop you. I'm guessing you didn't come here to start a row. Serafina's in the living room in her basket."

She carried Charlie through and settled him down alongside the cat. "I knew these two would get on. I bet Serafina soon got him in line." She stroked the cat and Serafina's purring grew louder.

"I gave her some sedative, so she's a bit soppy at the moment."

Laura looked up at him. "Looks like she's been up to some of her old tricks again. You spending enough time with her?"

"Ian Youde comes in to walk Charlie and they all keep each other company. I'm working, Laura.

On this murder in Port Sunlight, actually," Blake said, sitting in his armchair. "While I've got you, mind telling me what your involvement with Pro-Vets is?"

Laura gave Blake a mischievous smile. "Purely professional. A lot of their clients benefit from having pets and they have the same training needs as other pet owners. I was also doing some work around sourcing some therapy dogs for them..."

"Taking a hefty wage, by the sounds of it," Blake said.

Laura's cheeks coloured. "I value my services and I'm trying to build an actual business, Will, rather than a part time hobby job. So, yes, I charge a fee."

"Some would call it disproportionate..."

"I'm worth it. There isn't a penny of that money that can't be accounted for, Will."

"Which is more than can be said for some of the payments and transactions that have gone through Pro-Vets accounts, I believe."

Laura looked down at Serafina. "I imagine all those companies will be vanishing as we speak if they haven't already disappeared. Whoever was laundering their ill-gotten gains through Pro-Vets will have taken fright, I imagine, what with all the bad publicity it's been getting. I wouldn't waste your time chasing ghosts, Will. I'd look much closer to home."

"What do you mean?"

"Ask me no questions, I'll tell you no lies, as they say but someone had their fingers in the till."

"Quentin Ufford?"

Laura nodded. "And a friend, I suspect."

"Is that why you came here really? Did you want to send me off on a wild goose chase and distract the investigation away from Quinlan's dirty money flowing through the charity?"

Laura sighed and gave Will a sad smile. "No, Will. I came to see Serafina. And I told you, I'm doing things on my terms, looking after number one."

"What are you…?"

"Just listen. We can be friends but I realise now that we could never be anything more. I'm giving you this information as a friend. Don't waste your time and resources trying to link Pro-Vets and Kyle Quinlan; you'll fail. I just came to tell you about Ufford."

"We got that information already, thanks."

"Then you'll know that, whoever his accomplice is has transferred a whole load of cash from Ufford's account into their own and they're about to disappear."

"You aren't playing some kind of stupid, dangerous game with Quinlan are you, Laura? Because..."

"I'm not playing anything or anyone, Will. I can look after myself. What you need to do is forget Kyle for now and forget me. Catch whoever is about to do a flit with a huge chunk of Pro-Vets money."

*****

The back room of the Seraph was even smaller than the bar area if that was possible. It was shadowy and only managed to contain an old leather sofa, a low table and a couple of stools. The bare floorboards creaked under Jeff's feet as he walked in and he got a real sense of the pub's antiquity. He imagined dark deeds and underhand deals had been arranged here for centuries. The idea of writing a history of the pub flashed through his mind, only to be crushed by McClague's warning.

The woman cuddled up to Kyle Quinlan on the old leather sofa wasn't Laura and must have been half Quinlan's age. She wore a mask of make-up which Jeff found both attractive and confusing. Why would such a young girl plaster herself in slap when she didn't need it? Jeff planted the pint on the low table in front of Quinlan. The big, dark-haired man untangled himself from the young woman and picked up the drink. From what Jeff could see, Kyle didn't need another pint.

"Cheers, Jeff, you're a real gent," he said, his voice slurring. He turned to the woman. "This is Jeffrey Blake, Layla, he's an author."

"Wow," Layla said, smoothing out her short, sequined dress. "What have you written?"

Jeff felt a blush warm his cheek. "I don't think you'd have heard…"

"Go on Jeff, Layla's got 'A' Levels and everything."

"Quixote Junction?" Jeff said, hopefully. Layla looked blankly at him. "Cinnamon and Blue? It was a collection of short stories about people at a dinner party…"

"Ooh, hang on a minute. Yeah, was one of the stories called Crab Apples?"

Jeff blinked at her. "Yes. Yes it was…"

"Yeah, my English teacher was always going on about it. He bought me the book."

"He bought my book as a present for you?"

"Yeah, he was a good teacher," Layla said, giving Jeff a lipstick grin and stretching sinuously on the sofa. "I enjoyed it." For a moment, Jeff was uncertain whether she meant his book or something else.

"See?" Quinlan said, grinning madly. Jeff wondered if he was under the influence of something stronger than drink.

Jeff smiled and nodded, not quite sure what point Quinlan was making. Was the man trying to take credit for Layla's teacher giving her the book or the fact that Layla liked the book or what? "Great," Jeff said instead of asking any questions. "So, you said you'd give me some background on Josh Gambles, Kyle…"

Quinlan leaned forward, almost knocking the pint over. "I'd prefer it if you called me Mr Quinlan. It's just a matter of respect, Jeff. Hope you don't mind. People round here see you getting all pally and they'll start taking the piss."

Jeff pulled out his notebook. "Okay, erm, Mr Quinlan. So do you mind if I make a few notes? It just helps me remember."

"Fire away, Jeffrey, although, I'll warn you now, Gambles was a bit of a pussy, to be honest. Always hanging on my coat tails. I can't ever remember him pulling my fat out of the fire and he was always getting himself into scrapes."

"I can imagine. He speaks very fondly of you, though. Almost hero worships you…"

Quinlan puffed his chest out and Layla giggled, hugging onto him. "Well, that's understandable, I suppose," he said, then his face darkened. "It won't save him in the end though, you know,

Jeff. If he spends too much time poking his nose into other people's business, he's goin' to get it chopped off, isn't he?"

"Really?"

"Do you know where my ex-wife is, Jeff?" Quinlan said, changing the subject completely.

"No."

"At your brother's house feeding him a load of bullshit about Pro-Vets. She's a crafty one, that Laura," he said, he looked down at Layla and gave her a squeeze. "I must have a thing about girls with names beginning with 'L' mustn't I?"

Layla giggled again. "Stop it Kyle. You'll make me jealous."

"Do you think she still loves your brother, Jeff?"

Jeff felt his throat tighten. "I don't know. Judging from her actions and what she said on the phone the other day, I'd say not. She's got more sense."

Quinlan threw his head back and laughed. "Nice one. Still. I've got to keep an eye on her. She's just waiting for me to trip up, you know. She told me."

"I don't really know her that well but one thing I always thought was she's single-minded and smart. What you said about her keeping you on your toes the other day, that certainly makes sense in a twisted kind of way."

Quinlan nodded and tapped the side of his head. "You're wise, Jeff. You've got nous. That brother of yours, he's just a plod, really, isn't he?"

"I suppose you could say that," Jeff said, grinning briefly.

"He's still soft on her, though, isn't he?"

"None of us like rejection. I think he'll make a point of getting over her. Can we get back to Josh Gambles, Mr Quinlan?" Jeff said, trying to keep the edge out of his voice.

"We can," Quinlan slurred. "I reckon between you and me, we can make Joshy Gambles even more famous."

"That's a strange thing to say, Mr Quinlan," Jeff said.

Quinlan just tapped the side of his nose. That was the moment that Jeff realised that Quinlan was a powder keg and it was only a matter of time before he exploded.

Chapter 40

Noel Roscoe was worried. He'd watched Terry through the night. They were going to go and find Nicola last night but Terry had fallen into a seizure. Noel wasn't sure what to do and contemplated calling an ambulance but Terry had recovered and slept. He had a couple more seizures and managed to sleep a little. But when he came round he was muttering to himself and giving Noel sidelong glances. Noel didn't understand it, the boy had taken his medication so surely he'd be feeling better. Not that Noel was an expert. He'd worked for a guy once who took happy pills and reckoned they took a few days to kick-in. He didn't even seem very happy after that, to be honest. Maybe Terry's tablets were the same.

By the time Terry had woken, it was late morning. Noel rustled up some bacon and eggs for them and he watched Terry wolf them down with nearly half a loaf of toast.

"So what d'you reckon, Terry, should we go and find this Nicola today? See what she suggests you do?"

Terry stopped chewing and stared at Noel for so long, he thought the young man wasn't listening. "Yeah," Terry said, finally. He glanced over at his phone which lay, fully charged on the side. "Maybe I'll get some orders, too."

Noel licked his lips. "Have you ever thought, Terry, that whoever gives you those orders might not have your best interests at heart?"

Again, Terry paused. "What do you mean?"

Noel squatted beside the big lad. "I mean, Terry, that they're setting you up. Think about it. You get a call, it tells you to go somewhere and then you find yourself in trouble…"

"It's always like that in the army," Terry said, shrugging. "You get sent into danger…"

"Yeah, I can see that, mate, but this isn't the army, is it? Looks to me like someone's using you to cover their tracks."

Terry looked hard at Noel. "Who are you?" he said, slowly. "Really…"

Noel felt a flurry of panic. He could never out-run Terry, not with his bad ankle. He felt like he was trapped in a small box with an increasingly edgy lion. "I'm Noel, Terry, remember? Noel. I picked you up on the road the other day. I'm just an old man, done a bit of time for burglary and such. Just trying to help you. Okay?"

"Okay," Terry said, nodding. He rubbed his forehead. "I just wish I knew what to do. Who I could trust…"

"You can trust me, Terry. I think you're a good lad who's been treated badly, okay? I want to help you. I think we should find Nicola, don't you?"

"Yeah," Terry said, after a while. "Find Nicola. She'll tell me what to do."

*****

Even though it was early on a Saturday, the Major Incident Room lay almost deserted apart from Blake and his core team. Every hand possible had been drafted in to marshal and observe the horde of protesters headed towards the Wirral. The people of Liverpool had a history of containing and humiliating far-right groups who came to cause trouble. Only a few years ago, one group had to take refuge in the lost luggage kiosk in Lime Street station, such was their hostile reception. They'd jumped on the first train out once they were allowed.

But judging by social media, many people were coming to the area via Chester railway station. This meant that protestors only had to change platforms to join the Wirral Line rather than get kettled in the plaza as often happened at Lime Street. Some Cheshire Police Officers were keeping order in Chester but the bulk of the responsibility fell to Merseyside. Trains and stations were policed as was the route to the war memorial.

The first to arrive at the office after Blake had been DC Kinnear. He looked pale and sleep-deprived. "You okay, Andrew?" Blake asked.

"Yes, sir. Just a lot on my mind."

Blake nodded and glanced around. The room

was empty but he knew the others would be arriving any minute. "Jitters about the adoption?"

Kinnear gave Blake a guarded look. "Y-yes, sir, as a matter of fact," he sighed and sat down, heavily. "I mean, I want to and the idea of having Niamh in our lives is just so great, sir but I'm just not sure it's wise."

"I see. And how does Chris see it?"

"He's heart-broken but he understands, sir."

Blake squatted beside Kinnear and took a breath. "Listen, son, when I was your age, I was married and had a little girl. Then she was taken from me. Those few fleeting months were the best time of my life. That sense of loss never goes it's a weight I carry everyday but that brief time I had with my little girl, it was a treasure beyond value. If it's this job that troubles you, then don't worry. The world's a dangerous place whatever you do. You make the best of it and you don't let fear take your life away. Knowing what I know now, if I was in your shoes, I'd give little Niamh the best home and all the love I could and live."

Kinnear blinked at Blake with glittering eyes. "Th-thank you sir."

"Good," Blake said, standing up and coughing gruffly. "The others should be here any minute. Here's Kath now. Let's get busy."

Kath and Alex came in, followed closely by

Vikki. "Morning, sir. Looks like there are plenty of people going to the rally, sir," Kath said, dumping her bag on her desk. "It's not like there's even anything to protest about. I mean, Travis was killed by someone he knew. It's a murder plain and simple."

Blake shook his head. "That doesn't matter now, does it? Even Superintendent Martin going on TV and explaining that it wasn't a terrorist attack is dismissed as fake news or a mainstream media cover-up. It's madness, Kath. Despite his son having admitted that he fed his dad that terrorist bullshit, I bet you Lex Price stands up there on the war memorial and lies through his teeth to save face."

"He's bound over, boss," Kath said. "Surely he'd get picked up if he started rabble rousing."

Blake shook his head. "And then, what? He'd be a martyr in some eyes. Picked up for speaking the so-called truth."

"I just hope it doesn't hamper our investigation, sir," Alex Manikas said, settling into a chair next to Kinnear.

"It already has, Alex," Blake muttered. "Just think of the manpower wasted shepherding those people. They could have been out looking for Noel Roscoe and Terry White."

"One thing it does do, sir, is throw open the possibility of other suspects," Vikki Chinn said.

"I mean, if we're accepting that Terry White is being manipulated in some way, then it could be anyone. Barry Davies or Dave Jones could have climbed into the taxi that night in the full knowledge that White was waiting to pounce on Paul Travis."

"Maybe, but I'm not convinced by that story, Vikki," Blake said. "I mean if you wanted someone killed, how would you be certain that White would carry out the deed without being there to supervise him? He isn't the most reliable weapon. I mean, he can barely remember to tie his own shoelaces."

"But Terry White has been linked to the scene of each crime in some way, either through the toy soldiers or by his physical presence."

"It's convenient, isn't it?" Blake said. "Someone dies and White happens to be there but I don't think he's capable of that level of planning. He'd have to know when Travis was coming out of the pub, he'd have to get to Ufford's house. That's before we think about him gathering the weapons needed to cut someone's throat or the means to inject a lethal dose of heroin."

Kath looked dubious. "So somebody is just directing him to be at a certain location at a certain time, sir..."

Blake nodded. "Or even just taking him there. He leaves DNA and these bloody toy soldiers all over the place and then is told to run away."

"So he gets the blame," Kath murmured, considering the theory.

"Alex, has anything come from White's mobile records?"

DC Manikas flicked through a file. "Not many calls sir. Quite a few from an unregistered mobile…"

"Any around the dates of the murders?"

"Mainly clustered on those days, sir," Manikas said.

"It could be someone phoning orders through or giving White clear instructions about where to be and when."

"Someone would have to know him really well to achieve that, though, boss," Manikas said, looking pained. "I mean, really know what triggered him…"

"And how to get him to actually go to these locations," Blake said, archly. "You'd have to know exactly what was going on inside his head."

Vikki's eyes widened. "The only person who fits that description…"

"Is Nicola Norton," Blake said. "She has long periods of time with him. Time to convince him of things, to manipulate him. She may even have access to his medication. It doesn't take a huge leap of the imagination to see how she could seduce Ufford into stealing for her. I bet if we try to locate where those unregistered calls are coming from, it'll be Heswall and Port Sunlight."

Kath Cryer pulled a face. "But George Owens told you that whoever was laundering money through Pro-vets killed Travis…"

"Why would they do that, though?" Blake said. "And why in such a public way? They have nothing to gain from all the publicity and scrutiny, have they? No, if Travis had told the money-launderers, they would have quietly dealt with Ufford and we would have been none the wiser. Maybe Ufford and Norton were working on their own and once Ufford had become a liability, she dealt with him."

"She did this for money, sir?" Kath said, dubiously.

"It's a theory. Norton said Owens grumbled about the amount of money Paul spent on her services. Ollerthwaite said something about Pro-Vets spending a small fortune on their psychologist. What if she was putting in inflated invoices and Ufford was clearing them? What if George Owens was hinting that she was taking more than her fair share?"

"So Ufford wouldn't be hard to overpower, I agree, Sir, but Paul Travis was built like the proverbial brick crapper," Kath said. "How would

Norton take him down?"

"She's fit, ma'am," Vikki said. "Very athletic. I reckon she'd be capable of getting in a knockout blow with the baseball bat. She was a member of the medical corps too, so she'd have the know-how when it came to cutting his throat quickly and efficiently."

"We'd better find her then, right away. Kath and Alex, check her offices in Heswall, Kinnear, Vikki, you're with me. We'll check her house."

Chapter 41

Traffic choked the area around Port Sunlight. Cars were abandoned on grass verges or in shop carparks and streams of people marched along the pavements and roads, all going in the same direction. "What the hell's going on?" Noel muttered as he slowed the van down behind a queue of cars. "Is there some kind of event going on?"

Terry White twitched and stared out of the window, his knee pumping up and down like he was a rock drummer. "Too many people" he said. "What are we doing here?"

"We're going to find Nicola, remember, Terry? Nicola. Just hold on. She'll know what to do," Noel said, his heart thumping. Terry had been more and more anxious as they neared their destination. He'd been rambling about Corporal Graves and various other people. Noel felt sorry for the lad but he'd gone above and beyond the call of duty for him. There'd come a point where Noel was just going to have to bail out and he was getting close to it. The traffic ahead had just ground to a halt and Noel glimpsed a copper up at the front. His stomach lurched. He was definitely too old for this nonsense. Glancing around, he saw a side road and swerved the van up it.

"What are you doing? Where are you taking me?" Terry snapped.

"There was a copper stopping the traffic up there. I couldn't risk us getting caught, Terry," Noel said, trying to keep his voice calm. "Don't worry, I'll find us somewhere to park and we can walk the rest of the way. It'll be safer anyway."

Cars were double parked up this road, too and Noel inched the van along, searching desperately for somewhere to stop. Then Terry's phone rang.

Noel cursed and pulled the van onto the pavement, bumping up the kerb. Terry pulled the phone out of his jacket pocket. "Put it on speaker, Terry," Noel said. "So I can hear it too. Then I'll know you aren't going crazy, okay?"

Terry looked at him for what seemed like a century and then nodded, answering the phone. "Terry? Where are you?" A robotic voice said.

Probably the worst crime Noel ever committed was a kidnap. In his mind, it hadn't been that bad because the victim was a known drug dealer who had been filtering takings from his boss. They kidnapped the dealer to get the money back. He'd just been hired to drive but he remembered the boss using that kind of voice disguiser. Even though it had been deepened, he could tell it was a woman's voice.

"I-I'm in…" Terry looked helplessly at Noel. "Where am I?

"You aren't alone? That's against regulations, Terry. You've compromised the mission. There's only one option..."

"No, please..."

Noel was sick of listening. "Who is this?" he said. "Why do you have to disguise your voice from Terry if you're on his side?"

"Endgame, Terry. Endgame."

"No," Terry sobbed.

"It's a woman's voice, Terry. Who is she that she can tell you what to do? Your mum? Do you have a boss who's a woman? Think Terry. Why does she hide from you if she wants to help you?"

"Endgame, Terry. Endgame."

"Please," Terry whimpered, curling into a ball.

"Is this Nicola?" Noel said through gritted teeth. "Cos if it is, we're nearer than you think and we're coming for you."

"Endgame. That's an order." The phone went dead.

"Shit," Noel hissed. "Terry, we've got to..." He didn't manage to get another word out because a fist slammed into the side of his head, filling the world with stars and pain. Another blow fell on his shoulder but Terry was restricted by the cab of the van and his side-on position. Noel grappled with the door handle and fell out into the road on his hands and knees. A car blared its horn and Noel just had time to glimpse the red of its skirting and bumpers, a few letters of the registration plate before it ploughed into him, crushing him against the open van door before ripping it off and coming to a halt.

The world swam before Noel's eyes. He could feel the van door under him, digging into his back. Oddly, there was no pain as he lay there. That might come later, he thought. If there was a later. Terry White looked down at him, his face pale. "Run, Terry," Noel gasped. "Run, lad."

He heard Terry's voice as though through a thick blanket. "I-is that you, Graves?"

"No," Noel sighed. "Go and get the bitch. Get Nicola. She's your enemy now."

Terry vanished from view and darkness began to shroud Noel's vision. All he could hear was the slap of Terry White's boots on the tarmac as he fled the scene.

*****

Irked might have been one way to describe DI Kath Cryer's feelings as she approached Nicola Norton's office in Heswall. She didn't want to feel that way, but she felt side-lined by Blake. It was a stupid reaction, she knew, childish and unhelpful; the Heswall office was as important an element in this investigation as anywhere else but why didn't he send Vikki Chinn here?

Alex Manikas didn't seem bothered by the fact

that they were driving away from where all the action was likely to be. Kath shook her head. Why did she want to be near a source of potential danger anyway? She'd had enough excitement when she faced a shot-gun-wielding psychopath last year. She'd only just about recovered from that. She'd even tried to short-circuit the need to come out to Heswall by phoning but the number for the business just gave a continuous beep, suggesting it no longer existed. Under the circumstances, she had to go out and check.

They stood outside the mobile phone shop beneath the office. "Vikki said that the door to the office was round the back," Alex said.

"If she's so familiar with it, she should have come herself," Kath muttered. They walked round the back but the door was locked.

"Should we ask in the shop?" Alex suggested.

The shop was dingy and full of glass cabinets containing old phones, video games and keyboards. Kath wasn't a gambling woman but she'd lay a month's wages on some of this stuff being stolen. A balding, middle-aged man with thick glasses and a brown cardigan leaned on the counter watching them. Kath swore that he flinched when she produced her warrant card.

"I've got receipts for all of this stuff, I promise," he said. "If it's knock-off, then I wasn't to know, honest."

"Don't worry, sir, we're not here for you, we're looking for Nicola Norton. She has an office upstairs…"

The man looked even more despondent. "Yeah, well you won't find her up there, will you?"

"You tell me."

"No, you won't because she's moved on. I'm the landlord and she handed in the keys on Thursday. Shame, really, I quite liked her."

"She closed her office on Thursday? Did she say why?"

The man shrugged. "Said she was going away for a while. Didn't say where." But Kath and Alex were out of the door and heading back to their car.

*****

Blake hissed with frustration at the cars lined up in front of him. "Why are so many people still intent on going to this rally? It's for nothing." They'd been stuck for half an hour and were still not that far out of the tunnel entrance.

"I think it's touched a nerve, sir. I bet a lot of people going along just want to show that they respect what it stands for," Vikki Chinn said. "It's not so much the terrorist rumour as the idea of a murder on such a place that seems to have got people so exercised about it."

Kinnear sat in the back staring out of the window, lost in his thoughts.

Blake rubbed his forehead. "I sometimes think people care more about monuments than people. I know it's important but Paul Travis was a father and a husband. He wasn't a saint by any stretch but he was loved and will be missed. That should count for more. If people protested like this every time someone was unlawfully killed, we'd live in a better world. Maybe if they just picked up the phone to help us every now and then, I'd have a bit more respect for them."

Vikki gave a tight smile. "It's symbolic, I suppose, sir."

"Symbolic? I wonder if half the people going today have just come for some aggro," Blake snorted. "I'm sorry, Vikki. I don't suppose everyone going there supports people like Lex Price or even shares his views. It just winds me up."

"It's been a tough case, sir," Vikki said, keeping her eyes firmly on the road.

"Take a left here, we'll take the back roads," Blake said, pointing down a small street. They made progress, zigzagging through the smaller roads of Rock Ferry but as they approached Port Sunlight itself, the roads became busier again. Once or twice, Vikki had to flash the blue lights and give a blast of the siren to make the lines open up for them.

Blake's phone buzzed. "Nicola's not here, sir,"

Kath said. "She handed in the keys to her office on Thursday, said she was going away for a while."

"Jeez," Blake hissed through gritted teeth. "This just gets better and better. Notify Border Force, see if we can stop her getting out of the country and put a call for any transport police to keep an eye out for her but in this mess, I can't imagine that'll be easy."

They came to a dead stop. Vikki flashed her lights but the car in front had nowhere to go. The road was blocked with double-parked cars. "It'll take ages to sort this out, sir."

Blake opened his door. "It'll be quicker on foot. You keep trying to get to Nicola's, Kinnear, you're with me. We'll meet you there, Vikki."

"I'll notify any uniformed officers that you're heading that way, sir, in case you need back-up. Be careful."

Blake and Kinnear began running down the street. Praying that Nicola Norton hadn't already got away.

Chapter 42

Nicola Norton had not expected this kind of reaction to Paul Travis' murder. She watched the swarms of people meandering into Port Sunlight village as though heading for a picnic or open-air concert. They were a funny mix, too; some were the kinds of people she would expect to come to a rally like this, shaven-headed, with big boots and strange tattoos. Some even carried flags with symbols Nicola didn't recognise. Others looked like average punters, young and old. There were little kids, old ladies and even a few war veterans with blazers and medals on their chest.

The war memorial had been just another distraction to make the police think there was some kind of military link to his death. She didn't imagine for one second that it would spark so much outrage. It threw a spanner right in the works; she had to move fast. Not only did she have a flight to catch but she was worried about her call with Terry White. Somebody else had been with him and, by the sound of it, may have turned him against her. She didn't want to be here when Terry arrived with his new friend.

The chatter of the crowd and the sound of distant sirens filled the air as Nicola heaved the last of her suitcases into the back of the car. Somewhere from the centre of the village, a speech was being given over a PA system but she couldn't hear what was being said and, frankly, she couldn't care less. She just had to get her shoulder bag with the passport and tickets in and she would be away. She slammed the boot down and looked up. A large figure loomed over the crowds, striding up the street. So fixed on Nicola's house was he that Terry White had accidentally knocked a couple of people over. A couple of skinheads yelled abuse after him but thought better of having a go.

Nicola's heart thumped and she made a grab for the car door, then remembered her bag. She couldn't escape without the tickets and passport. She sprinted up to her front door, slamming it shut behind her. Where had she put her bag? She scanned the living room, searching for it. "No, no, no, no," she hissed as she ran around the house searching frantically. Tears of fear and frustration stung her eyes. "Where the fuck is it?"

As she stumbled down the stairs two at a time, she spotted the bag hanging in the hall. At the same moment All of Terry's massive bulk crashed against the front door, shattering the glass in the small window and splintering the frame. Nicola shrieked and grabbed the bag, dashing for the back door.

With a final crash, Terry flew into the hall, leaving the door hanging on one hinge. He tripped, and fell to the floor, cutting himself on the broken glass that lay there. "Endgame, Terry!" Nicola shouted.

"I know who you really are and what you're playing at, Graves," Terry panted, dragging himself to his feet. His eyes were wild and a manic grin cracked his face. "I'm going to finish you."

Nicola dragged the back door open and ran out, bag still clutched in her hand. Without looking back, she hurried through the small backyard and out into the alley behind. If she could lose White in the crowd, then double back to the car, escape would still be possible. She dashed into the main street and headed into the village, glancing back every now and then and ignoring the odd looks she got from some as she barged past them.

Terry emerged from the alley behind Nicola's house, she could see his bloody face as he craned his neck, searching through the crowd for her. She slowed to a brisk walk, trying her best to look normal. But when she looked back, she caught his eye and he stared right at her as though the crowd wasn't even there. He started running towards her. Nicola bolted too, knocking people aside and ignoring the yells of annoyance. She ducked and twisted, pushing herself between the crowd, totally oblivious to their protests as blind panic took over.

For a moment, she was uncertain quite where

she was in the village but then she saw the art gallery and the boating lake. If she could get to the war memorial, she'd be safe; there'd be police there and so many people that Terry wouldn't dare attack her, surely. She'd be able to talk him down or, even better, there may be armed officers there to take him down. A pushchair caught her ankle and she fell, screaming, her wrist cracking as she tried to break her fall.

Someone dragged her to her feet and she screamed for them to let her go, slapping out and with her good hand. "Steady on, love, you're okay…" someone said but Nicola gritted her teeth, tucked her throbbing wrist under her other arm and limped away as fast as she could. The crowd thickened but she knew White was gaining on her from the cries and shouts behind her.

She threw herself forward at the boundary of police officers who had formed a cordon around the memorial. Taken by surprise, one of them reached out to grab her. "Steady, Madam, can you…"

"Please. He's trying to kill me. You've got to help me!" Nicola screamed, pointing at Terry White as he pushed people aside and charged towards her.

*****

It was a little further from Vikki's car to Nicola Norton's house than Blake had estimated. His chest burned from the run and sweat soaked his back and forehead. Kinnear kept up with him but the weight he was carrying slowed him down. The front door dangled from one hinge, "We're too late, sir," Kinnear panted.

"The back door's wide open," Blake said peering through the house. Screams and shouts of anger rose from the streets behind the house. "Check inside the house and call for back-up, I'll check in the crowd."

Kinnear nodded and disappeared into the house as Blake ran round the side into the village itself and the surging mass of protestors. He waved his warrant card as he went. "Police, mind out!" Up ahead, he glimpsed Terry White's broad shoulders and, further in front, Nicola Norton's ashen face glancing back.

Some people swore at Blake, others stepped aside and pointed in the direction that Nicola Norton had gone. The punishment Terry White had given Blake earlier in the week and the damage to his ribs that he'd sustained in Scotland were beginning to take their toll on him and he had to pause. His head throbbed and he gasped for breath, wondering if it would have been wiser to let Kinnear chase after Norton.

Another scream up ahead forced him to start jogging again, holding his warrant card up once again. It looked like Nicola was heading for the war memorial. Blake headed for the edge of the crowd and began running on people's front gardens to skirt the mass of protestors.

Elbowing his way through the crush around the memorial, Blake forced his way to the front where, seeing his warrant card, the officer let him through. At the same moment, he saw Nicola Norton break into the memorial space, and turn to face the charging Terry White. The big man's bulk took two officers off their feet and he reached out, not stopping until he'd grabbed Nicola Norton, holding her like a rag doll under her armpits.

Blake ran forward and an officer fired a taser into White's back but the big man thundered on, propelling her forward. Then he stopped at the top of the steps, throwing Norton with all his might towards the statue of a soldier holding a rifle with bayonet fixed. Blake watched in helpless disbelief as the woman flew up into the air, then she stopped abruptly, looking down in shock at the bronze bayonet protruding from her chest, blood spreading across her pale sweater. Her head slumped and she dangled from the statue of the soldier.

It was only then that Blake realised that Lex Price stood on the memorial flanked by a couple of speakers and a microphone. He took one look at Terry White and swung a punch, sending the young man to the ground. Police officers piled onto the prone soldier and the crowd began to surge forward.

As if caught on a tidal wave, Blake lost sight of Price as he was swept by the sudden surge of the crowd towards the sides of the memorial. He could see what was coming but could do nothing to stop it and felt hard stone smack against his face and chest. He fell to the floor, a foot crushing his hand and a knee clipping the side of his head. Someone dragged him to his feet and he staggered, the press of bodies holding him up, now and propelling him along the wall of the memorial.

The police officers who had formed a cordon, were now trying to drag Terry's body onto the upper part of the memorial while some members of the public kicked at his body. Other officers were trying to get Nicola down and staunch the bleeding. Blake pushed forwards and grabbed an officer's arm, lashing out at anyone who tried to harm Terry. "You two, try and get the public back, we'll drag him to safety."

Many people were trying to get away from the crush now and hurrying from the area, others tripped over those running away in their effort to see what was going on. Sirens wailed as ambulances, fire engines and more police arrived.

"Stop!" Lex Price yelled at the top of his voice. Blake looked over his shoulder at the big man who now stood on the wall of the memorial with his hands in the air. "We've got to show these terrorists that we are better than them!" Lex continued. "Instead of fighting with our brave boys in blue, we should be helping them. Everyone back off!"

Given that many of the people at the rally had retreated from the violence, only a handful of skinheads with scarves around their faces remained and the police officers were forming ranks again. They did back away though and stood looking rather sheepish. The vacuum was replaced with a pack of journalists and photographers and Lex Price was swamped by people asking questions before Blake could intercept him.

"You okay, sir?" Vikki Chinn said, appearing next to him.

"Vikki, am I glad to see you?" Blake said, slumping onto the top step of the memorial. "Check and see if Norton's alive and if White's okay. He took quite a mauling there." Blake watched Vikki hurry off to the paramedics huddled over White.

Deirdre Lanham hurried over to him. "DCI Blake, have you got any comment on this outrage?"

"There'll be an official statement once we know exactly what happened…"

"A woman was assaulted, DCI Blake, right

under your nose. You must have something to say about it."

"There are many things I'd like to say about it and about the way this whole day was encouraged by shoddy reporting and emphasising social media over actual investigation. I'd love to say that the fact that your colleagues are interviewing that man over there and making a hero of someone who caused this chaos speaks volumes but that's just my opinion. I'll wait for the Media and Communications Manager to tell me what I can and can't talk about."

Blake dragged himself to his feet trying not to groan in front of the reporter and shuffled across to the ambulance where a paramedic sat him down and started looking at his injuries.

Vikki came back. "Nicola Norton is seriously injured, sir and in need of urgent surgery. We'll know more about how she is in a few hours. White has sustained head injuries but otherwise seems okay. They're taking him to A&E..."

"Get a shitload of officers to go with him. All big, anyone who can handle themselves. I don't want him walking out of hospital on us."

"Yes, sir."

Blake looked up at the paramedic. "Will I live?"

Chapter 43

In the bright light of the hospital ward, Terry White looked pale and weak. It was hard to imagine that he had powered through so many people and picked up Nicola Norton as though she weighed nothing. A large bandage covered his forehead and his face and neck were black with bruises. Blake sat by his bedside on a plastic chair that reminded him of his own injuries every time he moved.

"You'll be charged with the attempted murder of Nicola Norton, Terry, you do understand that, don't you?"

White nodded. "Is Noel okay?"

"Noel Roscoe. Was he the man who helped you, Terry?"

"Yes. He kept me safe for a couple of days and gave me a lift from Quentin's house. Is he okay?"

"He'll pull through. He was hit by a car when he got out suddenly. Nothing the driver could do to stop in time..."

"He was trying to get away from me," Terry said.

"You'd better wait until you have a solicitor with you Terry before you start telling me..."

"I hit him because he was saying that the commander on the phone was my enemy but he was right wasn't he? It was Nicola Norton."

"Yes, Terry, it was. She was trying to frame you so she could get away with murder and theft."

"I thought I'd killed Paul and Quentin."

"We think it was Nicola, Terry. We're trying to find any kind of physical evidence to link her to the deaths but she was clever."

"I was there that night," Terry said, quietly.

"When Paul was murdered?"

Terry nodded. "I was told to go to the war memorial just before midnight. I saw Paul was dead then I ran away. I think I stood in the blood…"

"You did, Terry. It's not your fault, mate. Nicola was setting you up. You have to remember that."

"But it looks like I did it."

"What evidence we do have is a load of Pro-Vets money in an account linked to her, so that's a start. We also have the mobile she used to contact you and we can pinpoint where she was using that."

"Will she go to prison?"

"She's regained consciousness after her operation and is recovering now but eventually, I'm sure she'll get some kind of prison sentence, yes…"

"I don't ever want to see her again," Terry whispered. "I trusted her. I thought she was my friend…"

"Don't worry, Terry, I don't think you'll be seeing her again. She's made quite a few enemies round here, some of them on the wrong side of the law, I suspect."

"I'm sorry I hurt you, Mr Blake," Terry said. "I was scared. I wasn't thinking right."

"It's all right, Terry, I understand. You weren't well. Hopefully, the doctors here will help you get your condition back under control, yeah?"

Blake stepped out of White's side ward and nodded to the guards that stood at the door. "Keep an eye on him, poor bastard," he said. "He's been through hell." He frowned at the figure stepping out of another side ward further down the corridor.

"Laura?" he said, hurrying towards her.

Laura Vexley turned and smiled at Blake. "Well, fancy meeting you here. You look terrible."

"Thanks," Blake said, touching his bruised cheek. "Do you mind telling me what the hell you're doing in Nicola Norton's room?"

"I know her. She tutored me when I was studying Psychology at university. I didn't know she was such a bad apple or I'd have steered clear."

"You're being sarcastic, I presume," Blake said, raising one eyebrow. "So what brings you here now?"

"Professional curiosity, a link with the past. She was quite surprised to see me."

"Really? There's a surprise! She's at the centre of a murder investigation. Are you trying to jeopardise the whole case?"

"No. If you're that worried about me being here, you'd better let me go."

"I should arrest you…"

"What for? Visiting a friend? Or do you think I've interfered in some way? In which case, please do arrest me and then let's see how that plays out. Not in your favour, Will. It was nice to see you, Will. I hope you heal. In all ways."

Laura stuck her hands in her pockets and sauntered up the corridor. As soon as she was out of sight, Blake hurried into Nicola Norton's room.

"I wondered when you'd turn up," she said, feebly.

"Laura Vexley. What did she want?"

"She was just passing. Called in to see how I was. I tutored her…"

"Yeah, yeah, cut the bullshit, Nicola. What did she say to you?"

"These painkillers," Nicola said. "They play havoc with your memory but she was curious about why I killed them…"

"Curious?"

"The psychology of it. I told her that it was purely a practical decision. Paul Travis had realised that money was going missing from Pro-Vets and he was putting pressure on Ufford. So I took him out of the picture and set Terry up..."

"And Ufford?"

"He was weak. He started to panic because George Owens was breathing down his neck. I could have killed George but actually, it dawned on me that killing Ufford would render me anonymous. Or so I thought. The truth is, they were all so weak, weren't they? You men are, though, aren't you? You're vain, violent, and greedy."

"That's a rather grim assessment," Blake said. "There are plenty of good men in the world. Vain or not, Travis gave lots of people a helping hand."

"Are you one of the good men, Mr Blake? I keep looking for them. I've killed before. Put men out of their misery on the battlefield after they been chewed up and spat out by politicians' wars. It's easy to be dispassionate about killing when it's a means to an end. The rent on my office in Heswall was a fortune and it needed a complete refit. I was broke when I stumbled across Pro-Vets. Maybe it was meant to be."

"And that's what you told Laura?"

Nicola Norton smiled but she looked at Blake with dead eyes. "No. I said I didn't kill them. That Terry White murdered them and that I had nothing to do with it."

"Then why are you telling *me* that you *did* kill them?"

"Because you're DCI Blake and I want to make a full confession. If you're quick and look in my next-door neighbour's bin, you'll find a bag of plastic soldiers. I tried to handle them carefully but you'll probably find my DNA on them somewhere. I threw the knife used to kill Paul in the Mersey but the sales assistant at the kitchen shop in Heswall will remember me. I think he had a thing for mature women and I flirted with him a bit. Probably shouldn't have, come to think of it but there you go."

"Why are you confessing?" Blake said. "I don't understand."

Nicola looked tired. "Remorse, DCI Blake," she said flatly, without a hint of emotion. "I'm overcome with guilt for everything I've done."

"What about Richard Ince?"

"Poor Richard. Quentin had been skimming off money from Pro-Vets for some time. He went boozing with Richard and inevitably got drunk and started bragging about it. Richard told me during a counselling session at Pro-Vets sometime last year. If he had gone to Paul then Ufford would have been sunk. I was desperate for money. Close to bankruptcy then. So I suggested we blackmail Quentin Ufford together."

"But you realised you could make more money by teaming up with Ufford and cutting out Ince altogether."

"Yes. Quentin couldn't believe his luck. He thought he was going to spend the rest of his life sunning himself on a Caribbean beach next to me. Then I sent Terry to get Ince drunk and waited at Ince's flat for him to come back. He thought I'd come with some blackmail money from Ufford. Once I was inside he drank himself unconscious. I just had to administer the heroin and leave the note."

"But why the plastic soldier?"

Nicola sighed. "Once I'd had to plan Ince's murder, I realised that other people might ultimately get in the way. It seemed quite clever to leave a 'calling card' and link it to Terry. It certainly distracted you and your team for a while." She yawned. "I'll make a full statement later but I'm very tired now and want to sleep."

"I can't believe you'd confess so freely. Especially when Terry White is in the frame for all the killings. What did Laura say to you?"

"Nothing much, Mr Blake. We were just catching up and she told me how well she was doing now, where she was living and who with. That was all. You don't mess with people like that, and you don't steal their money, do you?"

Chapter 44

The house was quiet and dark when Kinnear got home. After the initial excitement, he'd spent the rest of the day taking statements and talking to so many different colleagues that he hardly noticed the time. It was only when shadows began to fall that he realised the time. At that moment, he had felt weary and longed to go home.

Blake's words still tugged at Kinnear's heart as he got out of the car. He let himself in and savoured the quiet. In a few weeks' time, this place would be full of noise and love. A child was coming to stay, and he'd welcome her with all his heart and soul. It felt as though he got up the stairs in two bounds, he was so eager to tell Chris.

Life was precious. Life was to be lived.

*****

Serafina lay curled on Blake's lap, purring like a Rolls Royce engine while he sipped a steaming mug of tea. He sat in the living room enjoying the Spring sunshine that streamed through the window. It was clear and still cold outside, but the sun felt warm through the window. A promise of Summer.

"So, what'll happen to the young man who attacked you?" Ian Youde said. "Will he get a prison sentence?"

"Hard to say, Ian. He was badly manipulated.

I don't think he can get away from the damage he did to Ollerthwaite but his mental condition will have to be taken into account. The fact that Ollerthwaite is on the mend is encouraging and he's not a vindictive man. So who knows?"

"The lad needs some kind of support, though."

"Yeah, and hopefully, he'll get that. Norton wasn't treating him, she was manipulating him and making his condition worse. People call these ex-soldiers heroes and buy poppies every year but Terry White suffers every day. He shouldn't have ended up in the state that he did."

"True," Ian said.

"Prepare your hearts for Death's cold hand," Blake muttered. "That's Blake, my namesake. A War Song to Englishmen. Nobody prepares to end up like Terry, though, do they?"

"No," Ian said, staring into the distance. "And what about Laura Vexley?"

Blake shook his head. "God only knows, Ian. I can't decide if she's gone back to her old ways for good or is up to something else. Either way, I can't go anywhere near."

"Best way, mate. Stay clear of that whole business."

"I wish I could, Ian, but I think it's going to come looking for me whether I like it or not, someday." He looked down at Serafina. "Still, you seem much better... Jeez!" And to demonstrate her agreement, Serafina sank her sharp fangs into Blake's hand.

The End

Author's Note

My father joined the RAF in 1938 at the tender age of 18. Like many young men of his age at that time, he was patriotic and had no love for the Nazi regime that had taken power in Germany. He could see the writing on the wall and believed that war was inevitable. But his own father had died from wounds received in the Great War and he always told me that he wanted to be a trained soldier rather than a conscript.

To hear him talk, you'd be forgiven for thinking that my dad's war was a comedy of errors. He'd tell stories of the various cockups that had blighted his service; the time the USAF filled the only plane to take him home with salt water instead of aviation fuel, getting drunk in Cyprus and falling off a donkey, breaking his ankle, ditching an Avro Anson in the Mersey and finding out that the emergency dinghy had no paddle, being sent to Iceland with full tropical kit. I could go on but I suspect that my dad talked about these things rather than his other experiences.

I can remember only two occasions when he spoke about the horrors he'd seen. Once he told me about travelling up through Italy and described the rotting bodies of fallen soldiers. Another time, he described the RAF's policy of designating aircrew with what we would now call PTSD as Lacking Moral Fibre. He and his mates thought it was a disgrace. Needless to say, Remembrance Day was always observed in our household.

That last story resonated with me and I still think we, as a public, don't always recognise the traumatised and brain-injured amongst our veterans. I don't know what it must be like to be caught in violent conflict. I can imagine but I don't suppose it comes anywhere near the real thing.

About the Author

Jon Mayhew lives on the Wirral with his family and has done all his life. A teacher for many years, he enjoys traditional music and plays regularly in ceilidh bands and sessions. Jon is also an award-winning author. His dark children's books are published by Bloomsbury.

Find out more at www.jemayhew.blogspot.com

Find JE Mayhew on Facebook and twitter.

To keep in touch with Jon and get news about upcoming publications, what he had for dinner last night, and how his dogs and chickens are faring go to https://dl.bookfunnel.com/gs5oc6n68k There a free prequel novella waiting for you there, too...

Made in the USA
Las Vegas, NV
24 May 2021

23608389R00218